THE GREEN LINE

THE SAM LASKA CRIME THRILLER SERIES
BOOK 4

RICHARD RYBICKI

HOLLOW POINT

PRESS

For Bob Quaid
A good friend and one hell of a great copper.
Gone much too soon.

The world is a worse place for the murders that go unsolved.

CHAPTER
ONE

SAM LASKA WAS ALWAYS BETTER with faces than names but the face of the woman next to him was a mystery. He swiveled his barstool around to face her.

"Who are you again?" he said.

"I knew you wouldn't remember me," the woman said. "It was a long time ago. You were a police officer, a detective, back in Chicago. My father was murdered and you came to our home to deliver the news."

Laska searched his memory but found nothing. Over the years, he visited untold numbers of homes to deliver the same horrible news to devastated families. Sadly, there were too many to remember any single one. He needed more to jog his memory.

"I'm sorry, but I still can't place you. Where was your father...where did it happen?"

The phone in her hand dinged. She poked at the screen and slipped it into the back pocket of her jeans.

She leaned in a little closer. "On an 'L' train. The Lake Street line."

That was all he needed. He exhaled heavily and turned back to his drink. "I remember now. Walter Patterson. We never solved it."

The woman nodded. "It was sixteen years ago this April," the woman said.

"I'm sorry. I'm sorry about your father."

He looked back at the woman. His brow creased. "I remember you were very young back then."

"I was only twelve."

"That's too young to lose a parent."

"My mother is gone too. She passed away a few years later. I didn't understand back then but when I look back I think losing my father broke her. She gave up on life."

The woman took a sip from her glass and set it down on the bar. "You came by the house every week after that first day to let my mom know how the investigation was going. Then it was every couple of weeks. Before long, you stopped coming altogether.

"Those times you visited, when she saw you at the door, she hoped you'd tell her you caught him. That maybe, finally, her prayers were answered. When you didn't, it was like that first day all over again. All the grief, all the heartache, all the pain returned. She cried for hours afterward. Every time."

Laska stared at the glass in front of him.

"And now, you're here in Florida," she said. She crossed her legs and brushed back a lock of hair that had fallen across her face. "I know this sounds odd, but back then, I thought you were so handsome. If I'm being honest, I had a tiny crush on you."

Sam didn't know how to answer. He smiled, but it was a sad smile.

"But that was a long time ago," she continued. "I've done a lot of growing up since then." She emptied her glass and set it down. "You know, you're the same age now as my father was when he was killed."

Sam straightened up and turned to the woman. "How do you know how old I am?"

The woman's mouth curled into a little half-smile.

Laska now understood this meeting was not accidental. This woman didn't just happen to walk into this restaurant in a different city, a different state, and recognize a man from her past sitting at the bar with a face that, over time, should have faded into obscurity.

"You've been looking for me," Laska said. It was more a statement than a question.

"And I found you. Living the easy life here in Sarasota."

Laska shrugged. "I don't know that you could call it easy."

"You weren't hard to find. There's this thing called the internet." She leaned in even closer to him. "Would you like to know why I went looking for you?" She didn't wait for his answer. "I wanted to ask you what happened, why you couldn't catch my father's killer. Why you stopped trying."

Laska fiddled with his glass. "Some cases, some

homicides, there just isn't enough evidence. There aren't enough leads."

"My father was killed on a crowded train car during rush hour. There were dozens of witnesses."

"We couldn't find them. They scattered at the next stop as soon as the doors opened. They were probably scared out of their wits. And none of them ever came forward after that." He shook his head slowly. "There were a few that stuck around, but they were no help at all. We tried to find out who else was on that train, but no one came forward. We can't force people to help us."

"You promised. You promised my mother you would catch my father's killer. And you broke that promise. You gave up."

"I shouldn't have done that. I was wrong to make a promise. I thought it would help comfort your mother somehow, but I was wrong to do it. I know that now. But I tried, I really did. I did everything I could to keep that promise."

"No. You quit. You moved on. You transferred to somewhere else and dropped the case. You left it behind and never looked back."

"That's not what happened," he said. He turned away. He knew nothing he said from this point on was going to make any difference to this woman. She was hurt and angry. And she needed someone to direct that anger at. He would give her that. He would be that someone even though he knew it wouldn't help her.

"It is exactly what happened," she said as she stood. "Have you ever thought about my father once since then?" There was a chilling iciness to her voice now. She reached into her purse, took out a twenty, and tossed it on the bar. She turned back to Laska. "You're going to be a father yourself soon, right?"

Laska's head whipped around. "What did you say?"

"Your girlfriend, what's her name? Gabrielle Jones? She's due any week now. Maybe any day. It would be a shame if that child never got to meet its father."

Laska jumped to his feet and grabbed her by the wrist. He moved in closer, nose to nose. "Are you threatening me?"

With her free hand, the woman grabbed the thumb of the hand locked on her wrist. She wrenched it back against the joint. Pain ripped through Laska's hand and up his arm. He released her wrist as he tried to pull away. With her newly freed hand, she grabbed his bent elbow and jerked it upward and towards her as she increased the force on the joint of his thumb. Searing pain shot up his arm to his shoulder. His body twisted and his knees buckled. Nearly bent over backward, he dropped to the floor.

She bent down and whispered in his ear. "You have two weeks to keep your promise. Do it, or your child will grow up without you. That's my promise to you."

She walked out the door and was gone.

"Jesus, you let a woman beat you up?" Jack Hoke lounged in his chair, his feet propped up on his desk.

"That's not the part of the story I was hoping you'd focus on," Laska said.

Laska was sitting across the desk from Jack in the law offices of Hoke, Dunn, and Associates. He had been doing occasional investigative work for the firm for the last few months. When they needed his services – to find a reluctant witness, serve a subpoena, or whatever legitimate need they had – they'd call him.

He wasn't thrilled to be working for the other side - defense attorneys - but the money they paid was good. He assuaged his guilt by turning down cases when he felt the client was obviously guilty. The others he rationalized by telling himself the truth doesn't pick sides.

"But it's the best part," Jack said. "Tell me how she did it again."

"You're kidding, right?"

Jack Hoke grinned and sat up. He reached into a small wooden box on his desk and pulled out a cigar. "Yeah, of course. I'm just yanking your chain." He trimmed the butt of the cigar with a small silver clipper he drew from his pocket. "But seriously, tell me the whole story again. From the beginning."

"I was at a restaurant, One Love, over on Main Street."

"Nice place," Jack said.

"Yeah. I was sitting at the bar—"

"Day drinking? That doesn't sound like you."

"You gonna let me tell the story or not?"

"Yeah, sorry. Go ahead."

"And I wasn't drinking. I had a Coke and was

going to have lunch at the bar. Anyway, a girl, a woman, sits down a few stools away from me. I didn't pay attention to her until she looked up from her phone and said she knew me. It caught me off guard. She moved to the seat next to me and introduced herself. She said we had met before. She told me her name, but it didn't register with me. I didn't recognize her either.

"She said her father had been murdered in Chicago and I was one of the detectives who investigated the case. I asked and she told me where it happened. That's when it fell into place for me. We never solved it."

"You said she was the daughter of the victim?"

"Yeah, she was twelve years old when it happened."

"Jesus, that's tough. Poor kid."

Laska ran a hand through his hair and exhaled heavily. "Yeah. Then, she blamed me for never catching her father's killer, accusing me of giving up on it. I tried to explain that we didn't have anything to go on, but she wouldn't listen. I figured I'd let her vent, but it went sideways after that."

"How?"

"She threatened me. She threatened to kill me if I didn't solve the case. She said I had two weeks."

Jack Hoke perked up. He leaned in closer. "She threatened to kill you? Were there any witnesses? Did anyone hear her?"

Laska shrugged. "I doubt it. Maybe. I don't know. But I'm not going to make a police report, Jack."

"It would be good to do. You know, in case you

want to sue her. How's your arm? Did you see a doctor? I know a few good ones. We've used them before."

"My arm is fine. I'm not going to sue anyone, Jack. And I'm not going to have her arrested. Not yet anyway. Besides, I put my hands on her first."

"How did you put your hands on her?"

"She made the threat and started to walk away. I grabbed her by the arm. That's when she put me on the ground."

"You didn't hit her?"

"No, I just grabbed her."

"To stop her from leaving after she threatened you. We can work with that."

"You're thinking like a lawyer again."

"That's my job. What about the threat? What did she say? Exactly."

"She said my kid would grow up without a father if I didn't solve the case."

"You have a kid? I didn't even know you were married."

"I'm not married. And I'm not a father yet, but I will be soon. And, again, not what I want you to focus on."

"But how did she know?"

"That's why I'm here. She knew some things about me, personal things, and I want to know how."

"What things?"

"She knew the name of my…the mother of my kid."

"You think someone here talked to her? That wouldn't happen. No one here would give out personal info like that. And no one here knows you well enough to know that kind of thing anyway."

"I believe you, Jack. But there's something else. I want to find her."

"I wouldn't recommend you do that. File a police report. Let them handle it. Did you ever hear that old saying? Don't go looking for trouble or trouble will find you."

"I'm not looking for trouble. I'm not looking for payback or revenge or to get even because she—"

"Kicked your ass."

"—got lucky and caught me off guard."

"Yeah, right. Then, what are you looking for?"

Laska leaned forward in his chair, his elbows resting on his knees and his hands clasped together. "I want to talk to her again about her father's murder. Maybe—"

"You gotta be kidding."

"--maybe I should look into it again."

"That's nuts. You're not a cop anymore. It's not your job."

Laska dismissed Jack with a shrug and stood. "But before I can do that, I have to find her. Can I use your passwords to get on LexisNexis and Tracers?"

Jack's firm subscribed to several data provider websites. The providers were able conduct a comprehensive search of public records, consumer data, assets, and a host of other information sites. There was a fee but they were great for finding reluctant witnesses or for process service. The information they provided was essential to law firms, private investigators, and anyone else who was willing to pay.

"Sure, go ahead. Joyce has all the passwords."

Joyce Davis was the 'Associate' in Hoke, Dunn, and Associates. She was the firms' 'Girl Friday', the receptionist-slash-secretary-slash-paralegal for Jack Hoke and Larry Dunn's law firm.

"I'll tell her to give you a hand. Maybe she can help you find the woman. Joyce knows that stuff better than anyone. But, if you're asking for my opinion, you should just go to the police."

"Not gonna happen."

The phone in Laska's pocket began vibrating. He pulled it out and checked the screen.

"Hang on a minute, Jack," he said as he poked at the screen. "I have to take this."

He turned away and held the phone to his ear.

"Marley?" he said.

CHAPTER
TWO

GABRIELLE MARLEY JONES, the former fiancé and soon-to-be mother of Laska's child, didn't bother to say hello.

"What the hell, Sam? You started a fight in my restaurant?"

"That's not what happened."

"And with a woman?"

"Marley," he said, "that's not what happened. Can I explain?"

"That's what Joe said happened." Marley owned One Love, and Joe Trejo was one of her bartenders. Years ago, when she opened the restaurant, she explained to Sam that she picked a name for her place that represented their love, their promise to one another. There would be no one else for her, forever. One love. But that was before Sam screwed up and she broke it off.

"It's not what happened," Sam said. "Joe wasn't there for the whole thing."

"Are you saying Joe is lying to me?"

"No, I'm saying he's mistaken. Will you let me explain?"

"Okay, explain."

Sam went through the entire story again. He considered not mentioning the woman's threat but decided that if he ever had a chance of repairing his relationship with Marley, he needed to level with her. Always.

"She really threatened you?" Marley said.

"Yeah, but I don't think she really meant it."

"Why not? She was crazy enough to beat you up in a crowded restaurant. She could be crazy enough to follow through on the threat."

"She didn't beat me up."

"It kind of sounds like she did. What are you going to do?"

"I haven't decided. Not completely, anyway. Jack thinks I should make a police report and have her arrested."

"Jack?"

"Yeah, I told you about him. He's the lawyer I work for now and then. I'm here in his office. Anyway, I think that girl was just angry and venting. She's been stewing for years and blames me. I understand that in some way. But I don't think she'd really do anything like she threatened to do."

"You don't know that for sure."

"You're right. That's why I think I should try and talk to her again."

"Really? I mean, she already—"

"She didn't beat me up. Why does everyone keep saying that? And, yeah, I think it's the right thing to do. I think all she really wants is closure. Maybe I can help her find that. And if I talk to her again at least I'll get a better read on whether she intends to follow through on the threat. But to do that I have to find her first."

"How are you going to do that? Help her find closure, I mean."

"I'm working on it."

"You know, Sam, this stuff, this is why…" her voice trailed off.

Sam waited for her to finish her thought, though he really didn't need to. He knew what she meant.

He decided he'd better change the subject. "Are we still on for tomorrow?" he said.

"Tomorrow?" Marley said, "Yes, I'll meet you there. Good-bye, Sam."

And she was gone, without Sam getting another word in. He pocketed his phone and turned back to Jack who was already busy with something else, talking on the phone while tapping away on his laptop. Sam cleared his throat to get his attention, waved a 'thank you' and headed towards the door.

Joyce sat in her regular spot behind a U-shaped desk in the lobby facing the thick glass entry door. As Sam walked over Joyce, without looking up from her computer's monitor, said, "So, what's this chick's name?"

"Jack messaged you already?" Sam said, as he pulled a chair to the side of Joyce's desk.

"Yeah, he said you needed my help finding some girl that beat you up."

Sam didn't react except to exhale heavily. There was no point in explaining, he thought. Instead, he said, "You're probably busy. I can do it. I'm getting pretty good with those searches. I'll just grab a laptop and work in the conference room."

"I'm not busy," Joyce said. "And with your hunt-and-peck keyboarding, you'll be here all night. Just give me the name and let me get started."

Laska shrugged. "Beth Patterson. I think Beth is short for Elizabeth."

"You're not sure?"

"I'm pretty sure but not one hundred percent."

"Okay. How about a birthdate and address?"

"I don't know her exact birthdate but she's about 28 years old. Maybe twenty-seven. And I don't have a current address but sixteen years ago she was living on Kenilworth Avenue in Oak Park, Illinois. If I remember it right."

"So, she was what? Twelve or thirteen years old back then? You know her parents' names?"

"Walter and Amanda."

"You're not giving me a whole lot to work with. Do you know anything else?"

"Not really."

"How do you know this woman? What's the story?"

"She's the daughter of a murder victim. I was one of the detectives that handled the investigation back in Chicago."

"There's probably more in the police file, right? Like her birthdate and address. Maybe the school she attended?"

"I'm sure there is but no one is going pass me that info over the phone. Officially, anyway."

"Unofficially?"

"I can make a call."

"Okay, go make yourself useful. In the meantime, I'll get started with what we have."

Sam pulled out his phone and headed outdoors for privacy. April was a great time to be in Sarasota. The weather was near perfect. But the mid-day sun could still be a killer so he walked to a shady spot under a gnarly old live oak tree. He dialed a number from memory. The first call got him nowhere. The next two didn't fare any better. He stared at the phone in his hand. It was six years since he left the police department. He knew the longer he was away from the job, the fewer people there were around to remember him. He didn't like that, but he wasn't surprised either. People move on. They retire, get promoted, transfer to another unit, and some, unfortunately, die. New people come in and take those spots and the people that came before are forgotten. It's almost like they were never there at all.

But there were always one or two that stuck around. The ones who found that one spot they never wanted to leave. That spot that fit them and created a comfortableness they didn't want to give up. It took two more calls before Laska connected with one of those 'someones'.

"Area Four Detective Division, Sanders," the voice on the other end said.

"Brian, this is Sam Laska."

"Laska? Holy shit. That's a name I haven't heard in a while. How's it going? Last I heard, you were in Florida. You still there?"

"Yeah, Sarasota. What about you? I thought you'd be retired by now."

"Not until they force me to go. I've got an ex-wife and two kids I'm still paying for."

"Sorry to hear that. But it works out for me. I need a favor."

"What kind of favor?"

"I need some info on an old case I worked. Names, birth dates, address on the victim's family. That kind of stuff."

"What for? Are you getting sued or something?"

"Something like that. How about it? Can you do that for me?"

"Yeah, of course. I don't suppose you have the RD number?"

The RD stood for Records Division. The numbers were the Chicago Police Department's system of case numbering. Every report made in the city was given a unique number that allowed tracking the investigation from the first report to the last. Every police department did it and every police department called their system something different. Most just called it a case or file number, but Chicago loved being unique.

"No, I don't. I've just got the victim's name and the year it happened."

"Okay, give me what you have."

"Walter Patterson, homicide victim. April of 2006. Still open and unsolved."

"Where did it happen?"

"I can't remember the exact address used but it was on an 'L' train on the Lake Street line."

"The Green Line. Okay, give me a minute to punch it into the computer."

Sam held the phone to his ear and waited. He could hear the faint clicking of a keyboard as Sanders worked.

The clicking stopped. Sanders came back on and said, "Hang on a minute, Sam," and was gone again. Laska heard muffled voices, a back and forth someone else.

Sanders picked up again. "Bad news, man," he said. "I can't get into the file."

"What do you mean?" Sam said.

"It's locked. It's flagged 'Restricted Access'. Only a Deputy Chief or higher can get into it."

"What the hell? Why?"

"Hey, I don't know. I only work here."

"Shit," Sam said, more to himself than Sanders. "You can't get anything?"

"Just the RD number and address of occurrence, 3150 W. Lake Street."

"What about the hard copy? We always kept a working file on all open cases in the office."

"An old case like that will be back in the storage room. Are you really going to ask me to go look for it?"

"It's pretty important to me, Brian."

Sander's exhaled heavily, making sure Sam heard him. "Okay, hang on. This might take a while."

Sam heard a click as he was put on hold. He waited, holding his phone to his ear. He waited so long he thought he might have been cut off. He was ready to end the call and redial the number when he heard another click.

Sanders came back on. "Sam? It's not here."

"Are you kidding me?"

"No, man. I checked the 2006 open cases twice. I even checked 2005 and 2007 in case it was misfiled."

"Shit. You think Cold Case could have grabbed it?"

"Maybe, but they always insert a place holder and note that says they have the file. You know, those green card things. And that doesn't explain why you'd need a deputy chief's okay to pull up the file on the computer. They don't restrict a file just because Cold Case is working it. And don't even think about asking me to call to see if they have it. If I start poking around, some-body is going to want to know why. I'm probably even gonna get asked why I tried to pull it up on the computer in the first place."

"Damn, I'm sorry Brian. I didn't mean to cause you any grief."

"Don't worry about it. I'll just tell them a family member called looking for an update or something like that."

"Thanks again, man."

"No problem. Hey, What about your partner? Who did you work the case with? Maybe they kept a copy of the file for themselves."

"I didn't have a regular partner at the time, but they sent Dave Hermann out to the scene with me. We worked on it together for a few weeks until my transfer to Area Three came through. I could call him, I guess. Can you give me his phone number?"

"That won't do you any good. Dave Hermann is dead, Sam."

"What?"

"He bought a house on ten acres near Galena. He was gonna retire and move out there. A couple of months ago he took a few days off to work on the house. He never came back. He was found shot to death in the woods behind his property. I heard they ruled it accidental, hit by a stray shot during hunting season."

CHAPTER
THREE

LASKA ENDED the call and headed back to the office. He stopped just inside, turned, and stared out through the glass doors. Traffic was whizzing along Main Street. People hustled in and out of the courthouse across the street. People in business clothes mingled with those less formally dressed in the plaza fronting the building, talking, grabbing a snack from a street vendor, just waiting for a friend, relative, or for their own time to appear inside. A troop of seagulls wandered the sidewalk dodging the people while searching for stray morsels. But Laska wasn't paying attention to any of that. His eyes were fixed on some unknown point on the horizon.

The death of an employee wasn't uncommon in a large organization like the Chicago Police Department. There were nearly twelve thousand sworn police officers and who-knows-how-many retired employees. An insurance actuary could tell you how likely it was that disease, accidents, and even suicides were going to take a number of those people every year. But no one really needed an actuary to tell them people were going to die. The CPD was no different than any other segment of the population. These things happen. Everywhere, every day. Still, it was surprising, even disturbing, when it happened to someone you knew and worked with. Particularly when it was sudden or unexpected. Or weird like a hunting accident.

Sam wasn't close to Dave Hermann. He couldn't remember one time they talked about anything other than work. He had no idea if Dave was married or had children, if he was a Cubs fan or White Sox fan, if he drank Budweiser or Old Style, or if he drank beer at all. Dave Hermann was just another guy from the office. Sam's only real connection to him was that they worked on one case together sixteen years ago.

And that bothered Laska. If he hadn't met Beth Patterson a few hours ago, he might never have learned about Dave Hermann's death. And even if he had, he would have just thought to himself how sad it was and probably never given it another thought. Beth Patterson's appearance, and her threat, changed that.

"Hey," Joyce said.

Laska hadn't noticed that she had left her desk and was now standing next to him. She was staring out the glass doors also.

"What are you looking at?" she said.

"Nothing," he said. "I was just thinking."

"Did you get anything?"

"What?" The question confused him momentarily. He caught himself up and said, "No, nothing. No luck at all. How about you?"

"A little bit. Come on." She turned and headed back to her desk. Laska followed and stood next to her as she took her seat behind the computer's monitor. She gave the mouse a jiggle and a page of photographs, all individual headshots, popped up. It took Sam only a second to realize he was looking at a page from a high school yearbook.

"Here," Joyce said as she zoomed in on one single photo, "Elizabeth Patterson. Is this her?"

Laska bent over and studied the girl, unsmiling and staring through the camera's lens with a look that probably made the photographer shiver.

"Yeah, that's her. Younger, of course. But that's her."

"Fenwick High School in Oak Park, Illinois. Two-Thousand and nine. Her sophomore year."

"She'd be about fifteen years old then. What about her senior year picture?"

"I searched the next two years of yearbooks. Nothing. It looks like 2009 was her last year at Fenwick."

"And these yearbooks are all online?"

"Yep. Easy-peezy. You just gotta know where to look."

"What if she transferred to a different school?"

"I searched all the other schools in the area. There was nothing in any of the other yearbooks."

"Okay, so we have her at Fenwick until 2009. Did you find anything else? A birthday, address, anything?"

"Not a thing. And without a birth date it's near impossible to find her. LexisNexis and Tracers would do the job but without her birthday and at least some history of residences nothing I pull up will be reliable. There are a shitload of Elizabeth Pattersons in the Chicago area. If she even stayed there after…well, who knows when. Sometime after 2009, I guess."

"Yeah, I get it."

"I was hoping your phone call would turn up at least that."

"Did you check for a social media presence? Facebook and all that."

"Yeah, nothing. Which is a little strange for a girl in her twenties."

Laska straightened up and stretched his back. *Unless she didn't want to be found*, he thought.

"We could probably give Fenwick a call and try to wrangle a birth date from them," Joyce said. "Maybe even why she left there and where she transferred to."

"Hmm," was all he said.

Joyce looked up at him. He was staring across the small lobby and out the glass doors again. She continued to watch him as he walked around her desk and through the doors into the afternoon sun.

"Okay, I guess I'll handle that for you," she called out. "You're welcome."

But he didn't hear her.

• • •

Sam pulled to the curb in front of his father's house on Siesta Key. As he slipped the keys from the ignition, he realized he had no memory of the drive from Jack's office. He had been thinking about Beth Patterson. He sifted through all he knew and what he didn't. He turned it over and over again and finally came to the only conclusion he could.

There was nothing he could do here in Sarasota.

He walked into the small home, his dad called it a villa, and headed to his bedroom. Bruno Laska, his father, was standing over a cup of coffee in the kitchen and watched his son walk through the house.

"Hey," Bruno said, "you don't say hello?"

"Sorry, Dad," Sam said as he continued through the house. "What's going on?"

"Nothing," Bruno said, following his son. "How about you?"

Bruno stood in the bedroom doorway and watched as Sam opened the closet door and began rooting around.

"Whatcha looking for?" Bruno asked.

Without looking up, Sam said, "My gym bag. I don't remember where the hell I put it."

"You going to the gym?"

Sam stopped and looked at his father. "No, Dad. I'm not going to the gym. I've gotta leave town for a while."

"And you're gonna pack your clothes in that smelly thing? Just take one of my suitcases."

Sam looked back to the closet and exhaled heavily.

"Yeah, I guess I could." He turned to his father. "Can you get me one? I think the smallest will be okay."

"Sure," Bruno said and walked off to his bedroom.

He returned less than a minute later lugging a small grey carry-on bag. "Here you go," he said handing it to his son. "Where are you going?"

"Chicago," Sam said, tossing the bag on his bed. "Something came up with an old case."

Bruno leaned against a chest of drawers and crossed his arms. "You getting sued again?"

"No, Dad," Sam said as he pulled open one of the drawers and began tossing clothes into the suitcase.

"Just asking, son."

"Yeah, well, I'm just telling you."

Neither father nor son said anything. Bruno stood and watched as Sam packed the small suitcase.

Bruno broke the silence and said, "You need a ride to the airport?"

"I'm not gonna fly," Sam said. "I'm going to drive."

Bruno shook his head slowly. "I know you hate to fly but that drive is a pain in the ass."

Sam walked to the nightstand next to his bed and removed his pistol from its drawer. "I'm taking this," he said.

"Just pack it in the bag, declare it, and check the bag. No big deal."

"I don't want to advertise it and take the chance it gets stolen."

"Do you really need it? Just leave it at home."

Sam tossed the holstered pistol onto the pile of

clothes in the carry-on. He turned to his father. "I told you. Something came up with an old case. I need it."

Bruno, a retired cop himself, knew what that meant. "You wanna tell me about it?"

Sam continued packing the bag. "It's a long story, Dad."

"Okay" Bruno said. He waited a beat and asked, "Are you leaving tonight?"

"No, I've got to meet Marley at her doctor's office tomorrow."

"Everything okay with her?"

"Yeah, it's just a routine checkup."

"Good. Well, since you're not leaving tonight, how about we go out to dinner, and you tell me about this case?"

Sam tossed a heavy sweatshirt onto the pile of clothes in the suitcase. April in Chicago could be like January in Alaska or Nevada in August. You just never knew. "I don't know, Dad. It's been a long day."

"I'm buying," Bruno said.

Sam turned to his father. "Where're we going?"

CHAPTER
FOUR

BRUNO PICKED a local place on Siesta Key not far from his villa and across the street from the beach. Sam sat across from his father at a table near the restaurant's bar. Over dinner and drinks, he laid out the story.

"I gotta tell you," Bruno said when Sam finished, "I agree with that lawyer guy. Let the police handle it."

"What are they going to do, Dad? Fill out a report that she threatened me? If they do that much, that will be the end of it as far as they're concerned. They're not any more likely to find her than I am. And even if they do, if they arrest her, she'll be out only hours later and I'm no better off for it."

Bruno pushed his empty plate aside and took a sip of beer. Sam watched him and knew his father was working it over in his mind. Bruno set down his mug and said, "Okay, you're right about that. But do you really need to go to Chicago?"

"That's where the answers are. If I can find her, I'll

know how serious her threat is. And, I think, maybe… maybe I do owe it to her to try and find her father's killer again."

"Sounds to me like you're feeling guilty you didn't do it back then."

"Yeah, I guess I do."

Bruno nodded. "You want some company? We can split the driving."

"I don't think that would be a good idea."

"Why not?"

"Truthfully? I don't want to worry about you. This Beth Patterson could be a nut case, and if she really means to come at me, I don't want you caught in the crossfire."

"Yeah, I don't want that either. But I also don't want you hurt."

"I can handle myself."

"I know, Sam." Bruno took another sip from his mug.

Sam read his father's face. He knew the expression well. He had seen it before. It was a look of concern set against disappointment. He and his father had never been very close and often clashed over the pettiest of things. Always butting heads with neither father nor son giving an inch. But, whenever Sam needed him - most recently by taking him in when his life was a mess - his father was there for him.

"Dad, it's not that I don't want the company, and a second driver would be a big help, but I think it would be best for me to go it alone."

"You don't have to explain, son," Bruno said. "I get it."

Sam exhaled heavily. He looked at his father. Bruno was staring down into his beer, his shoulders slumped. "If you came with me," Sam said, "where would you stay? In Chicago, I mean."

Bruno looked up. "I figured we'd share a hotel room," he said.

"Different hotels would be safer."

"How about same hotel, separate rooms?"

"Not adjacent. Maybe even different floors."

"Deal," Bruno said.

Bruno spent the rest of the evening packing and loading his car. Sam agreed his father's Cadillac was the more reliable vehicle and didn't protest when his father offered it up. Sam passed the evening in the living room staring at the television. But he wasn't paying attention to it. His thoughts were occupied by Beth Patterson and Dave Hermann.

In the morning, Sam woke early and headed to the beach for a run. It was his daily routine for the last several months. After logging his three miles on the hard packed sand near the waterline, he trudged through the soft sugar-white sand and through a public access to Midnight Pass Road, the main drag on Siesta Key, and made the walk to his father's villa.

Bruno Laska was in the kitchen pouring himself a cup of coffee when Sam walked in.

"You take your shoes off?" Bruno said. "I don't want sand tracked all over my floors."

"Yeah, Dad. I left them outside."

Bruno put the carafe back on the machine's hot plate. "You want a cup? It's fresh."

"No thanks," Sam said pulling off his tank top. "I've gotta get in the shower. Maybe I'll take a cup to go on my way out."

"Where are you going? We're leaving today."

"I told you yesterday. I've gotta meet Marley at her doctor's office. Regular monthly check-up. Finish packing the car and we'll leave when I get back."

"Yeah, sorry. I forgot," Bruno said. He squeezed past Sam in the narrow galley kitchen and headed to the living room. "So, how's everything going with her?" he said.

Sam followed his father into the room. "Her blood pressure was running high last time. We'll see how it is today. Other than that, everything's fine I guess."

Bruno plopped down on the sofa. "I meant how are things with you and Marley?"

The last few years flashed through Sam's mind. It was nearly three years ago that he first met Marley Jones. She was working as a morgue assistant at the Sarasota County Medical Examiner's office and Sam was looking into a suspicious death as a favor to a friend. They began dating. One thing led to another, and he moved in with her a few months later. More things led to even more things and one day, a little over eight months ago, she told him she was pregnant. She left the ME's office and opened a restaurant. They began talking about marriage. Life was good and getting better. Then the worst happened. An old case came back to haunt him.

In an act of revenge against Sam, Marley was taken. Kidnapped by a former cop Laska helped put in jail. Marley escaped but Sam, instead of staying with Marley when she needed him most, left her in a pointless effort to settle the score. Blinded by rage and vengeance he ignored Marley's needs. He forgot what was most important and he lost her trust.

It all fell apart after that. Marley asked Sam to move out and it was weeks before she would even talk to him again.

"Well?" his father said.

"The same, I guess."

"Doesn't she want to get back together?"

"I don't know. We haven't talked about it."

"Why not?"

"Dad, I don't have time for this again. I can't be late."

Bruno pointed a finger at his son. "You better talk to her about it, Sam. I'm gonna have a grandchild and I wanna know if I'm ever gonna meet him or her."

"You will. Don't worry about that. Marley isn't the type to just freeze us out."

"Are you sure?"

"Yeah, Dad. I promise. One way or another we're gonna be a part of my child's life." Sam turned and headed for the bathroom. His father called after him. "What do you mean by that? One way or another?"

Twenty minutes later Laska was in his car heading towards Siesta Key's north bridge to the mainland. His cell phone began buzzing, rattling around in the console's cupholder. He checked the display and pulled over before answering the call.

"Marley," he said. "What's up?"

"Sam, are you at the doctor's office yet?"

"No, but I'm on my way. I'm almost to the north bridge."

"You're not talking and driving, are you?"

"No, I pulled over."

"Okay, good. Can you come and pick me up? I don't think I can drive today."

"Are you okay? Is something wrong?"

"No, I'm fine, I think. I'm just feeling worn out. And maybe a little dizzy."

"Dizzy? How dizzy? Should I call an ambulance?"

"An ambulance? No, of course not. I'm just a little woozy. I'll be fine. I just don't think I should drive."

"You're sure you're okay?"

"Yes, I'm sure. Now, please just come get me."

"Okay, I'll be there as soon as I can."

"Sam, don't hang up yet."

"What?"

"Don't go to the condo. I moved."

"What? You moved? When? Where?"

"A few weeks ago. I bought a townhouse. The address is—"

"I can't believe this. You actually moved and didn't...when were you going to tell me?"

"I just did. Can we talk about this when you get here, or should I call an Uber?"

"Okay, okay. Don't call a ride. What's your new address?"

Marley's place was the end unit in a block-long row of newly built townhouses on Cocoanut Avenue just off Third Street in the Rosemary District of Sarasota. The cookie-cutter town homes, cream colored stucco with red clay barrel tile roofs, were made up of two rows of homes. The two rows faced each other and were separated by a paved private road which served both as access and private parking for the residents.

Laska pulled in front of Marley's unit, double checked the address, and cut the engine of his aging Infiniti. Before he could step from the car the front door of the townhouse opened and a very pregnant Marley Jones stepped onto the poured concrete porch. She gripped the faux-wrought iron railing to steady herself and locked the door behind her.

Laska hurried over and bolted up the six or so steps to the porch. "Hey, let me help," he said as he took her arm. He hung onto her as she slowly made her way down the stairs and to his car. He held the passenger door open as she slowly and carefully backed into the seat with more than just a few moans and grunts. She looked up at him after settling back into the seat.

"Thank you, Sam," she said. Sam saw her eyes brighten a little and as she gave him a soft smile. "Hey," she said, "you look good. Thinner. Healthier."

"Thanks," he said as he carefully closed her door. He made his way around the car and settled behind the steering wheel. "I've been watching what I eat. Running on the beach too." He started the car's engine. "Now," he said looking around, "how do we get out of here?"

"You have to make a U-turn and go out the same way you came in. Did you give up bacon?"

He laughed as he turned the car around. "No, but I cut back."

"Good. I'm glad you're taking care of yourself."

"I am. Now, how about you? What's all this 'feeling woozy' stuff about? How long has this been going on? Did you talk to your doctor about it yet?"

Laska waited for Marley's answer as he pulled onto the street and began the drive to her doctor's office.

"Yes," she said, "I called him last week."

"What did he say? Is it normal? Is there something wrong with you or the baby?"

"He didn't seem overly concerned but he told me to take it easy until I see him today."

Sam glanced at her, looking for a sign.

"How do you feel now?" he said.

Marley exhaled and shifted in the seat to get more comfortable.

"Like I said, a little woozy but otherwise okay, I guess."

"What do you mean by 'woozy'? Tired, dizzy, feverish? What?" He glanced over to her again. He spotted a tiny trickle of blood on her upper lip. He yanked hard on the steering wheel and pulled to the curb.

Marley braced herself against the dashboard with a hand as the car jerked to a stop.

"What are you doing?" she said.

"You're bleeding. Your nose," he said as he geared into Park.

Marley dabbed at her nose with a finger. Examining the finger, she said, "It's just a bloody nose. Do you have any tissues?"

"I think there's a few napkins in the glove box."

Marley popped it open and sifted through several CDs, owner's manuals, assorted receipts, and scraps of paper, piling them on her lap until she found a few loose fast-food paper napkins. Sam unlatched his seatbelt and opened his door.

"Where are you going?" Marley said as she wiped the blood from her nose and lips.

Sam, standing outside his door, stooped to answer her.

"I'm coming around to your side."

"What for? Get back in the car. We don't have time for this. I don't want to be late."

"But—"

"Please get in the car. I'm okay. It's only a bloody nose. I've been getting them lately."

Sam climbed back into the car. He sat twisted in his seat towards Marley keeping his full attention on her. Marley wiped her nose and lip again. She took a clean napkin, wiped again, and checked the napkin. She looked over to Sam.

"See," she said, "all gone. Now, please can we get going? We can't be late."

Sam hesitated then said, "Okay, as long as you're sure."

He shifted into Drive and carefully pulled back into traffic.

"I was worried," he said.

"I know," Marley said, "thank you. But really, I'm fine."

Sam didn't believe her. If she was fine, why did she have him pick her up? But he knew this was not the time for an argument. If her blood pressure was the problem, it wouldn't be smart to agitate her.

Marley began stuffing the mess on her lap back into the glovebox. She stopped when she got to the compact discs. She shuffled through them one at a time, reading their labels.

"You've been listening to music?" she said.

Sam glanced over and then back to the road. "Yeah, I've been trying to educate myself."

"Good for you." She looked down to the disc in her hand. "Donny Hathaway. Very good."

She checked the next disc.

"Marvin Gaye. Excellent. Do you like him?"

"Yeah, I do. He's great."

"Next, Amy Winehouse. Logical progression from Donny Hathaway. And finally," she began laughing. "Katy Perry? What, are you a thirteen-year-old girl?"

"I like her voice," Sam said.

"Yeah, I'm sure that's it."

Sam smiled and glanced over to Marley. "I miss this," he said.

"What?"

"Us," he said. "Together."

"I know," was all Marley said.

CHAPTER
FIVE

MARLEY'S DOCTOR didn't seem very concerned with her fatigue or bloody noses. And only mildly concerned with her blood pressure. She told Marley to stay off her feet, bed rest was better, and stay away from work until the baby came. Her due date was about two weeks away.

On the way back to Marley's new townhouse, Sam asked if she was going to be okay.

"Sure," she said. "You heard the doctor. I'll take it easy, stay off my feet, and away from the restaurant. I'll be fine." She looked over at him. "Can I count on you if I need something? I mean, groceries and stuff."

"I was going to tell you. I'm leaving for Chicago today. I'll be gone a few days."

Sam waited but Marley said nothing.

"Marley, it's only for a couple of days," he said.

Marley turned away and stared out her window.

"Marley?" Sam said.

Without turning her head, she answered. "This is about that woman who threatened you?"

"Yes. Like I said—"

"I'll be fine. I'll call Aunt Vicky if I need anything."

"Marley?" Sam said. "Please look at me."

She didn't move. She only said, "Just take me home, Sam."

"What did you do after that?" Bruno asked his son.

Sam sat behind the wheel of his father's Caddy. He exhaled heavily. Sam took the first leg of the drive. It was a few hours into the trip, they were just south of Gainesville on I-75, when Bruno asked about the visit to Marley's doctor. Sam surprised himself by opening up to his father, something he rarely did.

"I drove her home, helped her into her place, got her settled into her bed, made her some tea, and left."

"Did she say anything else?"

"Not much."

"Sam, it's none of my business, but I know you love that girl. You gotta make things right."

"You're right," Sam said. "It's none of your business."

Bruno ignored his son. "Maybe we should turn around. This old case can't be more important than Marley."

"It's not. But I have to take the threat seriously."

Sam sensed his father was about to say something. He didn't give him a chance and changed the subject.

"I want to drive straight through, Dad. Only stops for gas and drive-through food. You should get some rest. Take a nap or something."

Sam kept them to his driving schedule. Switching drivers every few hours, they made it to Louisville, Kentucky a little after one in the morning. Sam crossed the Abraham Lincoln bridge spanning the Ohio river into Indiana and pulled into the first gas station he found. After filling the tank, he woke his father who was snoozing in the back seat.

Giving Bruno's shoulder a shake, Sam said, "Okay, Dad. Nap time is over. Your turn to drive."

Bruno straightened up, blinked a few times, and looked around. He said, "Where are we?"

"Indiana, Dad. We just crossed in."

"Damn, I hate driving through Indiana," Bruno said.

"Me too. Two lanes filled with trucks and potholes all the way to Chicago. Come on, let's get back on the road."

Bruno stepped out of the car and stretched. He looked over to the station's store. "They got coffee in there?"

"Yeah, Get behind the wheel and I'll bring you a cup."

The next five hours passed quickly for Sam. He fell asleep in the seat next to his father and came to when Bruno woke him with an off-key rendition of *Sweet Home Chicago*.

"Please don't do that," Sam said.

"I've got the voice of an angel, kid," Bruno said.

"It sounds like gravel scrapping across a blackboard."

Sam looked up and out through the windshield at the approaching Chicago Skyway bridge and the sign that read 'Welcome to Chicago'.

"You got any idea where we should stay?" Bruno said.

"Out near the airport, I think. There's a lot of choices for us. And I can rent a car at O'Hare."

Bruno glanced over to his son. "Why rent a car? You can just use the Cadillac."

"You're gonna need your car, Dad. I don't want you stuck at the hotel."

"Suit yourself."

Sam, using his phone, found a hotel midway between the airport and their old neighborhood on the northwest side of the city. After checking in, two separate rooms like Sam insisted, Bruno dropped him at the airport to rent a car. While Sam waited in line, he dialed Jack Hoke's office.

As his call was answered, Sam heard Joyce's voice. "The law offices of Hoke, Dunn, and Associates. Joyce Andrews speaking. How can I help you?"

"Joyce? It's Sam."

"Hey, where the hell did you go the other day?"

"Yeah, sorry about that."

"You didn't even say goodbye."

"I know. I had to work some things out. I kind of get lost in my head sometimes."

"No big deal, I guess. You coming in today? Did you find out anything else?"

"I haven't found anything yet and I'm not coming in. I'm in Chicago."

"No shit?"

"Yeah, I just got here a couple hours ago. I figured everything I need to know is here."

"Makes sense, I guess."

"Did you have any luck with Fenwick?"

"No, they wouldn't give me any information over the phone. I even gave them a line. I told them Beth was set to inherit a large sum and we needed to find her. They said to send them a notarized letter by certified mail or show up in person."

"Nice try. Too bad it didn't work out. But if I get what I'm looking for here we won't need them. I'm going to visit an old friend. He should be able to get me the file. If he does, I'll call with Beth's info and you can run her. Okay?"

"Sounds like a plan."

The line in front of Sam thinned out and the rent-a-car clerk waved him over.

"Listen," Sam said into his phone, "I gotta go. I'll call when I learn more."

"Good luck," Joyce said.

Sam slipped the phone into his pocket and stepped up to the counter.

• • •

Forty minutes later, Sam was steering his rented Toyota eastbound on I-90 towards downtown Chicago. The morning rush hour was over, but traffic was still bumper-to-bumper. That was the thing with the highways in the city, traffic was unpredictable. It hadn't changed a bit since he moved to Florida. No matter the time of day, weekday or weekend, the expressways could be packed or virtually empty for no apparent reason.

Content to creep along at fifteen miles an hour, he settled in. It was actually the first chance he had since arriving in the city to catch his breath. He shaded his eyes from the late morning sun hanging over the slowly nearing skyline at the heart of the city. He let his mind wander and his thoughts fell to his hometown.

Chicago didn't have the glitz of L.A. or the global presence of New York. It was a midwestern blue collar city. Burned to the ground and rebuilt bigger and better. It was scrappy and proud, and resentful of its status as the 'Second City'. Nelson Algren said loving Chicago was like loving a woman with a broken nose. Laska believed he meant that you might find a more beautiful city but despite all its faults, maybe because of its faults, you couldn't help but love Chicago. As with any real love, you looked past the flaws, forgave them, accepted them, and maybe even knew that the imperfections made the rest all the more beautiful.

Sam missed his hometown and was glad to be back, if only for a little while.

For no known reason, as he reached the exits leading

downtown, the traffic eased. He soon passed 31st Street and moved to the right lane. He exited the highway at 35th Street in the shadow of Guaranteed Rate Field, the ballpark the White Sox called home. Turning eastbound, he saw his destination ahead, the headquarters building of the Chicago Police Department.

CHAPTER
SIX

SAM WALKED into the building and down the hall that held the Honored Star Case, a wall covered by a much too long glass display case containing the stars worn by the police officers killed in the line of duty since the beginning of the CPD. He slowed his pace and gazed at the exhibit as he walked. He couldn't help but feel a deep sense of remorse and respect for the police officers represented by each star. Some of whom he knew personally.

He passed the end of the display, and the star belonging to Officer Casper Lauer, the first Chicago police officer killed in the line of duty and made his way to a circular reception desk set in the middle of the large concourse. The desk was manned by a single uniformed police officer and displayed a sign that demanded all non-police visitors to the building check in.

That was him now, he thought. He was no longer one of 'us'. He was now one of 'them'.

Sam handed his retired CPD identification card to the uniform and asked to see the Chief of Detectives.

"Do you have an appointment?" the man asked as he checked Laska's ID with a listing he pulled up on his computer terminal.

"No," Sam said. He was about to explain but the officer didn't give hm a chance.

"I'm sure the Chief is pretty busy. Without an appointment, I doubt he'll have time to see you. Can I ask what this is about?"

"Just a social visit. He was my partner way back when."

The officer said, "Why didn't you say that from the jump?" and grabbed a telephone receiver. He punched a series of numbers in and told whoever it was on the other end he was sending up a visitor.

The officer handed Sam his ID card and a visitor pass attached to a long lanyard. "The Chief's aide will let you know if he's got a few minutes for you. Take the elevator to the Fourth floor."

"Thanks," Sam said, "I know the way."

He hung the visitor's pass around his neck and, minutes later, was stepping off the elevator on the fourth floor. He made his way down the hall and to the Chief's office. He stood in the hallway in front of the door. He knew what was on the other side of the door, an anteroom manned by the chief's assistant, but gave a courtesy rap on the door anyway. Without waiting for an answer, he opened the door and walked in.

A uniformed sergeant sat at a desk trying to look busy. He was expecting a visitor but didn't know who that visitor would be. For all he knew it could be a business leader, alderman, or some other politician. As Laska entered, he looked up and said, "Can I help you?"

The sergeant was familiar to Sam, but he couldn't place him. And from the look on the sergeant's face, Sam could tell he felt the same about Laska.

"Yeah, Sarge. My name is Sam Laska. Retired a few years now. The chief was my partner back in Area Four and I was wondering if he had time to see me."

The sergeant stood. "I thought you looked familiar. I was in Area Four Burglary. You left the Area a few months after I got there."

"I thought I knew you too. Good to see you again." Laska approached and shook the sergeant's hand.

Laska looked at the brass nameplate on the sergeant's shirt. It read 'Williams'. It clicked for him then. "Roy Williams, right?"

"Yeah," Sergeant Williams said. "This is just a social visit, then?"

"Pretty much," Sam lied.

"Great. Let me buzz the chief and see if he's busy." Williams sat and grabbed his desk phone's receiver. He looked up at Laska and said, "You're in luck. I don't think he's got much going on for the next few hours." He punched a single button.

After a short conversation on the phone, Sergeant Williams pointed to the door to his right. "Go on in," he said.

Sam thanked Williams with a nod and walked through the door and into Chief of Detectives Gene Kroll's office.

Chief Gene Kroll was behind his desk and already standing when Sam walked in.

"Sam," he said with a smile on his face. He walked around his desk to Laska and extended his hand. "How are you? It's been a while."

Sam took his hand and said, "Good to see you, Gene. Yeah, a few years, huh?"

Kroll motioned Laska to a chair with a sweep of his hand and took his own seat behind the desk.

Laska bounced himself on the well-padded chair as he sat. "Pretty nice," he said. "Whose dining room did you steal this from?"

Kroll extended his arms, palms up, and looked around the large office. "Rank has its privileges. They tossed out all the old furniture and other crap when they built this place and moved out of the old HQ on State Street."

Laska looked around and wondered how many cherry trees gave their lives for the furniture and bookcases in the office.

"You look good, Sam," Kroll said.

"Thanks. You too. But you've gone grey."

"And wide." Kroll patted his stomach. "Tell me,

you're still in Florida, right?" Kroll leaned back in his chair and crossed his legs.

"Yep."

"And you're back here on vacation? I'm asking because I remember your last trip to Chicago didn't go well." Kroll's tone was casual but there was tension underneath it.

Kroll was referring to a shootout in front of the Peninsula hotel which resulted in the tragic death of a deputy U.S. Marshall and the serious wounding of another. During the incident, Marley was kidnapped and only narrowly escaped. That was the beginning of the end to Sam's relationship with her.

"Nothing like that, Gene."

"Then this is just a social visit. I'm glad."

"I didn't say that."

Kroll rolled his chair closer to the desk and leaned in. "What *are* you saying, Sam?"

"I need a favor."

"What kind of favor?"

"An old case is haunting me. A murder I couldn't close."

"It happens to us all. How long ago did it happen?"

"Sixteen years, in 2006."

"After I got promoted to sergeant and left the unit. Who did you work it with?"

"Dave Hermann."

Kroll arched his eyebrows at the mention of Hermann's name. "Did you hear about Dave?" Kroll asked.

"Yes."

"Horrible accident."

"What did you hear?" Sam asked.

"Same as everybody, I guess. Killed in a hunting accident near his new home. His body had been there awhile before he was found. Someone said the animals got to it. A real bad scene."

"Did they ever find who shot him?"

"No, I don't think so."

Sam watched Kroll carefully. He saw nothing to indicate Kroll believed Dave Hermann's death was anything but an accident.

"Anyway," Kroll continued. "Sixteen years ago, that's a long time. Are you sure it hasn't been cleared since then?"

"I'm positive. I called in another favor and checked."

"Are you asking me to have it looked at again? I certainly can do that. I can get Cold Case to evaluate it today."

"That would be great, but that's not what I'm asking."

Kroll crossed his arms on his desk and leaned in. "What exactly do you want, Sam?"

"I'd like to take a look at the file."

Kroll kept his eyes on Sam and didn't move. Laska could see the wheels turning in his head. After what seemed like minutes, he said, "You don't work here, Sam. You're a civilian now. Why would I do that?"

"It's personal, Gene."

Kroll sat back and crossed his arms across his chest. His demeanor and posture changed. Sam knew he was no longer talking to good old Gene. He was now talking to Chief of Detectives Kroll.

"Let me ask you this," Kroll said, "the favor you called in earlier, when you learned the case was still open. Why didn't that person give you a look at the file?"

"He couldn't get into it. It's locked, flagged 'Restricted Access'. Only a Deputy Chief or higher can open it."

"What about the working file they store in the Area?"

"Misfiled or missing."

Kroll's eyes widened momentarily but he caught himself quickly. He sat forward and turned to the keyboard and monitor on his desk.

"Do you have the RD number?"

CHAPTER
SEVEN

KROLL TYPED in the RD number and stared at the monitor's screen. He began typing again entering his private access ID. He propped his elbows on the desk, folded his arms, and hunched closer to the screen. The monitor was angled such that Sam couldn't see the display. He kept his eyes on Kroll's face hoping to get some clue as to what his old partner was reading.

Kroll frowned, his eyebrows forming a deep vee.

"What?" Sam said.

Kroll glanced at Laska then back again to the screen. He said nothing.

"Come on, Gene," Sam said.

Kroll swiveled his chair to face Laska. "Jerry Robinson put the restricted access flag on this."

"I don't know the name," Sam said. "He's a deputy chief?"

"He was. He retired some years back. Took a job in the private sector."

"How many years back?"

"I don't remember. I'd have to look it up. But I think I remember there were some rumors."

"What kind of rumors?"

"Personal problems of some kind. But like I said, those were just rumors. You know how coppers love to gossip."

"Yeah, I remember. Do you have any idea why he locked the file?"

"Not yet. I want to read more. Nonetheless, it's pretty strange."

"Why?"

"He was one of the deputy chiefs in the Patrol Division."

"What business would a deputy chief of Patrol have flagging a Detective Division homicide file?"

"Good question," Kroll said. He turned back to the monitor and said, "Make a fresh pot of coffee, Sam." He pointed to the machine on a credenza in the back of his office. "It's gonna be a while. I want to finish reading this file."

Sam drank two cups by the time Kroll had finished reading. Kroll's coffee sat cold in his cup.

"I don't see anything that warrants restricted access," Kroll said turning away from the screen. "Usually that tag is only applied to sensitive investigations. Something with political implications or involving some celebrity or scandal. Something we don't want just anyone in the department pulling up and reading."

"And maybe selling to the media," Laska said.

Kroll frowned. "Yep, we've been burned too many times in the past. Moving to digital record keeping took care of that."

"But, in addition to restricting who gets to see the report, you can also tell who has seen it, right?"

"Not only that, but we can also tell who has printed it out."

"So, are you going to let me have a look at it?"

Kroll folded his arms on his desk again. "Are you going to tell me why you have such a keen interest in this all of a sudden?"

"I told you, it's been haunting me."

"Don't bullshit me, Sam. What's the story?"

Sam drew his head back and stared at the ceiling. He needed a few seconds to make sure he got the words just right without giving away too much.

He looked at Kroll. "The victim's daughter came to me. She asked me to look into it again."

"Sam," Kroll said.

Laska didn't give him a chance to continue. "She's looking for closure, Gene. I want to help her find it."

"Closure is a lie, Sam. You know that. The world is full of people who can't get over things. There is no closure and there is no peace. All we can offer them is some meager measure of revenge through the knowledge that the bad guy is going to suffer the rest of his life behind bars."

"Maybe that's enough." Laska moved to the edge of his seat, hunched forward, and rested his elbows on his knees. "I remember something you once said. We had only been working together a short time. We had a reluctant witness in the interview room, and we were trying to convince him to cooperate. At one point, you told him helping us was the right thing to do because no one should get away with murder. You used those exact words. No one should get away with murder."

"I remember."

"And we all believe it, Gene. Deep inside, every cop does. We don't often say it out loud, but we believe it. It is our mission."

"As I recall, it didn't convince the witness to cooperate."

"No, it didn't. But it doesn't matter. All that matters is that we keep trying. All that matters is the mission."

Kroll locked his eyes on Sam and began drumming a finger on the desktop.

"You have no standing, Sam."

"Screw 'standing'."

Kroll stopped drumming his finger.

Laska dropped his head for a moment. He looked up again and said, "I'm sorry. What I meant to say is that I promise not to step on any toes. I won't act on anything. I'll just turn over whatever I find."

The telephone on Chief Kroll's desk buzzed. He pushed a button on the telephone and, without using the receiver, spoke. "What is it, Roy?"

The voice of Sgt. Williams came on. "Don't forget your appointment with Commander Cornish in Area Two, Chief."

Kroll checked his watch. "How much time do I have?"

"Forty-five minutes, boss."

"Alright, thanks Roy. Why don't you go down and get the car and I'll meet you in front?"

Kroll pushed another button on the phone and looked at Laska. Sam tried to give him his best puppy dog face.

Kroll shook his head and exhaled heavily. He picked up a pen and scribbled a telephone number on a yellow note pad. He pushed the pad and pen across his desk to Laska.

"That's my personal cell phone. Take it and then write down your number and where you're staying."

Laska took it as a good sign. He grabbed the pad and pen and quickly complied.

Kroll took back the note pad and pen and turned to the computer's keyboard. He punched a series of keys. The large printer next to his desk hummed to life.

Kroll stood. "The entire file is printing, along with a list of people who have accessed and printed the file. I don't know what good it's going to do though. From what I read, you and Hermann covered every base. There just wasn't any more to go on. And now, sixteen years later, I don't see how that's going to change." Kroll checked his watch again. "You can stay here in my office and read the entire file, but I can't let you take it out of here. If something really is sideways about this, I might have to prove I kept the printed copy."

"I understand. Thanks, Gene."

"I'm only doing this because we were partners once. Don't make me regret it." Kroll nodded to a copy machine next to the printer. "And don't even think about burning a copy." He pressed a toggle switch on the copier and it sprang to life. "This copier needs an access code to work. And it would be pretty careless of me if I slipped and told you I used my old detective star number as the code."

Kroll walked around his desk and stopped at the door. "You can show yourself out, Sam. The doors will lock behind you. And don't forget, you take no action. You hand over anything you turn up."

"Thanks, Gene," Laska said.

Kroll nodded. "And don't lose my phone number."

CHAPTER
EIGHT

IT TOOK Sam a full five minutes and several failed entries before he remembered his old partner's star number correctly. Back when they worked together, he must have typed it a thousand times on the reports they submitted together. But that was a long time ago. Without reading any, he copied all the reports in the file. There would be time for reading later. He left the originals on Kroll's desk and headed back to his rental car.

As he settled behind the wheel of the Toyota, his phone dinged. He dug it out of his pocket and checked the screen. It was a text message from a blocked number. The message read:

Glad to see you took me seriously. Any progress?

Laska quickly thumbed in his response:

Who is this?

And then the reply:

You know who I am.

Sam did know, and he wasn't happy about it. He thumbed a question:

How did you get my number? How do you know where I am?

He waited for a response but received none. He tossed his phone on the seat next to him and started the car. He didn't put it in gear. He had more questions for Beth Patterson. He picked up his phone and began texting.

Why did you threaten me? I might have helped you without the threat.

The response came quickly:

It worked. Didn't it?

She had him there. He typed one more question:

What happened to Dave Hermann?

Laska waited a full minute before the response came:

I'm sorry about Dave. I warned him.

Sam felt his jaw tighten and a burning rising up from his chest to his neck and face. He threw his phone onto the floor, put the car into gear and sped out of the parking lot.

Despite his suspicions, he had hoped Dave Hermann's death was just a coincidence, that it was just what everyone else believed it was. Just an accident. Now, he didn't suspect. He was sure that it wasn't. Beth Patterson texts confirmed what Sam did not know, that she knew Dave Hermann. She had gone to him before she approached Sam in Sarasota. And now, Sam was beginning to believe that she killed Dave Hermann because he couldn't or wouldn't do what she wanted. And that changed everything.

The mission had been to help Beth Patterson and solve her father's murder. Sam thought her threats were just a manifestation of her frustrations. She had been a girl who suffered a horrible loss at a young age and had been unable to cope with that loss. Who could blame her? She had carried that burden all these years and finally decided to do something about it. Only, Sam thought, she did it the wrong way. Instead of asking for help she lashed out and demanded it, using a seemingly empty threat against the only person she knew to blame.

But Laska was beginning to think he had been wrong. The threat was not empty. Beth Patterson wasn't looking for closure. She was looking for revenge. And as long as she couldn't exact that revenge on the true killer, she would get it from those who she believed failed her.

As he steered his rented Toyota westbound along the expressway through the city, he felt his rage morphing into somber determination. The mission had changed. His mission now was to find the truth about Dave's death and if that truth was that Beth Patterson murdered Dave Hermann, so be it.

Moving further from the center of the city, he saw the sun was getting low in the sky. He checked the clock on the dashboard. It was nearly five in the afternoon and his stomach reminded him he hadn't eaten all day. He exited the expressway near his hotel and pulled into the lot of a clean looking diner. Still sitting in the car, he retrieved his phone from the passenger's side floor and dialed his father. He surprised himself by thinking he wouldn't mind some company.

———

Marley's Aunt Vickey carried a tray holding her dinner up the stairs to the bedroom. Marley was lying on the bed propped up on a stack of pillows reading a book.

"What you reading, darling?" Vicky said as she walked into the room.

Marley looked up from her book. Her aunt's Jamaican accent always made her smile. Her aunt's family including her brother, Marley's father, left the island over fifty years ago but the accent stuck despite all those years in the States.

"Just some trashy romance novel," Marley said. She folded over a corner of the page she was on and closed the book. She looked at the tray in her aunt's hands. "Thanks for making dinner."

"My pleasure, child. We havin' lasagna tonight."

"You made Italian food?"

"Frozen, Marley. The microwave did the cookin'."

Vickey set the tray on the bed next to Marley and picked up the book. She scanned it front and back, made a face, and tossed it back on the bed.

"Trash is right. That ain't romance. That's a dirty book for lonely housewives."

Marley, with a mouthful of lasagna, just shrugged.

Vickey pulled a chair over to the side of the bed and sat. Marley looked over to Vickey. "Aren't you eating?" she asked.

"Later, I want to talk."

"What about?"

"You and Sam."

"Aunt Vickey—"

"Hush. You gonna hear what I have to say." Vickey skooched her chair closer to the bed. She looked at her niece. "When you gonna stop torturing that man? He loves you and you love him. That's all that's important."

Marley set her fork down and folded her hand across her belly. "I don't know if I can forgive him for what he did."

"You love him, right?"

"Yes, I do."

"Then you forgive him. What he did, he did for you. He did it to protect you. He did it because he loves you more than his own life."

"He could have been killed."

"So, you wanted him to stay to protect him and you're angry because he did the same for you? Do you hear yourself?"

Marley dropped her head back onto the pillow. She looked over at her aunt. "There's more to it than that. It's what he does, what he wants to do. His work."

"What about it?"

"I don't know if I can live every day not knowing if…something bad is going to happen to him."

Vickey nodded. She knew what Marley meant. Her husband, Nosmo, was a detective in Sarasota.

"How do you live with it?" Marley asked.

Vickey sat back and exhaled heavily. "You're right. It's not easy. I kiss your uncle good-bye every morning and again when he comes home and I try not to think of the in between."

"I don't know if I can do that."

"You can't ask him to give up doing what he does, Marley. What he does is who he is. It's what made him who he is and the man you fell in love with. Don't force him to be something he isn't."

Vickey stood and pushed the chair back to its place. "That's all I've got to say. Now, you think about what you really want. For yourself and for Sam." Vickey headed to the door. "I'll be back in a while to get the tray."

CHAPTER
NINE

SAM WALKED out of the diner after eating dinner alone. His father never answered his call. Sam figured he was either taking a nap or catching up with friends. He stood just outside the doorway and shivered in the cold April evening. It was after six and already dark. There was nothing left to do tonight but head to his hotel room.

He spent the next few hours lying on the bed and reading through the Walter Patterson homicide file. This was the first and most basic step in any cold case investigation. In any investigation, but particularly homicide investigations, the file was everything. Every known detail was recorded in the reports. Every thought of the investigators was preserved in their notes, evidence and its analysis was recorded, and the scene was preserved in photographs and video. Even every detail of the victim's body was documented in the autopsy report. The process of getting up to speed can be daunting and sometimes confusing to a detective picking up the case years after it happened. Laska's advantage was that he was the original investigator and only needed to refresh his memory.

On the second page of the first report – what was called the scene report – was the information Sam deemed most important to him now: the birthdate of Elizabeth Patterson and her address at the time of the murder. He circled these with the pen courteously provided by his hotel. He would call Joyce in the morning and see if she could work any magic with them.

But finding Beth Patterson wouldn't be enough. He had to prove she killed Dave Hermann, if she killed Dave Hermann. He knew her text message wouldn't fly in court as an admission. Plus, they would have to prove it was her on the other end of the messages. He needed to get more. And that meant he would need to work her father's murder until he did. He was obviously being watched by Beth Patterson and he needed her to think he was following her marching orders.

As he read through the reports, first once and then a second time while taking notes, the memory of the night Walter Patterson was killed came back to him. Small, nearly forgotten, details returned. The memory of his past actions, the timelines, and interviews became clearer.

But there was a problem with the copy of the file Kroll gave him. Since the year 2000, all Detective Division paper reports were discontinued and were replaced by digital reports, entered into a software program rather than typed on paper. But that was only for the formal reports. The handwritten notes, crime scene photos and videos, evidence and inventory reports, and other such paper records such as copies of subpoenas, phone records, and autopsy reports were all still hard copies. The department was only beginning to digitize these records when Sam retired. The file he held in his hand did not contain a digitized copy of those paper notes and reports. They were kept in the working file. In this case, the missing working file.

The digital reports the detectives submitted were always a thorough and comprehensive summary of the investigation. They were a 'just the facts, ma'am' summary of the scene details and actions taken by the detectives and police officers. They needed to be as they were the backbone of any future prosecution. They would be poured over by state's attorneys, defense attorneys, and judges. But they were, for lack of a better word, a simplified account of the facts. They didn't contain the thoughts, theories, and impressions of the detectives. Nor did they contain the forks in the road or dead ends that didn't pan out. Those were in the notes the detectives made during the course of the investigation.

Sam wanted the entire file: the scene photos, the autopsy report, evidence reports, and, most of all, his notes. He leaned back against the bed's headboard, closed his eyes, and thought about what he had read.

Walter Patterson was killed during a robbery gone

bad. A random victim caught in a tragically random event. The classic wrong place, wrong time. Patterson left work, walked to the Lake Street 'L' station, and boarded a train. The same train he took every day to go home to his wife and daughter. None of the witnesses could state when or where the offender had boarded the train but, as the train was moving, he approached random passengers and moved in close, displayed a handgun, and demanded cash. He confronted several passengers, taking cash from each, until he arrived at Walter Patterson. It is unclear, according to the witnesses, if Walter resisted the robbery. The assumption was that he did. The offender pointed the handgun at Patterson and fired twice at close range. Panic on the train car ensued with passengers rising from their seats and rushing to either end of the car away from the offender and Patterson who had collapsed onto the floor. As the train pulled into the Kedzie Avenue station and the doors opened, there was a rush to the doors. The offender escaped in the crowd of people.

The witnesses, there were only three who remained on the scene after the shooting, all stated they did not notice or pay any attention to Walter Patterson until shortly before his murder. They seemed to pay even less attention to the offender as only one could offer more than a cursory description.

Only three witnesses, Laska thought, *a horrible shame.* He imagined a typical 'L' train car and tried to count the seats in his head. There must have been at least fifty people in that car alone. Six-forty-something in the evening on a weeknight. The back end of rush hour. And only three people bothered to wait for the police. Fear will do that, he thought.

He picked up the pages with the names of the three witnesses. Ronald Burke, Mae Lin Chan, and Darryl Wilcox. He scanned their addresses and wondered if, sixteen years later, they were still there. Hell, he thought, they might not even be alive anymore.

He picked up his pen and circled their names and addresses. He'd ask Joyce to check them out as well.

He set the pen down and rubbed his eyes. He checked the clock on the nightstand. It read 11:52 pm. He gathered up the papers scattered over the bed, put them back in order, and set them on the desk across the room. He headed to the bathroom to shower. He was feeling pretty ripe since his last one was two days ago.

It was only after he climbed into bed that he realized how exhausted he really was. He hadn't had a decent night's rest since Florida. The naps on the drive to Chicago certainly didn't hack it. Yet, tired as he was, he felt energized. He was back in the game, working murders again instead of boring PI work. He didn't even care that he wasn't getting paid for any of it. It was never about the money. No one ever got rich solving murders. Payment came in another form.

He drifted off, wondering if he did the right thing by agreeing to early retirement instead of fighting the allegations against him.

CHAPTER
TEN

SAM WOKE to the sound of a telephone's ring. He sat up and swung his legs over the side of the bed. The room was dark, but he could see daylight peeking through the space between the curtains. He grabbed his phone off the nightstand. "Yeah?" he said.

"Rise and shine, son," his father said.

"Morning, Dad."

"Yeah, 'morning. How about we get some breakfast?"

Sam looked at the alarm clock next to the bed. "It's barely seven o'clock, Dad." *Why did old people get up so early?* he thought.

"Yeah, we're burning daylight. Come on. I'll meet you down in the lobby. I'm driving."

Sam exhaled heavily. He probably wouldn't be able to fall back asleep anyway. "Yeah, okay. Give me fifteen minutes."

• • •

Sam and his father ended up at the same diner where Sam ate the night before. The two men made small talk as they ate. Bruno told Sam how he spent the previous day and how he tried catching up with a few old friends only to learn most of them had passed away.

"I even stopped at a wake last night," Bruno said. "Billy Simpson. You remember him? He was at the old house a few times."

"No, I don't think I remember," Sam said as he munched on a piece of toast. "How did he die?"

"I don't know exactly, but he was a heavy smoker. He looked pretty bad lying there in the casket."

"Well, he was dead, Dad."

"Wise ass. I meant, even for being dead. If I had to guess, I'd say cancer."

"That's too bad. How'd you hear about the wake?"

"From Woz. I stopped at his tavern for lunch. I figured a bunch of the old crew might be there."

"Were they?"

"Nope, just old Woz behind the bar. And he looks like shit too."

"I'm sorry, Dad."

"Why? It was inevitable. They're old. I'm old." Bruno shook his head slowly and exhaled heavily.

Sam figured he'd better change the subject, but his father beat him to it.

"Anyway," Bruno said as he pushed his empty plate to the side, "how about you? Did you get anywhere on the thing with that girl?"

Sam took a sip of coffee. "Elizabeth Patterson," he

said. "Yeah, I did. I got a copy of her father's homicide file."

"How'd you do that? I thought it was locked or something like that."

"Yeah, it is. But an old partner of mine is now the Chief of Detectives. Gene Kroll. I paid him a visit and talked him into letting me have a copy."

"That's great. That'll make it easier for you. Did your old partner tell you why it was locked?"

"He didn't know, and I could tell he was surprised it was. He read the file and couldn't find anything that warranted the tag."

"Well, who the hell tagged it?"

"That he did know. He said some deputy chief in the patrol division did it. Jerry Robinson."

"Jerry Robinson? Skinny black guy?"

"I don't know. I don't know the guy or what he looks like. I don't know anything about him. He must have come up after I left the job."

"No, if he's the same Jerry Robinson I know he's probably a little older than you. He was a new sergeant when I was in the 17th District. A real asshole. Very ambitious. He'd step over any copper to get ahead. He was promoted to Commander by the time I retired."

Sam pulled out his phone and began tapping on the screen. His father leaned over the table to get a look. "What are you doing?" he asked.

"I'm doing an internet image search for Jerry Robinson. Maybe I can find a picture," Sam said. "Kroll told me he left the job a while ago, but the internet never forgets."

Bruno dragged his chair around and sat next to Sam, his eyes locked on the tiny screen in his son's hand as Sam scrolled through pages of pictures on the internet.

"Stop," Bruno said hitching himself closer, "back up. I think I saw him."

Sam slowly scrolled back. His father pointed to the screen. "There. There he is. That's Jerry Robinson."

Sam double tapped the small picture. It took him to a page featuring a larger picture and an article about Jerry Robinson.

"Yep," Bruno said, "I was right. That's him."

Sam scanned through the article as his father sat back and smiled.

The article was from the business section of the Chicago Tribune. Only a few sentences long, it announced Jerry Robinson's early retirement from the CPD to form his own company, Truncheon Security and Risk Assessment. The included photo was a head and shoulder shot of him in his CPD uniform, obviously taken from the police department's photo gallery of exempt bosses. He checked the date of the article, November 10th, 2008, more than two years after the murder of Walter Patterson.

"You're right, Dad," Sam said. "This has got to be him. Thanks, you gave me a direction to go in today."

Bruno moved his chair back across the table from his son and sat. "What are you gonna do, Sam?" he asked. "You gonna talk to him?"

"Yeah, of course. I want to know why he tagged the Patterson file." He did a quick search for Truncheon Security on his phone. "According to this website," he said, "their office is on Fulton just off Racine. I think I'll pay them a visit today."

"Are you going to call first? How do you even know he's in today?"

"I don't. But better tells and better reads come from face-to-face meetings. And I don't want him to know I'm coming. I want him unprepared. I want that chance to read him when I ask him why he flagged the file."

"How do you know he'll see you without an appointment?"

"Because he knows who I am, Dad. Or, at least, he should know my name. It's on every report in that file."

Bruno pushed his chair back and stood. "Alright then. Let's go. I'll drive."

Sam cocked his head and looked up at his father. "You want to come with me?"

"Yeah," Bruno said. "I've got nothing to do today. What do you say? It'll be fun."

Sam stood and shrugged his shoulders. "Okay, why not? But I'm not sure how much fun it's going to be."

"Good," Bruno said. "You get the check this time. And don't forget the tip."

Sam had his father stop at their hotel before taking the highway into the city. He wanted the Patterson file and the included list of people who accessed it, and when they did. He had scanned the list the night before and knew Jerry Robinson was on that list more than a few times. Now, he wanted an exact count, including the dates he did.

Jerry Robinson had accessed the file ten times and printed it twice. The first time was the day after Walter Patterson's murder and then once every week for the next four weeks. Laska knew from reviewing the time-line in the file that the four-week mark was pretty much the point where the case went cold. There were no more leads to follow up. There were conflicting descriptions from the witnesses and nearly no physical evidence of any worth. The case had hit a stone wall. Laska was transferred out of the unit shortly thereafter and it was obvious Dave Hermann did next to nothing on the investigation after Laska left. Not that there was anything else that could be done.

Robinson opened the file a few more times in the months that followed. The last time he pulled it up was November 6th, 2008, only days before he left the CPD and moved on to his own business, Truncheon Security.

There was only one more entry on the list. Dave Hermann tried to pull up the reports in late February, just about two months ago, but was denied. He never got, or apparently asked for, a deputy chief's permission.

The highway was virtually empty and Sam and his father sped along arriving less than twenty minutes later. The address Sam pulled from the internet was a long squat yellow brick building with a fenced and gated parking area adjacent to it. The few windows along the perimeter were protected with rusty steel grating, evidence of the once rough neighborhood. Now, however, the neighborhood had seen a resurgence. Undoubtably due to its proximity to downtown, easy highway access, and the new United Center a few blocks to the west.

There was plenty of street parking and Sam's father pulled to the curb in front of the only door.

"Wait here, Dad," Sam said. "I'll try not to be too long."

"You don't want me to go in with you?"

"No, it's better if I go alone." Sam jumped out of the car before his father could argue.

The entry was an imposing windowless steel door, its grey paint was scratched and scuffed. The name, Truncheon Security, was painted across the front at eye level in simple block letters. He tried the door handle and, as he expected, the door was locked. He looked around, above and to each side of the door. Two security cameras were mounted high and to the right and left and pointed at the door. To his right was an intercom. He pressed the push-button and waited.

"Can I help you?" came a voice over the intercom.

"I'm here to see Jerry Robinson," Sam said and waited.

After a more than a few seconds, the voice came back on. "You need to hold the button in to talk."

Sam looked up at one of the cameras and nodded.

He held in the button and repeated himself. "I'm here to see Jerry Robinson."

"Name?" said the voice.

Sam held in the button. "Sam Laska."

"One minute."

Over a minute passed. Sam turned and looked to his father in the car. Bruno was looking back at Sam. He held up his hand in a 'what's up?' gesture. Sam answered with a shrug.

The intercom crackled and the voice said, "You don't have an appointment. What's your business?"

Sam pressed the button and said, "Tell Mr. Robinson it's in reference to Walter Patterson."

Sam waited again.

The door buzzed. He pulled it open and walked inside.

CHAPTER
ELEVEN

THE ROOM WAS UNEXPECTED. Considering the look of the outside of the building, Sam was expecting a dim and dusty open warehouse-like space with high industrial ceilings and outfitted with fluorescent lights and ancient fixtures. Instead, the space had been partitioned into smaller spaces by clean white walls and lit by recessed fixtures in a dropped ceiling. Facing him as he entered was a long built-in desk running the length of the room. It was slightly higher than his waist and reminded him of the front desk you'd find in any police station in the country.

Security cameras were positioned in all four corners of the room and cardboard boxes were stacked to one side. Nail holes dotted the walls and framed photographs and large posters leaned against the back wall.

A linebacker sized man in uniform stood behind the desk watching Sam as he approached. He had a pistol strapped to his waist and a gold badge on his breast. The patches on the shoulders of his shirt read Truncheon Security,

As Sam bellied up to the desk the guard said, "You got ID?"

Sam removed his Florida driver's license and handed it to the man who ran it through a small card reader like you'd find in a doctor's office. He handed the license back to Laska. "Mr. Robinson is on the phone, and he asked that you wait here." He pointed to a grouping of contemporary-style chairs and sofa across the room. "You can take a seat over there."

Sam nodded and picked a chair with a view of the entire room. As he settled in the guard answered a buzz on his phone. With his ear still glued to the receiver, he looked over to Sam. "Mr. Robinson will see you now." He hung up the phone and waved Sam back to the desk. He had Sam clip a visitor ID to his shirt and escorted him through a door and down a hall lined with steel doors. They turned at an intersecting hall and then another. The guard finally pointed to an unmarked door and said, "In there. Knock first." He left Sam standing there alone.

Sam watched the guard leave, turned back to the door, and rapped twice.

"Enter," a voice said from the other side.

Sam walked through the door into a modestly proportioned room. Jerry Robinson was standing behind a large oak desk. Aside from three chairs, one behind and two in front of the desk, the room was bereft of furniture. More cardboard boxes were stacked to the side and the putty-colored walls were bare.

Robinson walked around his desk and extended his hand. "Mr. Laska," Robinson said, "how can I help you?"

Sam took his hand and said, "Thanks for seeing me." He looked around the room again. There were no security cameras here. "Moving out?" he said.

Robinson smiled, his perfect teeth bright against his dark skin. "Relocating. Our new facility is just about ready for us."

"New facility?"

"Yes," Robinson said as he walked back around his desk. He motioned Sam to a chair with his hand as he said, "We're moving out to DuPage County. We've been fortunate to see great growth and we built a new campus closer to our clients."

"A campus? More than one building?"

"Yes," he said as he sat. "Aside from the required office space, we've built a training facility which includes classrooms and a dormitory."

"You must be doing very well," Sam said.

"As I said, we've been very fortunate." He leaned forward and crossed his arms on the desktop. "But, enough of that. You mentioned Walter Patterson to my people. That got my attention."

"I thought it might. I'm sure you recognize my name as the lead detective assigned to his murder."

"I didn't. At least not until I did a little research. But

you're not any longer, are you? A detective, or a police officer I mean."

"No, I've been retired for a few years."

"You retired under duress, correct?" Robinson sat back. A corner of his mouth curled up slightly.

"Yes, I was given that option and I took it."

"So, what interest could you still have in the investigation?"

"It's never been solved. I've been asked to look into it again."

"By whom?"

"That's private."

"Fair enough. But why come to me?"

"When you were still with the department, as a deputy chief, you accessed the file several times. Ten to be exact. Why?"

"You know how many times I looked at the file?"

"Yes. I still have friends on the job."

"Pretty powerful ones it sounds like."

"That's debatable. Anyway, I'd like to know what interest the Deputy Chief of Patrol for Area Five had with the investigation."

Robinson scooched his chair closer and again crossed his arms on his desk. He leaned in. "I had a personal interest in the investigation. I knew Walter Patterson."

That bit of information caught Sam off guard and Robinson saw it on his face.

"I see you're surprised, Mr. Laska," Robinson said. "Let me elaborate. I wouldn't call him a friend, but we were acquainted. One of the perks of rank in the CPD is that you get to hob nob with politicians, businesspeople, and other movers and shakers in the city. Mr. Patterson was one of those movers and shakers. I met him a few times at dinners and parties."

"Well, that makes sense. Your interest was nothing more than curiosity."

"A little more than that, but yes."

"A little more?"

"I had been planning to start my own business for a while. I needed help, of course. I didn't have a whole lot of business smarts, but I knew I needed a good lawyer. Incorporation, taxes, all those things. Since I was a little familiar with Mr. Patterson, I had consulted with him several times and was planning on establishing a permanent relationship with his firm for representation."

"Okay, I get it now."

"There was nothing nefarious in my interest, Mr. Laska."

"I never said there was."

"But you thought there might be. I would." Robinson sat back again. "Is there anything else I can help you with? I hope I can. I was disappointed you were never able to solve the murder. I hope you'll have better luck this time around."

"I really have only one more question. Why did you lock the file?"

"I did what?"

"You locked the file. You restricted it. It can only be

opened with the permission of a Deputy Chief or higher."

"Did I do that?"

"Yes."

"That must be a mistake. I never intended to do that. I must have hit the wrong key or something."

"You're saying the restricted tag is a mistake?"

"It has to be. I wouldn't do it intentionally."

"Alright, I guess that answers all my questions," Laska said, standing. "Thank you for meeting with me."

"Of course," Robinson said. He stood and walked around his desk. "Again, good luck to you. I hope you're successful." He walked Laska to his door. "By the way," he said, "I saw that you have a Florida driver's license. Are you a licensed PI down there?"

"Yes, I am," Sam said.

"There is no reciprocity with the State of Illinois when it comes to Private Investigator's. If you like, I can probably get you a license here in Illinois. In fact, I could even put you on our payroll. You'd be working under our license."

"I don't think that's necessary. But thanks for the offer."

"I hope you'll consider it. I can offer you a lot of help. People, tech, that sort of thing. I'd like to see Walter Patterson's killer finally caught."

"So do I. Your offer is interesting. I'm good for now but I'll think about it. Thanks again."

. . .

Sam settled into the seat next to his father.

"How'd it go?" Bruno said.

Sam thought before answering. He turned to his father then back again. He said, "I'm not sure."

"What do you mean?"

"He said he knew Walter Patterson, but only casually." He looked at his father again, "He also said he consulted with Patterson professionally a few times."

"What for."

"For this." Sam nodded towards the building. "He needed legal advice for the start-up. He said that's why he checked the reports."

"But why did he do that restricted thing?"

"He said that was a mistake. He claimed he didn't realize he did it."

"That sounds like bullshit, son."

"Yeah, I thought so too." Sam replayed the conversation in his head. Robinson was good, he thought. He had no tells Sam picked up on. That is, if he was lying.

Bruno started his car. "What are you going to do?" he said, pulling from the curb.

"I'm going to check out his story." Sam looked into the sideview mirror and the building fading in the distance. "And Truncheon Security."

"How are you going to do that?"

"I'll talk to Patterson's law partner. See if he can verify anything Robinson said. I was going to talk to him anyway, so I'll just add a few more questions to the list. As for Robinson's business, I've got a call to make."

CHAPTER
TWELVE

"DO you want to go visit that lawyer now?" Bruno asked.

The question confused Sam momentarily. He was reviewing the Patterson file and collecting his thoughts before he called Joyce. Bruno's question clicked and he said, "The law partner? No, I think I'll call and make an appointment. I don't need to ambush him. Plus, I want to review his original interview in the file."

"Okay, then where are we going?"

"Head back to the hotel. You can drop me there."

"What are you gonna do there?"

"Like I said, I've got a few calls to make."

"And then?"

"I don't know. Maybe I'll wait and see what answers I get from the calls I make. Maybe I'll try to track down the witnesses who were on the 'L' train."

"You want me to wait for you?"

"No, Dad. You go on and do whatever."

"You don't want my help?"

Sam saw where this was going. "Dad, I appreciate you driving this morning. And I appreciate the offer to help. But some of this I really have to do on my own."

"Yeah, sure. I get it."

Sam heard the disappointment in Bruno's voice. "How about we get dinner together later tonight. I'll fill you in on anything I find out. You really helped figuring out who Jerry Robinson was and maybe there's more you can help with."

Bruno perked up. "Yeah, okay. Dinner. I'll try to think of a good place."

Sam sat at the desk in his room and dialed the number for Jack Hoke's office. It took five rings before Joyce answered.

"The law offices of Hoke, Dunn and Associates," Joyce answered. "How can I help you?"

"Joyce? It's Sam. Are you busy?"

"Hey, Sam. Not at all. How are you doing? You finally got some info for me?"

"Yeah, I do. In fact, I've got a whole list of stuff I'm gonna ask you to do, if you can."

"Sure, no problem. It's been a little busy around here but I think I can squeeze in your stuff. What do you have?"

"Let's start with Beth Patterson."

After filling Joyce in on Elizabeth Patterson, he gave

her the details on the three witnesses, Ronald Burke, Mae Lin Chan, and Darryl Wilcox.

"I need to locate them," Sam said. "It's been sixteen years so there's a good chance they're not at the same address they gave us back then."

"Alright. I'll dig up current addresses and employment histories. Anything else?"

"Yeah, one more. Jerry Robinson. I don't have a birthdate or address but he's a former deputy chief with the Chicago Police department and he now owns Truncheon Security here in town."

"Do you know if his first name is Gerald or Jerome?"

"I don't think it's either. I think it's just Jerry."

"Okay, got it. I'll give you a call when I have something."

"Do me a favor, do Elizabeth Patterson first and call me as soon as you have something."

"Will do, Sam."

He thanked Joyce again and ended the call. He set his phone down on the desk and stood. He looked around the room and down at his phone again. He picked it up and put it in his pocket. He walked to the bathroom and splashed water on his face. Walking back into the bedroom he thought he was wasting time waiting for Joyce to call back. There was no telling when she'd call back. Something might come up and she wouldn't get to it for hours.

He thought about what he could do while he waited. He could try the witnesses, but that might just be wasted effort. He'd wait until Joyce called with their current information. Next on the list was calling Walter Patterson's law partner. He walked back to the desk and double checked his name, Malcolm Burnett.

At the time of Patterson's murder, their law office was located on Washington Street near City Hall and the State of Illinois building. He checked the telephone number he had in the file and wondered if it was still good. There was only one way to find out.

He dialed the number. It was answered on the first ring.

A woman's voice said, "Law offices of Burnett, Styles, and Price."

"Hi," Sam said, "I'd like to make an appointment with Mr. Malcolm Burnett."

"Are you an existing client of Mr. Burnett's?"

"No, but—"

"I'm sorry, Mr. Burnett is not available for appointments, but we have several associates available for consultation. I can set you up with any one of them."

"No, I'm not looking for representation and I think Mr. Burnett will want to see me. Tell him this is in reference to Walter Patterson."

Silence.

The woman came back on. "One moment please."

Sam heard a click and then a smarmy Muzak version of "We've Only Just Begun".

He listened to half of the song before hearing another click.

"This is Malcolm Burnett. To whom am I speaking?"

"Mr. Burnett, this is Sam Laska. You might remember I was the detective who originally interviewed you regarding Walter Patterson's murder sixteen years ago."

"Yes, Detective, I remember. Of course, I remember. I'll never forget that horrible day. It's been so long without hearing anything. Do you have some news?"

Though Burnett addressed him as Detective, Laska was not going to correct him. At least not yet. "I think it would be best if we had this conversation face-to-face. Is there a time that would be convenient for you?"

"How soon can you get here? Or would you rather we meet somewhere else?"

"Your office is fine. Depending on traffic, I can be there in about thirty minutes."

"I'll make sure my people know to expect you. There are still a few people who were here…who remember Walter."

"I'd rather we keep this confidential for now, sir."

"Oh, of course. Alright then, I'll just let my assistant know to show you right in."

"Thank you, sir. See you soon."

Laska picked up on the black Chevy Tahoe in the hotel parking lot as he walked to his car. It was parked more than twenty spaces from his rental, and he wouldn't have paid it much attention except it was backed into its spot. The dark tinted windshield making it impossible to see inside sealed the deal. He climbed into his rental and made his way to the expressway heading into the city, making sure to check his mirrors regularly. The Tahoe followed him the entire trip downtown, several cars back, changing lanes, and generally trying to be inconspicuous. Sam thought about shaking the tail but figured, for now, it was enough for him to know he was being watched. And the list of people it could be was short: Elizabeth Patterson or Jerry Robinson. He hoped it was Jerry Robinson or his people. That would mean Robinson was a liar and Sam shook the right tree.

He pulled up to the building on Washington Street and realized he should have taken public transportation. Living in a small town for the last six years had made him forget. There was no parking downtown unless you paid for a spot in a lot. And that would cost him upwards of fifty dollars. He decided to take a chance and slipped into a loading zone around the corner.

The second mistake he made was not double-checking the address of the law office with Malcolm Burnett. Again, it was sixteen years ago, and a growing firm would likely move to bigger offices, if not a more prestigious address. But luck was with him and Burnett's firm was listed prominently on the building directory in the lobby.

He took the elevator up to the tenth floor. He stepped out and found himself in an opulent reception area with walls paneled in dark oak, overstuffed leather chairs and sofa, and plush carpeting. On the wall facing him were large oil portraits of three men. The three partners whose names headlined the firm, Laska assumed.

Before he took another step, he was greeted by a woman in business attire. A conservative length skirt, white blouse and jacket, and her dishwater blonde hair tied up in a loose bun.

"Welcome to Burnett, Styles, and Price. How can I help you?"

"I'm here to see Mr. Burnett," Sam said. "My name is Laska."

"Yes, Mr. Burnett said to show you right in, sir. Please follow me."

The woman led Sam through a door and down a long wide hall to a set of double oak doors. She rapped lightly and opened the door, allowing Sam to step inside. The room he entered was larger than his father's entire home. The wall opposite from him wasn't a wall at all but floor to ceiling nearly seamless glass. The view looked east towards Lake Michigan. The other walls were paneled in the same dark oak. To the left, at the far end of the room, sat an older man. He had a head full of gray hair and wore wire framed glasses. The wire was so thin and the glass of the spectacles so clear it looked as if he were wearing none at all. He sat behind a long dark wood desk and rose as Sam entered the room. Walking around his desk, he said, "Detective Laska, thank you for coming." He looked over to the blonde woman, "Thank you, Christine, you can go now."

The woman left, closing the large door behind her.

"Come, Detective," Malcolm Burnett said. "Please sit."

Sam crossed the room and extended his hand as he approached Burnett. "Thank you for seeing me, Mr. Burnett."

Burnett shook Sam's hand and pointed to a chair. "Of course, of course. Please sit." He walked back around his desk and slowly lowered himself into his chair. "To say I was surprised is an understatement but I'm glad to finally hear Walter's death hasn't been forgotten." He leaned forward, crossing his arms on the desk. "I'm excited to hear what you have, Detective."

Sam settled into the red leather Queen Anne-style chair. He never liked Queen Anne chairs. Their backs were too high and too straight for him. He could never figure out how people felt comfortable in them.

"Please call me Sam. You don't need to address me as detective, Mr. Burnett. I'm no longer with the police department."

"I don't understand."

"I left the department several years ago. If I'm being honest, I was asked to leave."

Burnett sat back. If he was surprised, his face didn't show it.

Sam continued, "But, because I was originally involved, I have been asked to take another look at Walter Patterson's murder."

Burnett expression didn't change. "By whom?"

"Respectfully, I'm not going to answer that."

"Was it Elizabeth, Walter's daughter?"

Sam expected the question. "Again, sir, I'm not going to say."

"Was it the police department? Would they do that?"

"No sir, they would not. They have plenty of capable detectives and wouldn't ask a retired detective to re-investigate an old case."

"I understand. Can you answer this? If they have so many capable detectives, why has the police department not been investigating Walter's murder?"

"This is what I know. Sixteen years ago, I was the lead detective on the case. My partner and I followed every lead and talked to every witness. We studied every bit of evidence there was. We hit a wall. There was nothing more we could do. The investigation, as per standard procedure, was reviewed by my sergeant and lieutenant and probably up the chain of command to the Chief of Detectives. Everyone agreed there was nothing more to be done until and unless further information was forthcoming. The investigation was stalled. And it stayed that way, open and unsolved, until recently when I was asked to take another look at it."

"Is there new information then?"

"No sir. Not yet."

"Then why did you agree to investigate it again? I assume you're being paid for your work. Is it the money?"

"I'm not being paid."

Burnett sat back and nodded. "Then I must believe your motivation is pure. Good. How can I help?"

CHAPTER
THIRTEEN

"AFTER SIXTEEN YEARS," Sam said, "I need to re-familiarize myself with the investigation. I've read the reports and the statements of the people interviewed, including you. But to be thorough, I'm speaking with everyone again."

"Do you expect everyone to remember anything after sixteen years?"

"You yourself said you'd never forget that day. Walter Patterson's murder was a traumatic event for everyone involved. Those events don't easily fade away."

"But sixteen years? Being an attorney, I have some experience with this. I wish you luck."

"Time can blur the memory, but sometimes it can crystalize it."

"Fair enough. Ask your questions, Mr. Laska."

Sam asked Burnett to re-tell the events of the day Walter Patterson was murdered as he remembered them. He allowed Burnett to tell his story without interruption, saving any questions to fill in the gaps for later.

Malcolm Burnett told Sam it was a fairly typical day at the office for both he and Patterson. They each had their own office, and they each spent most of the day there. They had no business interaction that day, save one. A meeting to discuss the status of cases they were handling and the general state of the practice. This meeting was common and took place every week or as needed.

After the meeting at the end of the day, Burnett left the office while Patterson stayed behind. He told Burnett he had a few things to handle before the end of the day.

"And that's it. That was my day. Until I received the phone call telling me Walter had been killed," Burnett said.

"Who called you?"

"Amanda, Walter's wife."

"What time was that?"

"I don't remember exactly but I was in bed. The phone call woke me up."

"What time did you go to sleep that night?"

"Pretty early if I remember correctly. I had a few drinks with dinner and was pretty worn out."

"So, ten? Eleven?"

"Oh, no. Earlier. Probably about nine."

"Okay. So, you went home after work—"

"No, I met my wife, my ex-wife, for dinner at a restaurant. Home after that."

"You're divorced?"

"And re-married. It didn't work out with Evelyn. My fault, I guess. Too many hours at the office. I neglected her."

"I'm sorry to hear that."

"Don't be. It happens every day."

Sam nodded. He knew well the pitfalls in relationships.

"Just a few more question, Mr. Burnett. How long had you been in practice with Walter Patterson?"

"We established our practice about a year before his death. We both were working at different firms and decided it was time to strike out on our own."

"How did you know one another?"

"We were classmates in law school. Northwestern Pritzker School of Law."

"Wow, Northwestern, huh? Even I know that's a great law school."

"The best. And Walter was a brilliant student. Much better than I." Burnett shook his head slowly. "And he became an outstanding attorney. It's a horrible shame. The good he could have done."

Sam waited for Burnett to continue, maybe to add more. Experience had taught him when you allow people to talk, they do. And it was in those moments that people revealed their true thoughts and feelings. Questions gave a person time to think, to formulate an answer. Answers were usually calculated in a sense. But when a person stopped calculating, formulating a response, and their emotions joined the conversation, they laid themselves bare.

Burnett did not disappoint. "We had such great plans together," he said, his eyes wandering to the view out his window wall. "We were going to become the premier law firm in the city. Maybe in the country. We had just secured our first big client. And it was actually funny how it happened. We represented a client in a discrimination suit. The respondent company offered a substantial settlement, but Walter told our client he thought his case was a winner. The client agreed and Walter took the case to trial. Naturally, he won and the award was ten times the settlement offer.

"The client was ecstatic. But the respondent, a very large corporation, was even more impressed. They approached Walter and wished to put us on retainer to represent them in all their legal needs and dealings. Representing them was going to put us on the map, so to speak." Burnett turned back to Sam. "The original client in that litigation was not our first big fish. The company we sued was going to be." Burnett's head dropped and his eyes closed. "Damn him," he said, nearly in a whisper, "why did he..." His voice trailed off.

"Why did he what?" Sam said.

Burnett raised his head. His eyes open. He looked at Sam. "I'm sorry, Mr. Laska. I think I got lost in a memory."

"No, that's okay, Mr. Burnett. You said 'why did he' but didn't finish. What were you going to say?"

Burnett took a breath. "Why did he have to die, of course. It still angers me."

"I understand. Do you still represent that company? The one you sued?"

"What? Oh, no. Once Walter was…gone, they went with another firm. It was really Walter they wanted. And I certainly understand that. But, as you can see, we survived and have done quite well since then."

"Yes, congratulations. But I'm sure you wish Walter Patterson was part of that success."

"Yes. That's true."

Sam shifted in his seat. He felt his back stiffening in the uncomfortable Queen Anne. "How close were you with Walter, Mr. Burnett? Did you socialize outside of work?"

"Oh, yes. As I mentioned, we knew each other from law school. We became good friends. We were nearly inseparable back then. Even when we took positions at different firms after graduating and passing the bar, we would usually have dinner every weekend. I even introduced him to his wife."

"Amanda, right?"

"Yes, that's right." Burnett sighed. "It was sad to lose her also."

"She died a few years after Walter's murder. Do I have that right?"

"Yes, that's correct."

"And what of Walter and Amanda's daughter?"

"Elizabeth. She adored her father, like every man's daughter does I suppose. They say fathers and daughters have a special relationship. She took his death hard. Her mother's death also."

"What happened to her after Amanda died?"

"I'm not sure. I think she went to live with Amanda's relatives."

"In the area here?"

"I'm sorry, Mr. Laska. I really don't know." He cocked his head slightly. "I suppose those questions mean that it wasn't Elizabeth who asked you to revisit her father's death."

Sam shrugged.

"I'm sorry," Burnett said, "I shouldn't have asked that question. I understand client confidentiality is important."

"I've already forgotten about it."

"Are we done then, Mr. Laska?"

"Almost. I have one last thing. Do you know Jerry Robinson?"

"Who?"

"Jerry Robinson. He's a former deputy chief from the police department and currently owns a security company, Truncheon Security."

"The name is not familiar to me."

"Mr. Robinson told me he was acquainted with Walter and was trying to establish a professional relationship with him. I thought you might have met him as well."

"I'm sorry, I don't remember meeting him. I'm actually a little surprised I don't remember. Walter and I had a habit of meeting each other's clients. Is it important? How does this man figure into all of this?"

"I don't know that he does." Sam stood, happy to escape the Queen Anne chair. "Alright then, Mr. Burnett. I think we're finished. Thank you for seeing me."

Burnett pushed himself out of his chair. "You're welcome. But it is I who should be thanking you. I pray you are successful in bringing Walter's killer to justice finally."

"I'm going to give it my best, sir."

Sam assured Burnett he could find his own way out and left the man alone in the large empty office.

Sam found his car unmolested right where he parked it. He half expected it to be gone, towed to an auto pound somewhere or at least tagged with a parking ticket. Neither was true and he was happy for his good luck.

He sat behind the wheel and checked his phone. There was nothing yet from Joyce. He debated calling her but dismissed the idea. She'd call when she had something and, knowing Joyce, pushing her might only piss her off.

He dropped his phone into a cup holder in the console, fired up the Toyota, and was about to pull out of the loading zone when his phone dinged. He shifted back into Park and checked the message. The display read *What did Burnett say?*

Sam looked up and around the car through every window. He checked every mirror. The street was crowded with foot and vehicle traffic. Cars and trucks lined the street, jammed into loading zones and every available parking spot. She could be anywhere, he thought.

He considered ignoring the message but instead tapped out a response:

I'd be happy to fill you in. Let's meet.

The response came quickly:

Only after you catch the killer. Or don't.

Sam felt his blood pressure rising. He wasn't going to play this game any longer. He keyed his last response:

Don't bother me again until then.

He switched his phone to silent and pulled the car into traffic.

CHAPTER FOURTEEN

THE TEXT from Beth Patterson was confirmation she was still watching Sam. Driving back to his hotel, he was careful to check his mirrors often. He didn't pick up on any tail. The black Tahoe was nowhere to be seen. He was now fairly convinced Beth Patterson was behind the wheel earlier. For now, though, he felt he was in the clear.

As he pulled into the hotel's parking lot, his phone began rattling in the cup holder. Hoping it was Joyce, he pulled into a spot and answered without checking the display.

"Sam," Bruno said, "It's me."

"Dad?" he said, "What's up?"

"Hey kid, you about ready for dinner?"

Sam checked the clock on the dashboard. "It's only four o'clock, Dad."

"Yeah, but it's five o'clock back home and I skipped lunch. How about you? Did you eat?"

"No, I missed lunch too. How about you give me time to clean myself up, take a shower, and I'll meet you in the lobby?"

"Okay but hurry up. I picked a good place."

"You can tell me later, alright? I'll see you soon."

Sam ended the call and headed inside. He had a thought and stopped just outside the door to the lobby. He turned back and walked the entire parking lot checking out the cars. Nothing struck him as unusual. He walked over to his rental, got down on his hands and knees, and checked the wheel well, bumpers, under the hood, and everywhere else he could think a GPS tracker could be attached. He found nothing and headed to his room.

Sam stepped out of the shower and heard his phone ringing. He ran to it, still dripping wet, and dug it out of the pocket of his pants on the bed. The call had already gone to voicemail. It was a number he didn't recognize. He briefly debated calling a number he didn't know but curiosity got the best of him. He dialed it back, but it was busy. Realizing he needed to wait for whoever to finish leaving their message, he toweled off and got dressed. He passed on listening to the voicemail before hitting redial.

"Sam? You busy," Joyce said.

"No. I just got out of the shower. Where are you? I didn't recognize the number."

"Sorry, I'm at home. I couldn't call back sooner. We

got pretty busy around the office and I kind of forgot about you."

"That's okay. I understand. Did you get anywhere with any of that stuff though?"

"Yeah, I did like you asked and checked on the Patterson chick first. I never got to the others though."

"Hey, you will when you can. What did you find out?"

"Okay, this might seem a little disjointed because I'm reading from several pages I printed out. Here we go."

Sam heard papers rustling through the phone.

"First," Joyce said, "Elizabeth Ashley Patterson. That's her full name. Or rather, was."

"Was?" Sam asked.

"I'll get there. After her mother died her aunt and uncle were granted custody because she was still a minor. The aunt and uncle are Jennifer and Joseph Adamowski. Jennifer was Amanda Patterson's sister. And here's why Elizabeth left Fenwick High. Her aunt and uncle live in St. Louis. The town of Kirkwood actually. It's a suburb of St. Louis."

"Missouri?"

"You know another St. Louis? Anyway, she graduated from a high school there and then kind of fell off the grid."

"What do you mean?"

"Well, I couldn't find anything like college, or employment, or even a credit history. Then it popped. I found adoption records online. Her aunt and uncle adopted her. Her legal last name is Adamowski. Once I found that out, all kind of shit fell into place. Get this, she joined the Army after high school."

"You're kidding?"

"No, she did two tours."

"Holy shit."

"Yeah, I guess that's where she learned how to kick your ass."

"I'm gonna let that slide because you're helping me out. When did her service end?"

"A year ago, last September. Honorable Discharge."

"Anything else? Address, phone number?"

"Nothing. She's been a ghost since getting out of the service. No address that I found, no credit history, and nothing on social media with the new name."

Joyce had nothing else, and they ended the call. Seeing as she hadn't yet researched the witnesses to Walter's murder or Jerry Robinson, Sam had a new plan for the following day.

Bruno picked an old neighborhood restaurant for dinner, the Gale Street Inn. It was a small family-owned place that had been around forever. Nothing fancy, just good food. Growing up, it was one of those places Sam considered a big treat to visit with his parents.

After ordering, and over drinks, they talked. Bruno started the conversation.

"Did you get anywhere on that murder?" he asked.

"Nothing to speak of. I just interviewed Walter

Patterson's law partner."

"Did he say anything interesting?"

"Not really. He doesn't know anything about the murder. I was just trying to get some background again. You know, maybe there was something I missed the first time I talked to him."

"Did you?"

"I don't think so. Well, maybe. He talked about a big new client they were about to make a deal with, but it fell through when Patterson was killed."

"The partner lost money because Patterson died?"

"Yeah, I guess so."

"So, he's not a suspect."

"I never thought he was. Dad." Sam took a sip of his cocktail, an Old Fashioned. He was getting into bourbon lately. He set down the glass and smiled. "You're getting into this, huh? My work?"

"Well, yeah. It's interesting."

"Actually, most of it is boring, tedious leg work."

"You think?"

"I do."

"Then why do you do it?"

"Because someone brought me up to care."

"Well, that must have been your mother because I don't remember doing it."

Sam raised his glass. "Here's to mom," he said.

"To your mother," Bruno said, and clinked his glass to Sam's.

Bruno drained his glass. "I miss her," he said.

"Me too, Dad."

For the second time, Bruno changed the subject before Sam could. "What are you gonna do next? What's your plan?"

"I've got a few things to follow up on, but I was thinking I might put them off. I'm going to drive out to Galena tomorrow."

Galena, a small town in Jo Daviess county in northwest Illinois, was best known for its charming 19th century buildings and scenic countryside. With a Main Street filled with taffy shops, souvenir stores, and antique shops it had become a favorite get-away for Chicagoans looking to escape the city for a weekend or two.

"What's out there?"

"I'm going to meet up with an old partner of mine." It was only sort of a lie, Sam thought. "How about you?"

"It's opening day at Wrigley. Woz got tickets and asked me if I wanted to go with him."

"You're going, right? You can't miss opening day."

"You bet your ass I'm going. It beats Galena any day."

They spent the rest of the evening eating and talking baseball. Bruno had a few more cocktails and Sam ended up driving the Caddy back to their motel and seeing his father safely into his room.

Back in his own room, Sam checked the time. It was just a little after nine, ten o'clock Sarasota time. He took out his phone and dialed Marley. He stretched out on the bed and listened as the phone rang.

"Sam?" Marley asked as she answered his call.

"Hi," he said, "am I bothering you?"

"No. No, you're not."

"You sound sleepy. Are you sure? I can call back tomorrow."

"No, it's okay. How are you? Are you getting anywhere on your case?"

"You don't really want to hear about that, do you?"

"No, I don't."

Sam nodded to himself. "So, how are you feeling?"

"I'm okay. I'm getting tired of doing nothing. And I just want this baby out already."

"I can only imagine. Has your aunt been there much?

"Every day, all day. I'm getting tired of that too."

"She's not there with you now, is she?"

"No. She's downstairs. Probably watching some housewives show. She gives me the update on all of them every day."

Sam chuckled. "I'm glad she's there with you."

"I guess. Listen, Sam. I'm really beat. I'd like to go to sleep now."

"Okay, I'll let you go. I'll call again later."

"Okay. Thanks for checking on me. Goodbye, Sam."

"Goodnight, Marley."

"Sam?"

"I'm still here."

"I love you."

And she was gone before Sam could answer her.

CHAPTER
FIFTEEN

IT WAS an early start for Sam. He was out of bed and showered by seven. He dressed, retrieved this Beretta from his room's safe, tucked it into the small of his back, and covered it with his sweatshirt. A to-go cup of hotel coffee in his hand, he scanned the parking lot as he walked to his rental. Confident he was alone, he hit the road, heading northwest bound on I-90.

The trip would take almost two and a half hours and he figured he'd get to the Jo Daviess County Sheriff's office by ten-thirty. Maybe later if he stopped along the way for breakfast.

He was in a good mood. The call to Marley was a big part of that. Particularly the way it ended. But he was also energized by Joyce's phone call. The stuff she dug up on Beth Patterson - he couldn't yet wrap his head around her new last name - wasn't a great revelation, but it helped refocus him. He still wanted to work Walter's murder but proving Dave Hermann's death was a murder – and finding out who did it - was his primary goal.

The first step was to get a look at the sheriff's reports and, hopefully, talk to the detective who handled the scene and the medical examiner. Everything else would follow from what he learned from them.

Beth's time in the Army was evidence she had the skills to take Dave out and make it look like an accident. Particularly when he didn't know when or where it was coming from. It also made Sam feel a bit better that she put him on the ground so easily.

He ended up skipping breakfast and only refilling his coffee cup when he stopped for gas just west of the city of Rockford. He doubled checked the directions on his phone and was back on the road in twenty minutes. An hour later he was pulling to the curb near the Jo Daviess County Sheriff's office.

It wasn't a new building, but it wasn't very old either. A two-story light brown structure built of rough faced concrete block set on a gradually sloping hillside. Sam had visited the town of Galena plenty of times in the past but somehow forgot it was nestled in the only part of Illinois that wasn't flat. Wooded and hilly and set on the banks of the Galena River, Galena was a town almost forgotten by time.

Sam pulled open the smoked glass double door and walked up to the front desk. Clean and modern inside - the county obviously believed in investing in Law

Enforcement - it was as bustling as any police station in Chicago.

Several deputies stood or sat behind the desk busy doing something or another. Sam parked himself in front of a deputy who was sitting and talking on the phone. He glanced up at Sam and held a finger up.

The deputy, finished with his call, looked up at Sam and said, "Can I help you?"

Sam handed him the ID card he was issued by the CPD when he retired. It was identical to the active police department ID except it had the word "Retired" in big red letters printed across its face. Police and sheriff's deputies always took care of you better when they knew you were or once had been part of the brotherhood.

The deputy looked over the card and handed it back. He nodded in acknowledgement of that bond.

"I'm hoping to talk to someone about a death investigation your department handled."

"What's the name?" the deputy said, turning to a computer monitor and keyboard.

"Hermann," Sam said. "David Hermann. I was told it was a hunting accident."

The deputy began typing. He stared at his monitor and looked back to Sam.

"Are you related to the deceased?" he asked.

"No, he was my partner in Chicago." Sam didn't see the need to elaborate.

"Hang on a second." The deputy picked up his desk phone and punched two numbers. He spoke into the phone. "This is Halloran at the desk. I've got a retired cop here asking about one of Hatfield's cases. Is he around today?"

Deputy Halloran nodded into the phone and hung up. He pointed at a staircase to the right of the desk and said, "Second floor. Ask for Detective Hatfield."

Sam sat across a desk from Detective Earl Hatfield. His desk was located in the middle of a sea of similar workspaces in a large room. Each desk was separated from the others by movable partitions covered in gray fabric. Hatfield's partition was dotted with notes and various other pieces of paper, each pinned to the fabric of the partition.

"You're a retired copper from Chicago?" Hatfield said. "We get a lot of you guys up here. They retire and move as far from the city as they can while still being close enough to go back and visit."

"Yeah, well, I moved a bit farther. I live in Florida now."

"Yeah? I've been only once. Took the kids to Disney. Never again."

"Why's that?"

Hatfield chuckled. "Too damn expensive. I could have bought a new pickup for what I spent on that trip."

Laska smiled and nodded as if he knew the poor guy's troubles.

"So," Hatfield said, "you were David Hermann's partner?"

"Yeah, I was."

"A real shame, going out like he did. I understand he was close to retirement."

"Yeah. He was going to move out here, like you said."

"Do you know if he had any relatives? A wife or kids?"

"No, I don't. You can't find any?"

"No. We called the CPD Personnel section too. They have nothing either," Hatfield said. "In fact, you're the first and only person who cared enough to come asking about him."

"I'm sorry to hear that."

"Yeah, it's a shame." Hatfield sat back. "Now, what can I tell you?"

"Well, I only heard about his death a few days ago. I was wondering if you could tell me what happened."

"It's kind of simple really. He was walking near the woods on his property and was hit by a stray shot. A hunting accident."

"How long ago was that?"

Hatfield checked the report on his desk. "It happened on March third or so. The ME couldn't determine an exact date. His body was found a few days after. You know how that goes. Time and date of death is a guess at best after a while."

"Who found the body?"

"A family from Chicago. They were on a nature

hike. Their poor kid, a little eight-year-old girl. Talk about traumatizing."

"I'm sorry to hear that. It must have been a bad scene. I was told animals had got to the body."

"That's right. But it wasn't as bad as it sounds. The body was pretty much, well, intact."

"What about the wound? What can you tell me?

"Entry in the back of the chest. The ME found pieces of the projectile imbedded in the body. It hit a bone. Unsuitable for comparison. The lab guessed the round was a probably a .233. Typical for some hunting rifles."

"Was March even hunting season. What would someone be hunting?"

"No, not any hunting season. Well, like deer or such. But nuisance animals like coyote and skunk can be hunted all year."

"And I guess you don't know what direction the shot came from?"

"No. The body was moved, dragged a bit by the animals. No way of telling after that."

"And you never found the person who shot him?"

"No one came forward. We put out a public service announcement asking if anyone knew anything and got no response."

"And you're sure it was an accident?"

"I know where you're going with that question. I get how you might want it to be more than just a tragic accident. He was your friend and a cop and all. But there's just no evidence it was any more than that. Do you have any information that might change that? Was he working on something that might have led to someone—"

"I don't know," Sam said. He didn't want anyone thinking he might be taking a closer look at Dave's death.

"Listen," Hatfield said. "I'm sorry your friend was killed. But unfortunately, these things happen."

"What about neighbors? Did they hear anything?"

"His nearest neighbor was three miles away and heard nothing."

Sam thought about what else he had on his 'ask-them-about' list. "What about his personal effects?"

"The medical examiner's office has everything that was on the body. Well, almost everything. He had a badge case with his badge and police ID. We called your department and they asked us to mail it to them."

"That's it? No one came out to get it?"

"Nope. Just wanted the badge and ID and a copy of the report and death certificate."

Sam sighed, disgusted at the impersonal request. He pointed to the report on Hatfield's desk. "Can I get a copy of that?

"I don't see why not. It's public record." He stood and picked up the papers. "I'll make you a copy. Be right back."

Hatfield returned minutes later and handed a copy of the report to Sam. "Is there anything else?"

"Just one more question. Did you go into his house?"

CHAPTER
SIXTEEN

DAVE HERMANN HOUSE was on a partially wooded ten-acre lot in an unincorporated area east of Galena. Hatfield said that, after the body was found, responding deputies did enter Dave Hermann's house. The back door was unlocked leading them to assume Hermann intended to return and wasn't concerned anyone else would enter while he was gone. He said there was nothing found that indicated anyone else had been there before them. Aside from a few dirty dishes in the sink, the house was in good order. They used Dave's keys to lock up the place.

Hatfield also told Sam that since they couldn't locate any relatives, the State would probably take possession of the house. That's how it worked in Illinois. You die with no heirs, everything you own now belongs to the State.

Sam walked over to his car, sat on the hood, and used his phone to search for the county ME's office. He got the address of a funeral home – it was common for some rural counties to use funeral homes for autopsies - about ten miles from the city. He checked the map and turn-by-turn directions.

Before he got into his car, he checked the street, up and down. He didn't spot any tail all the way from Chicago, but he didn't want to chance the possibility he was still being followed. He gave himself the all clear and headed off.

After following the directions on his phone, he arrived at Miller's Funeral Home. A white colonial style building bookended by two large parking lots and a drive in front of the building connecting both.

He drove a long access road from the highway to the building The place looked deserted, so he parked on the driveway in front of the entry. Trying the door, he found it locked. A buzzer was set to the right of the door. It took several rings before he saw someone approaching through the door's window.

A short balding man wearing coveralls and a rubber apron opened the door only part way. A clear plastic facemask was pushed up over his face and he wore yellow elbow length rubber gloves. He stuck his head out.

"Can I help you," he said.

"I hope so," Sam said. "I wanted to talk to the ME."

"What about?"

"David Hermann. Hunting accident?"

"Oh," the man said, "we were hoping the sheriff would find someone." He pulled the door fully open and stepped aside, making room. "Please, come in. I'm Will Miller, the funeral director."

Sam walked in and stopped in the foyer. The smell of formaldehyde and disinfectant and some kind of scented candle filled his nose.

"Excuse my appearance," Miller said, "I'm in the middle of an embalming."

"Don't think twice about it. Are you the medical examiner also?"

"I'm not. That would be Dr. Edwards."

"Is he around? I'd like to talk to him."

"Sorry, but no. I can call him though. But before I do, are you a relative of the deceased?"

"No. Just a friend."

"Then what exactly did you wish to speak to Dr. Edwards about?"

"The autopsy. I'd like to get a few details."

Miller shook his head slowly. "I don't think that would be a good idea. The descriptions can be very graphic, very upsetting for someone who knows the deceased."

"I was a homicide detective, Mr. Miller. I've attended more autopsies than I care to remember. I promise you, I won't be upset."

"I understand. I'll give Dr. Edwards a call. Please, find a comfortable seat and I'll be right back."

Miller walked to the back of the building and disappeared down a hallway. Sam walked from the foyer into a large wide central room. Four doorways, two on either side of the central room, led to more rooms.

Showing rooms for wakes, he guessed. Paths were worn into the plush carpet leading to each room. Oil paintings of serene landscapes hung from every wall. He peeked into one of the viewing rooms. Rows of wood folding chairs filled the room and worn, over-stuffed sofas lined the side walls. Brass lamps sat atop dark wood end tables between each sofa and tall vases and brass candle holders surrounded an empty space at the far end of the room.

Sam walked back to the foyer and gazed out the window. Funeral homes depressed him. He dealt with death all throughout his career and he was able to, for the most part, treat it in a clinical, scientific manner. But funeral homes hit him personally. They reminded him of his mother, grandparents, friends, and co-workers. The people that he lost. The people who touched him personally.

As he started to turn away he caught a streak of black flashing across his vision. He whipped his head back and his eyes caught the tail end of a large black SUV speeding down the highway in the distance. The vehicle disappeared behind a stand of trees that lined the road and was gone. He stood staring at the highway, almost willing the SUV to come back.

He wondered if it was a coincidence. There are plenty of black SUVs in the world. And he couldn't be sure it was the same one that followed him yesterday. He couldn't tell if it had tinted windows. He couldn't even tell if it was a Tahoe, much less a GMC product. But he didn't like coincidences.

"Sir?" Miller's voice came from behind Sam. He turned to face him. Miller was walking through the room to Sam. His gloves, facemask, and apron gone.

"Yes?" Sam said. "Is Dr. Edwards on his way?"

"No sir. He's at the hospital and unable to meet you. I explained your request and he said, considering your familiarity with the deceased and your experience, it would be okay for me to give you a copy of his autopsy report."

"I guess that would be alright."

"He also said that, if you had any questions after reading it, you could give him a call. I can give you his phone number."

"That would be great. Thanks."

Miller led Sam to an office in the back of the building. He pulled Dave Hermann's autopsy report from a file cabinet and made a copy for Sam after scribbling Edward's number at the top of the first page.

As he handed Sam the report, he said, "Is there anything else, sir?"

"Yes, just one. His remains, Dave's remains. Is there a process for me to claim them? I'd like to give him a proper funeral and burial instead of seeing him in some county grave."

"Mr. Hermann was cremated, sir. We don't bury unclaimed bodies anymore."

"Alright. What about his ashes? Can I get those?"

"I think we can do that, seeing as we can't locate any blood relatives. You'll have to sign for them, of course."

"Not a problem."

"You should know, the ashes are stored in plastic bags. That's how you'll be receiving them unless you wish to purchase an urn."

"How much is your least expensive urn?"

"Forty-five dollars."

"I can do that. One more thing. His personal effects? Can I get those?"

"Yes. We'd be happy to make a little more room in our storage space."

Sam walked out of the funeral home carrying Dave Hermann's ashes in a simple steel urn and a plastic bag holding Dave's wallet, keys, cellphone, and twenty-six cents in change. He placed the urn and bag on the seat next to him and flipped through the autopsy report.

It was the same as every other autopsy report he read during his career. It was a clinical explanation of Dr. Edward's examination. Just as Detective Hatfield told Sam earlier, Dave suffered a single gunshot entering his back a few inches right of the midline. It ripped through his heart, hit a rib in his upper left chest and shattered. Several shards of the projectile apparently exited his upper left chest as several small exit wounds were observed. Two fragments of the projectile remained imbedded in the musculature of the chest.

Sam skimmed over the injuries suspected to be caused by animals and moved right to Dr. Edward's determination of the cause and manner of death: Gunshot wound to chest and heart / Accidental.

He set aside Dave's autopsy and grabbed the report he got from Det. Hatfield. He checked the location of Dave Hermann's property and entered it into the map on his phone. Dave's place was east of Galena. The fastest route was through the middle of the town but it would still take over thirty minutes to get there. He checked the time on his phone. It was already past two in the afternoon and he hadn't eaten all day. He'd find a place in Galena and stop before heading to Dave's property.

CHAPTER
SEVENTEEN

SAM FOLLOWED his phone's map onto Main Street in Galena and picked a sports bar for his lunch. He sat at the bar sipping an iced tea as he waited for his burger. He saw her in the mirror behind the bar as she walked in, her ponytail bobbing left and right as she walked. He spun around on his barstool to face her as she drew nearer.

"You've got some balls," he said as she sat next to him.

"I don't, actually," Beth said.

"You know what I mean."

She smiled.

The bartender came over and she ordered a light beer. "You wanted to meet," she said after the man left to fetch her drink. "We're meeting."

"What changed your mind?" Sam said.

The bartender returned and set her beer down. He stood there waiting.

Beth nodded towards Sam. "Put it on his bill."

Sam nodded his assent and the guy left.

"I'll ask again," he said. "What changed your mind?"

"You're being followed."

"I can see that."

"Not by me. Well, not only by me."

"The black Tahoe?"

"That's the one," she said as she took a sip of her beer.

"I picked up on them yesterday. But I didn't see them around today."

"They've been laying pretty far back. They must have you on a tracker."

"I checked my car and didn't find anything."

Beth shrugged. "Then you missed it."

"Not likely."

"Yeah, okay." She looked at him like he had a mouse sitting on his head.

Sam ignored the look. "Why would someone else be following me?"

The bartender came back and slid Sam's burger in front of him. Beth reached over and stole one of his French fries.

"You could ask first," he said.

Again, Beth shrugged and continued munching on the stolen fry.

"I asked you why someone else would be following me," he said.

"Why else? You're asking questions about my father's murder."

"Okay, I'll admit it looks that way. But I haven't found anything that says your father's murder wasn't anything but a simple robbery gone bad."

"You must have scared somebody."

"Let's put that aside. Let's talk about Dave Hermann."

Beth looked at Sam and then his burger. Sam pushed the plate over to her.

Beth took a monster bite out of the burger. Gulped more than chewed then took another bite and another. Sam handed her his napkin and said, "You have catsup on your chin."

She took the napkin and, with a mouth half full of Sam's lunch, mumbled a thank you. Sam waved the bartender over and ordered a second burger for himself. He turned back to Beth who had already demolished most of the sandwich and was working on the fries.

"When was the last time you ate?" he asked.

She wiped her mouth again. "Yesterday," she said.

"Why? Don't you have money or something?"

"I've got money. Enough for lunch, anyway. I just haven't had time to stop."

"Because you've been watching me."

She smiled and took a slug of her beer.

"Back to Dave Hermann," Sam said.

"Not here," she said. "Let's go somewhere quiet."

"This place is just fine." He leaned in closer to her. "I'm gonna look really hard at his so-called accident.

And if I find out you killed Dave you're going to spend the rest of your life in prison."

"I guessed that's why you came out here." She crossed her arms on the bar. "I didn't kill Dave. I knew you'd find out he was dead and I wanted you to think I did it."

"Bullshit."

Beth looked around the pub. "Do we have to do this here? Can we go someplace without so many ears?"

"No one is listening to us."

"Do you know who's following you? Do you know what they look like? They could be sitting right over there." She nodded to an older couple sitting a few stools away."

Sam looked over to the couple and back to Beth.

"Okay, not them," she said. "But they could be somewhere in here."

"And I'll bet you have someplace else in mind?"

"You pick the spot," Beth said.

"Fine. The Sheriff's Department."

"You're kidding, right?"

"No. We'll both go in your car. You drive and keep your hands on the steering wheel the entire time we talk. We'll park and talk in the car."

"Hands on the steering wheel? Really?"

"You could be armed. You threatened me, remember?"

"I do, and I am. It's in the glove compartment. You can check when you get in my car. Anyway, what are you afraid of? You're carrying too. That bulge in the small of your back isn't fooling anyone."

"I just don't trust you, Beth. Do we have a deal or not?"

"Yeah, we have a deal. Pay the check and let's get going."

"No. I've got a hamburger coming. I'm not leaving until I eat. And neither are you."

Sam climbed into the passenger's seat of Beth's Jeep Wrangler. Beth, as instructed, gripped the steering wheel, her hands at ten and two.

"Check the glove box," she said as Sam closed the door behind him.

Sam pulled the latch and the door popped open. Nestled inside was a Sig Sauer 9mm pistol.

"There it is. Just like I told you," she said.

Sam took the weapon, removed the magazine, and racked the slide to eject the round sitting in the chamber. He returned the gun to the glove box but held onto the magazine and cartridge.

"That's a little extreme," Beth said. "Don't you think?"

"No, I don't," Sam said.

"If you say so."

"Start the car. Drive over to the sheriff's department. You're going to take a left up ahead."

"I know the way," she said.

"And on the way you can explain how you got my phone number and how you know about Marley."

"I thought you might bring that up," she said as she pulled into traffic.

"Your phone was easy," Beth said. "I cloned it as I was sitting next to you at the bar."

"Back in Sarasota?"

"Yeah," she chuckled. "I didn't think it would be that easy but you left your Bluetooth on. That gave me the in with your phone. I saw every text and phone call you made and I was able to track you with your phone's GPS."

"That's how you knew I was in Chicago."

"I followed you all the way."

"What about Marley? How did you know about her?"

"I was in Sarasota for two weeks before I approached you. Following you, watching you, working on my tan now and then. I still have a little afterglow, don't you think?" She smiled. Sam didn't. She continued. "You like to eat at her restaurant a lot so I figured people there would know you. I started chatting up the bartenders when you weren't around." She glanced over to Sam and then back to the road again. "Guys like to talk to pretty girls who seem interested in them."

"Joe."

"He likes to gossip too. That's how I heard about you and Marley. By the way, why doesn't she use her first name, Gabrielle?"

"How did you know that's her first name. Everyone knows her by Marley."

"I followed her too. When I saw where she lived it was just a matter of checking the county real estate records. She apparently uses her real first name on official stuff." She looked over at Sam again. "Are you going to get back together with her? I think you make a cute couple."

Sam looked a question at her.

"I told you," she said, "Joe likes to gossip."

They drove in silence until they pulled up to the sheriff's department. Sam pointed to a spot across from the front entrance. "Pull over there," he said, "and turn the engine off."

Beth did as she was told. She turned to Sam.

"Hands back on the wheel," he said.

She frowned but complied with his order.

"Tell me about Dave," Sam said.

"I didn't kill him."

"Then who did?"

"I don't know. Whoever didn't want him asking questions."

"What questions?"

"He was helping me find my father's killer. I went to him a few months ago and asked him, actually pleaded with him, to re-open the case."

"Murder investigations are never closed until they're solved. One way or another."

"But no one was working on it. What do you people call it? A cold case?"

"Why pick him? Why not just go to the Area and talk to one of the sergeants?"

"He worked on it with you. And you weren't around. You were already retired."

"You remembered our names?"

"No. My mother saved everything. She had papers and letters from the county's victim assistance program."

Sam nodded, satisfied with her answer.

Beth continued her story. "After Dave was killed, I got scared. I didn't know what was going on or who killed him. I didn't know what they knew about me and if I was next. I needed to leave for a while so whoever killed Dave would think they scared me off. I knew you were in Florida so I thought I'd go to Sarasota and find you."

"You did and you threatened me."

"I needed you to come back and work on my father's murder. I didn't want to give you the option of saying no."

"I probably would have done it if you just told me the truth."

"I didn't want to take the chance. I'm sorry, but I'm not sorry. I wanted you to take my threat seriously. And that was to protect you. The threat was supposed to make you more careful, on edge and watching your six. I didn't want you to end up like Dave."

"End up like Dave, huh? You used his death to intimidate me. That's pretty shitty."

"No, I used his death to protect you and keep you looking over your shoulder."

"I'm not buying that line right now." Sam leaned back against the door. "Let's pretend for a minute you didn't kill Dave. How do you know his shooting wasn't just a hunting accident like the sheriff's office says?"

"I can't say but come on. That would be a hell of a coincidence, right? He starts asking questions about a sixteen year old murder and just happens to die in an accident."

"It happens. I haven't seen any proof one way or the other."

"And you've got no proof I did it but you suspect me anyway. What about the black Tahoe following you? Just another coincidence, right?"

Sam shrugged. He sat, thinking. Deciding.

"Do you believe me? About Dave, I mean?"

"I haven't made up my mind yet."

"Will you still help me find my father's killer?"

"Yes, I will. But if you did kill Dave, I'll take you down too."

"I believe you," Beth said. Her hands fell from the steering wheel onto her lap. "Now what?"

"Take me back to my car," Sam said.

"What are you going to do?"

"I'm headed over to Dave's property. I want to scope it out and look through his house."

"What for? What do you think you'll find?"

"I don't know. I'll know it when I find it."

"My father's file?"

Sam stiffened. "What do you know about the file?"

"I have it. It's in my trunk."

"Where did you get it?"

"From Dave. Dave's house actually."

"When?"

"The day they found his body. I was there."

CHAPTER
EIGHTEEN

"TELL ME," Sam said.

"Dave had been working on the case for a few weeks already, Beth said. "He called me almost every day to give me updates. One day, he called and told me he was going on vacation. He was still going to work on the case, going over the file and stuff, but he would be in Galena at his new house. I guess he was working on that too. You know, getting ready to retire out there. He promised to call me every day, though."

"But he didn't," Sam said.

"The first day he didn't call I didn't think anything of it. When he didn't call on the second day, I tried calling him. He didn't answer and that was strange. He always answered my calls. On the third day, when he still didn't answer any of my calls, I jumped in my car and headed to Galena."

"How did you know where his place was at? Did he ever tell you?"

"County real estate records. Same way I found your girlfriend."

Sam nodded.

"When I got close to his place, I could see the flashing lights. A sheriff's car blocked the access road to his property. I pulled up and asked the cop what was going on. He told me there was an accident. That's all he said. But I knew there was more going on because I could see more flashing lights deep into the property past a house I figured was Dave's.

"I drove down the highway a bit so the cop couldn't see me and I pulled over. I got out of my car and started walking. I cut through some woods and got closer. There were more cop cars, an ambulance, and one of those black station wagons funeral homes use."

"A hearse."

"Yeah. I watched them for a while from the woods. I saw them take a body away and a couple of cops go into Dave's house. They were in there only twenty minutes or so and after they left the house, I went back to my car and waited. It was a few hours before they all cleared out. That's when I went in."

"You searched his house?"

"I wouldn't call it a search. I looked around, opened a few drawers, checked the closets, and stuff like that."

"That's called a search. Where was the file?"

"In a drawer of a desk in the living room."

"Did you find his gun?"

"No, and I was looking for that. When I didn't find

it I figured he had it on him when he was killed and the police took it."

"They never mentioned his gun to me. Could they have taken it when they were in the house?"

"Maybe, but I didn't see them carrying anything out of the house. But I was kind of far away. I could have missed it."

"I'll give the detective a call and find out."

"So, what? We're going to Dave's place now?"

Sam reached over and pulled the keys from the ignition.

"Hey," Beth said, "you can't leave me here."

"I can if I want to," Sam said. "But I won't. I want to get the file from your trunk."

"You don't need my keys for that. Just pop the glove box and hit the trunk release."

"I intended to. I just don't want you driving off while I'm out of the car."

"You don't trust me yet?"

"I'm getting there." Sam opened the glove box and pressed the release button. He picked up the Sig Sauer and stuck it in his waist. "But not yet," he said.

Sam retrieved the file, a stack of papers and reports bound by metal prong fasteners and sandwiched between blue pressboard covers. In Los Angeles, it was called the murder book but the Chicago homicide units weren't that clever. They just called it the homicide file. He returned to Beth's car and sat next to her. "This file was missing," he said. "No one knew Dave took it."

"Was he supposed to tell someone?"

"Yes. The homicide files are never supposed to leave the office. There's a tracking form he should have signed and left as a place holder."

Sam paged through Walter Patterson's homicide file while Beth drove him back to his car. He had her let him out a block away. He told her he didn't want his tail picking up on her car. They may have already, he told her, but there was no reason to take any chances.

"Are you going to follow me there or should I meet you there?" Beth asked.

"Neither one," Sam said. He stepped out of the car still holding on to the homicide file.

"You don't want me to go?"

"You're going to drive us both there. Just in case I did miss a tracker on my car."

"Then let's just go now. Why are you going back to your car?"

"I have Dave's keys in my car. I picked up all his personal effects from the funeral home. His ashes too."

"You have his ashes in your car?"

"I just said I did. Can we talk about this when I come back?" Sam didn't wait for her answer. "Don't move," he said and closed the car door.

Sam half expected Beth to be gone when he returned, but there she was, right where he left her. He climbed into the car, shoved the file he still held under his seat, and said, "Let's go."

The drive took longer than he expected mainly because Beth kept slowing down looking for the right turnoff. Sam kept checking the sideview mirror along the way and was relatively satisfied they weren't being followed.

Beth slowed again and said, "I think this is it." She turned onto a dirt and gravel road. "Yeah," she said, "we're here."

As she drove along the road she pointed out an area heavily forested by pine and birch trees. "That's where I watched them from. And there," she pointed ahead past a house a few hundred yards or so in front of them, "those woods way over there is where I saw the cops and ambulance."

"Where they found Dave," Sam said.

"Do you want me to pull up over there?" Beth asked.

"No, let's go to the house first. We can walk over later."

Beth parked the car on the gravel driveway near the garage attached to the house. As Sam stepped from Beth's car, he scanned the house. It was more of a large cabin than a house, with painted grey clapboard siding and a bright red door set back along a long covered porch that stretched the length of the building. His shoes crunched on the gravel as he and Beth walked. They climbed the two steps onto the porch and Sam pulled Dave's keyring from his pocket. He picked out a key and slipped it into the lock.

"Hey," Beth said, "you got it on the first try."

"Lucky guess," Sam said as he unlocked the door and swung it open.

They stepped in and stopped just inside the doorway. An old familiar feeling gripped him. He felt it many times in the past when he entered the homes of the dead, the murdered. It was a feeling of violation, of intrusion into the spaces no longer occupied by the owner. He was the uninvited visitor. The unexpected guest.

"You okay?" Beth said. She had walked into the center of the room, a great room people called them now. A large central room with no wall separating it from the kitchen and dining areas.

Sam looked over to her. "Yeah, why?"

"You were just staring off into space somewhere."

"I was just taking it all in," he said.

Beth gave him a little half shrug and continued wander around the room. Looking at nothing and everything, picking up a book and putting it down, pushing papers around on the desk, and generally looking like a disinterested homebuyer than anything else. She looked over to Sam again. "What's your plan here?" she said.

"I'd like to search the place. Hopefully we'll find Dave's gun."

"Anything else?"

"Yes."

Beth waited for more from Sam but he said nothing. She followed him from the great room down a hall. "What else?" she said.

"I'll know it when I see it."

"What does that mean?"

"It means there could be something here that's important that we have no idea about."

"Like what?"

Sam walked into a large bedroom. Beth followed and watched as he scanned the room.

"I don't know," Sam said. "I'll know it when I see it."

Beth shook her head and looked at Sam like he had that same mouse on his head. Sam began searching the room, starting with the obvious and lifting the mattress from the bed. "Let me ask you something," he said. "What did you do during your two tours in the Army?"

"You know about that?"

"Yeah, I did some checking on you too." He glanced at her standing at the foot of the bed. "Maybe you can help me search instead of just standing there while you think of your answer?"

Beth moved around to the other side of the bed and began looking through a nightstand's drawers. "Why do you want to know about my Army life?"

"Because you don't act like the bad ass battle hard-ened combat veteran you acted like when we first met."

"You mean when I put you on the ground? I was on the staff of a full bird colonel. I was basically a glorified secretary. I never saw combat. Unless you want to count punching out a horny second lieutenant who got handsy with me."

"Why did you join up?

"I wasn't a very good student in high school. I had no ambition for college after that. I didn't want to stay with my aunt and uncle any longer, I assume you know about them too, so it seemed like it was either the service or working behind the cosmetics counter at Macy's for the rest of my life."

"How old were you when you enlisted?"

"I just turned twenty."

"What did you do after high school for those two years before the Army?"

"I was nineteen when I graduated. I lost a year when my father was killed. Then I took a job—"

"Behind the cosmetics counter at Macy's."

"Exactly."

"And after the Army?"

"I bummed around California for a while, ended up in LA. I started taking some classes at a community college but all the while I kept thinking about my dad. I finally decided to do something about it and came home."

"Criminal Justice classes?"

"How'd you guess."

"It wasn't a big leap."

Sam finished his search of the bedroom having checked every nook and cranny. He looked in and under every drawer, the closet, and every pocket in every garment, under the bed and other furniture, and behind the dresser mirror. He rolled up the small area rug and even peeked under the lampshades. Satisfied, he next moved to the bathroom.

He had Beth follow him and recheck every place he looked. It took nearly an hour and a half in the small house to finish the search. Sam stood in the kitchen over the sink and cupped his hand under the faucet for a drink.

Beth plopped down on a beat-to-shit recliner. "Well," she said, "did you find what you didn't know you were looking for?"

"No," Sam said, wiping his hands in a paper towel. He walked around the large island that separated the kitchen from the great room. He gazed across the space and out a pair of sliding glass doors that led to a small outdoor deck and fields of tall grass. At the far end lay the edge of the forest where he knew Dave Hermann died.

The sunny early spring day was gone. The once bright blue sky was now gunmetal grey. Wind whipped the long grass of the field into an undulating sea of green. The branches of the pines in the distance bobbed and weaved like an inflatable tube man on a used car lot.

"Now what?" Beth said, knowing where his eyes were fixed. "Go over there?"

"Yeah," Sam said, "but first I want to check the garage. We haven't searched there yet."

CHAPTER
NINETEEN

BETH FOLLOWED Sam to a small mudroom off the kitchen and through a door leading to the garage. The garage was lit by a single miserly bulb hung from the center roof rafter. Sam checked the wall and found the switch for the overhead door. The door creaked and clanged in its runners and the daylight, what was left of it, spilled into the garage.

The space was dominated by a Dodge Ram Pickup and old green riding mower. Tools and jars of odd screws and bolts were strewn haphazardly on a work bench. A pile of garden tools were stacked in a far corner.

Sam had Beth look around the garage while he concentrated on the truck. The search didn't take him long. Dave was obviously pretty meticulous when it came to taking care of his ride. Aside from registration papers, an insurance card, and the garage door remote, Sam found nothing. Not even any loose change.

He climbed out of the truck. "Find anything?" he asked Beth.

Beth stood at the tool bench along the back wall. "Only spiders and dirt," she said.

Sam walked around the pickup and stood on the garage's apron looking out towards the highway in the distance. The air had turned cooler and the wind carried the scent of approaching rain.

Sam heard the plunk of metal on metal against the truck's tailgate before he heard the crack of the gunshot.

"Get down!" he yelled to Beth as he dove onto the concrete.

He looked over and saw her sprawled across the floor in the back of the garage. "Are you okay?" he called out.

"Yes," she said. "You?"

"I'm good." Sam crawled along the floor on his belly to her. With the truck between them and the open garage door, he sat up and pulled his pistol.

"Give me my Sig," Beth said, reaching out.

"It's in your car. I put it back in the glove box after you got out."

"What the fuck, Laska?"

"Get your phone out. Call 9-1-1."

"It's in my purse."

"Where's your purse?"

"In my car."

Laska dug his phone out and passed it to her.

"What do I tell them?" she said.

"Someone's shooting at us. What the hell do you think?"

She began punching in the numbers. She paused. "Where are we? I don't know what to tell them."

He told her to check his search history for the address. She tapped away on the phone, paused to read, and then finished dialing. She held the phone to her ear and waited. She looked over to Sam. "We have to move, get back into the house."

"No. We have cover. We stay here and wait for the police."

"The house is better cover. And easier to defend."

"This pickup is great cover. They have a rifle. Most likely with a scope. We'd be easy targets if we expose ourselves."

Beth was about to say something to him but turned away and began talking into the phone to the 9-1-1 operator. She finished and handed the phone back to Sam. "Okay," she said, "they said they're on the way."

Sam nodded to her.

"Where did the shot come from?" she said.

"I'm not sure but I think I caught a flash out the corner of my eye. Over by the trees to the right of the access road."

"That's where I was watching the cops from the day Dave was found."

They sat still, waiting for the sheriff. The minutes ticked by.

"Where the hell are they?" Beth said, breaking the silence.

"It's a long way from there to here," Sam said.

They waited. More minutes passed. They both heard it. A car in the distance. It's engine growling as it accelerated.

"Is that them?" Beth said.

Sam moved along the flank of the pickup truck towards the garage's open doorway. He took a breath, poked his head out and back again.

"Shit," he said.

"What?" Beth said from the back.

"It's the black Tahoe." Sam checked his weapon. "Beth," he said, "come around to this side."

"Why?"

"Take Dave's keys from me and get in the pickup. I'll lay down some cover and you get out of here."

Before she could answer, the whoop-whoop yelp of a siren pierced the air. Sam peeked out again. The Tahoe was over one hundred yards away and barreling towards them on the access road. Blue lights strobed from behind its front grill.

"Sirens," Beth said. "Is the Tahoe leaving?"

"The Tahoe is the police," Sam said.

Sam stood but stayed behind the protection of the Dave's pickup. The Tahoe crunched to a stop on the gravel drive, the strobes still flashing. Sam held his ground, his pistol at the ready. Two men jumped from the black SUV, weapons drawn and holding up their IDs. Chicago Police stars.

"The shot came from those trees," Sam called out, pointing.

"Anyone hit?" the passenger asked.

"No," Sam said.

"How many shots?" the driver said.

"One," Sam answered and walked over to the two men. To the passenger, he said, "Stay with her." He nodded to Beth who was peeking out from behind the pickup truck. Sam turned his head to the driver. "Take me over there. He again pointed to the stand of trees near the highway.

The driver looked over to his partner who nodded.

The Sheriff's police began arriving, sirens screaming, as Sam and the driver pulled up to the tree line. Three one-man cars. Sam identified himself as the caller - well, his friend called - and gave them the short version. Two of the deputies headed to the garage while one, a corporal, stayed with Sam and the driver.

The corporal, Clayton was the name on his uniform shirt, pointed to the police star now hanging from a lanyard around the driver's neck. "What are you guys doing here?" he asked.

"Protection detail for him," the driver said, throwing a thumb over to Sam.

Sam shook his head, turned, and walked into the stand of trees. "Anyone want to help me look for the shooter's spot?"

The driver and Clayton followed. The driver stayed close to Sam while Corporal Clayton wandered the area kicking at the low brush as he walked.

"Protection detail?" Sam said to the driver as he scanned the ground.

"It was the best I could come up with," the driver said.

"What's your name?"

"Marcin. Joe Marcin," the driver said. "You didn't look too surprised to see us. When did you know?"

"Not until I saw the flashing lights," Sam said. "I picked up on you guys at my hotel and knew I was being tailed, but I didn't know by who."

"Chief Kroll assigned us to follow you."

Sam looked up from the weedy ground. "I puzzled that out." He went back to the search. "I had you all the way from my hotel to Washington Street downtown, but never saw you again. I checked my car for a tracker and didn't find one. I guess I missed it."

"You've got a rental car. They install a tracker on their cars' computers. They're happy to cooperate with us. It took us a day to get the subpoena though."

Sam nodded. "You learn something new every day. Did I lose you when I switched cars back in Galena?"

"Yeah, we were on the outskirts of town. We never had a visual. We just stayed on your car's tracker."

"You were monitoring the sheriff's radio band and heard the 'shots fired' call, I assume."

"Yep. But I'm surprised we beat them here."

Marcin kicked at a spot on the ground. "Don't," Sam said. "We're looking for flattened and crushed weeds. The shooter was probably lying on the ground."

Marcin looked back to the corporal who was

wandering deep in the trees still kicking at the brush. "We should tell him."

"Don't bother," Sam said. "Let him think he's doing something useful. The shooter was nearer to the front of the stand. Too many trees and bushes back there. He wouldn't have a clear line of sight."

The pair keep searching the ground, moving slowly and carefully.

"Here," Marcin said and pointed at a spot to his left.

Sam moved closer. "I think you found it."

CHAPTER
TWENTY

"LET'S BACK AWAY. We'll let the sheriffs do their thing and take a closer look here," Sam said.

"What about the ejected casing?" Marcin said.

"Let them look for it." Sam called Corporal Clayton over and showed him the spot. "It's your scene," he told Clayton.

"What do you want me to do with it?" Clayton said.

"Your job," Sam said.

"You don't know the shooter was here," Clayton said. "It's just a patch of crumpled weeds."

"And you don't know that he wasn't. There could be evidence around. Maybe he spit out a wad of gum, maybe he dropped a cartridge, maybe he even left a fucking note. Get your techs out here to do what they do." Sam turned to Marcin and said, "Take me back to the garage."

Back in the Tahoe, Marcin said, "Left a fucking note?"

Sam chuckled. "Best I could come up with."

The techs showed up a half hour later along with Det. Hatfield. Hatfield guessed the shooter pulled to the side of the highway and walked through the trees and brush before setting up in his spot. He also probably took off right after missing his first shot. Laska couldn't argue. It made the most sense. He couldn't risk sticking around knowing Sam and Beth probably had cell phones to call for help.

The techs moved in and took their photos, dug a .223 round from the tailgate of Dave Hermann's pickup truck, and, surprisingly, found the expended cartridge in the stand of trees. Det. Hatfield told Sam it was about twenty feet to the right of the trampled patch of weedy ground Marcin and Sam found.

"Twenty feet?" Sam said. "Did we get the spot wrong?"

"We don't think so."

"What rifle ejects a round twenty feet?"

"A Ruger mini-14. They're over gassed. Up to thirty feet isn't unusual. And they chamber a two-two-three. Lots of farmers and hunters use them around here. It's a good varmint gun."

"Are you trying to say this was another hunting accident?"

"No, not at all. From the statements you and Miss Adamowski gave and the evidence we have, I believe you were targeted. I just don't know why."

"You and me both brother. Beth - Miss Adamowski - thinks it's because I've been looking into a cold case. Her father's murder. But I've hardly started. I've only talked to her and two other people. One of them is a retired boss from the Chicago Police department."

"If I were you," Hatfield said, "I'd be talking to them both again."

"It's on my list," Sam said. "Are you going to take another look at Dave Hermann's death again?"

"Was Hermann looking into the same case as you are?

"Yes."

"Then you lied when I asked you if you knew about anything he was working on."

"I did. I'm sorry. But if I had told you, would you have reopened his shooting?"

"Probably not, not until I had more proof his death was connected to that case."

"So, no harm, no foul."

"You still shouldn't have lied to me."

"Fair enough. How about this? I'll give you what I have. I'll make a copy when I get back to Chicago and send it to you."

"I'd appreciate it."

"Are you going to reopen his shooting?"

"As soon as I find a connection."

"And I promise to let you know if I do."

Hatfield looked over to the tree line where the shooter took aim at Sam. It was well over two hundred yards away. "You know why he missed you?" he asked.

"I'm guessing the wind. I'm no expert but I know the wind can affect a shot over that distance."

"You'd be guessing right. You got lucky." He nodded a good-bye to Sam and walked over to the deputies standing inside the garage.

Det. Hatfield and the others wrapped up their work and cleared out. The overcast sky had turned black as the early evening became night. A light ran fell, driven nearly sideways by the wind. Sam and Beth were left alone with Marcin and his partner who sat in the Tahoe. Beth headed back into the house and Sam walked over and stood next to Marcin's window. Marcin lowered it only half way.

"I expect you'll be driving back to Chicago tonight," Sam said.

"We're not leaving," Marcin said. "Not until Kroll gives us the okay."

"Your cover is kind of blown. I don't see any point in hanging around."

"Our job is to keep tabs on you and report back. That's what we're going to do."

"It's up to you," Sam said. "Tell the Chief I'll be giving him a call." He turned and left them sitting in their Tahoe.

He found Beth inside, curled up in her spot on the recliner again. In her hand was a bottle of beer.

"Any more of those in the fridge?" Sam asked.

"Yeah," she said, "a few."

Sam grabbed a beer and twisted off the cap. He leaned against the kitchen island. "There's a few things we have to talk about," he said.

"Yeah, I know," she said. "Me first. Why were cops from Chicago following you?"

"Remember that first time you texted me?"

"You were at the police headquarters building."

"Yeah. Well, the Chief of Detectives is an old partner of mine. He let me take a printout of your father's file, the reports. He was kind of giving me permission to look into your father's case. He told me to stay in touch and let him know if I found anything. Apparently, he didn't trust me and put a tail on me. They're tracking me using the rental car company's GPS they install in the cars."

"Why doesn't he trust you?"

"He a cop. We, I mean, they don't trust anyone."

"I guess we actually got lucky with that. What about Dave's gun? Did you ask the detective about that?

"I did," Sam said. "He said they don't have it. It wasn't on his body and they didn't find it when they checked around the house. Okay, my turn now." Sam took a swig from the bottle. "We have to figure whoever shot at me knows about you. Whether they knew about you or not when they killed Dave, they know now."

"You finally believe me."

"Yeah, I had that 'come to Jesus' moment in the garage. And that means we both have to look over our shoulders now."

"I always have."

"Good." He took another drink and set the bottle on the island. "Because of that, I think we should stay here tonight. It's a long way back to Chicago on long stretches of highway with only light traffic. There are plenty of spots they can set up an ambush. Even with the police following us back there, it's better to be careful." He looked around the room and saw that Beth had already closed all the curtains and pulled the shades.

Beth said, "I'm way ahead of you. I'm taking the bedroom."

Sam looked over to the couch. "I've slept in worse places." He turned back to Beth. "Tomorrow, you drop me at my car and we follow each other back to Chicago. Okay?"

"Sure."

"Where are you staying?"

"At a motel not far from yours."

"I think you should switch. Stay at my hotel."

"I can't afford that. The motel I'm staying at is a low rent place. It's more for the afternoon delight crowd. Hourly rates, you know?"

"Yeah, well I still think we should stay close. How about if I cover the hotel for you?"

"You don't have to ask me twice."

"It's not charity. You're going to pay me back when you can."

"You're going to be waiting for a while."

"You know where I live. You can send me a check whenever."

"Sure. Anything else?"

Sam spotted her purse on the floor next to the recliner. "You got your Sig from the car?"

"Yeah."

"You reloaded?"

"Of course."

"Keep it close."

"Duh."

"One last thing. Your last name? Adamowski or Patterson?"

Legally, Beth told him, it was Adamowski. But she preferred Patterson and when she had the money for a lawyer she would have it changed back.

Beth left Sam for the bedroom and, after retrieving the homicide file from her car, he spent the next few hours on the couch reading. He bypassed the reports he had already read and moved straight to his handwritten notes.

He read his notes twice. He read the notes on the interviews he and Dave Hermann did with the witnesses three times. His notes were nothing more than an abbreviated version of the witnesses' statements written in his own shorthand. Dave's notes were no different.

After going over them all, he found nothing. No startling revelations, no missed clues, no key to unlock the whole mystery. There was nothing that led him then, sixteen years ago, or now to think Walter Patterson's murder was anything more than a robbery gone bad.

He flipped through the evidence report. It took him

fifteen seconds. Evidence recovered were two projectiles, bullets, removed from the chest of Walter. Both projectiles were submitted to NIBIS, the National Integrated Bullet Identification System. The database stores ballistic markings created by firearms used in past crimes. There were no matches in the database.

The only other evidence recovered was Walter's clothes. They were only important because of the powder burns which showed the gun was pressed tightly against Walter's chest when it was fired.

Sam closed the dark blue folder and laid it on the floor next to the couch. His cell phone told him it was already after two in the morning. He got up and walked down the hall to the bathroom. On his way back, he peeked in on Beth. She was curled up on the bed. Her rhythmic breathing told him she was asleep. He left the light on in the bathroom and the door ajar and walked back to the great room. After he double checked all the doors and windows, he plopped down on the couch. He stretched out, tucked his pistol between the cushions, and closed his eyes. He tried to clear his mind and give himself to sleep.

It didn't work. Getting shot at can do that to you. When he finally did doze off, he dreamt he was in Dave's garage again. But it was Marley with him instead of Beth.

CHAPTER
TWENTY-ONE

SAM WOKE to the smell of coffee. He heard Beth before he saw her.

"Hey, sleepy head. How was the couch?"

He slowly pushed his legs over the edge of the couch and sat up. He yawned, grimaced, and stretched his back. "Lousy," he said. He looked over to Beth, again camped out on the recliner, a cup of coffee in her hand and her father's file in her lap.

"You shouldn't read that," he said.

She looked down at the file and back to Sam. "I haven't. Not yet. I want to but I'm afraid to. Does that make sense."

Sam stood. "It makes perfect sense." He moved to take the folder from her but she dropped a hand on it to stop him.

"I'll give it back to you when you're ready," he said.

"You promise?"

"I promise." He pulled at the file and she let him

take it. He walked over to the kitchen island and set it down. He poured himself a cup of coffee and returned to his spot on the couch.

"You still look tired," Beth said.

"I was up late," he said after a sip from his cup.

"Reading?"

Sam nodded.

"Anything good?"

"Not yet. But I'll find something."

It was Beth's turn to nod. She set her empty cup on a side table. "Now what?"

"Like I said last night. You take me to my car and we head back to Chicago. We move you out of your motel and check you into mine."

"Do you still want to look for the spot where Dave was found?"

"No, after sleeping on it, I don't see any point. It's been months. There will be nothing to find. We wouldn't even be able to tell what direction the shot came from."

Beth nodded again and pushed herself out of the recliner. "I'm going to go clean up and get ready. Just let me know when you want to leave."

He watched her walk back down the hallway. When he heard the bathroom door close, he got up, walked to the island, and began leafing through the file. He wasn't looking for anything in particular. And he was more wrapped up in thinking about the investigation rather than reading any of the pages he flipped through. He started with the first page, turning each over one by one. On the eighth page, the page that included the summary of Darryl Wilcox's original interview, he found a yellow sticky note. It was stuck directly beneath Wilcox's statement.

Sam detached the note and paged ahead to Hermann's notes. He examined Dave's handwriting and tried to compare it to the note. He couldn't see a match. There was no way he could. The only thing written on the note was a question mark.

He left the file but took the note to the desk in the great room. He rummaged through the drawers and found a pad of yellow sticky notes. He took the pad to the kitchen and held it up to eye level. He angled the pad, twisting and turning it in the light. And there it was, lightly impressed on the pad. A question mark. Nothing else.

Sam went through the remaining pages but found no other notes. He closed the file and stood there thinking. Dave wrote the note and he wrote it here. Sixteen years after Water Patterson was killed.

"Ready when you are," Beth said.

Sam hadn't heard her come into the room. He told her to give him fifteen minutes and headed to the bathroom.

Beth dropped Sam at his rental. He followed her out of town and to the highway back to Chicago making sure to let her get no more than a few car lengths ahead of him. The four lane highway, two in each direction, cut through a countryside of farms and fields sitting ready for planting. He settled in for the drive, looking forward to the break from company. It would give him time to think. And he had a lot to think about. He started by making a list in his head.

First, like he told Beth, they would check her out of her motel. Next, check her into his hotel. Third, he would head back to the airport and return his rental and rent another from a different company. It wasn't so much to ditch Kroll's guys as he didn't care about them. It was more about losing the shooter. He had to believe he had another tracker on his car. It was the only way Sam could figure the shooter found him.

Next on the list was to call Joyce. He was a bit surprised she hadn't called him back yesterday. In fact, he thought, there was no time like the present. He pulled out his phone and hit the speed dial for Jack Hoke's office.

"Hoke and Dunn," Joyce answered, "please hold."

Sam put his phone on speaker and slipped it between his legs. He waited. It was a long wait. Finally, Joyce came back on. "Hoke and Dunn," she said, "how can I help you?"

"Joyce, it's Sam."

"Damn, I knew you'd call. I'm really sorry I didn't get back to you sooner."

"That's okay. I've been busy. Have you found anything?"

"Some. I'm still working on other stuff though."

"Well, can you give me what you have?"

"Yeah, hang on." Sam heard papers rustling. Joyce came back on. "Jack's been a pain in my ass lately. That's why this is taking me so long."

"What's his problem?"

"Nothing important as far as I'm concerned. All of a sudden we're busy as hell. We're handling everything but stuff is piling up."

"Well, I appreciate you doing this for me."

"Yeah, yeah. Okay, I found it. You ready?"

"Yeah, go ahead."

"Okay, first, Ronald Burke. He's dead.

"No kidding?"

"Yeah, about five years ago. I have a copy of the death certificate. Natural causes it looks like. A heart attack."

"Okay, anyone else dead?

"No. Moving on. Mae Lin Chan. I've got a couple of addresses and phone numbers. One of them is a business. A nail salon. You ready to copy?"

"No. I'm in my car. Can you text them or can I call you back later?"

"I'll text everything. Next, Darryl Wilcox, he's a piece of work. I have a couple of addresses, the last one from over ten years ago. I have no way to tell if he's still there. No phone either. And he's got a criminal record but I can only get it through the Illinois State Police website. There's a fee attached. Do you want me to run it?

"How much does it cost?"

"Twenty-five dollars."

"Don't bother. Way back when, we ran all of our witnesses. There's a copy of his criminal history in the file I have. But it's sixteen years old. I didn't read it again but if I remember correctly, it's mostly petty stuff."

"Let me know if you change your mind."

"Okay. Do you have any employment history on him?"

"No, I don't."

"Let's move on. What about Jerry Robinson and Truncheon Security?"

"That's the stuff I'm working on."

"Robinson should be easy."

"Yeah, he is. But the company is tricky."

"Why?

"I don't want to say until I have more."

Sam's phone buzzed. He checked the display. Beth was calling. "Hey," Sam said, "I've gotta go. I have another call."

"Yeah, go. I'll text you that stuff and call you when I have more on Robinson and Truncheon. Bye."

Sam punched at his phone. "Yeah, Beth?"

"I'm gonna need gas soon and I'm hungry."

"Pick any spot you like. I'm right behind you."

Beth passed two gas stations until she found one with a mom and pop diner next door. They gassed their cars then headed over to the restaurant. The place was like every other small, family run diner way out in the sticks. The main features were a local clientele with the occasional trucker, mismatched furniture and dinner ware, and good coffee.

They picked a table in the back, away from everyone else, for privacy while they talked. The locals didn't seem offended in the least. They put their orders in with the disinterested waitress and sipped their coffee.

"Can I ask you something?" Beth said.

"About your father's…about the case?"

"No, a personal question."

Sam fiddled with his silverware. "I guess. Go ahead."

Beth smiled. "Can you get the check for breakfast?"

Sam laughed. "Sure. I'll add it to your tab."

Beth took a sip of coffee. "Did I break the tension?"

Sam's eyebrows formed a deep vee. "Was there tension?"

"I kind of felt some."

"You're wrong. I just get lost in my own head sometimes and forget other people are around. It happens when I'm working a case."

"Okay, good. I was hoping we're okay now. You know, after I kind of played you."

"Kind of? Yeah, you played me. But we're past that."

"Good." It was Beth's turn to fiddle with her silverware. "You haven't told me anything about my father's investigation yet."

"What did Dave tell you?"

"Not much at all. He was a lot like you. He kept

things to himself. He said he'd tell me when he had something solid."

"Old habits die hard. As cops, we never shared with the victim's family."

"Why not?"

"False hope. We get leads, they don't pan out. We get more leads, they don't pan out. If we told the family every time we thought we had something we'd be putting them on an emotional rollercoaster."

"I can see that." She looked down at her silverware as she played with it. "Will you tell me anyway?"

"Do you want me to get the file out of my car so you can read it now?"

"No, I don't think I'm ready for that yet. Can you just tell me what's going on? Like, do you have any suspects yet?"

"I talked to a couple of people. One of them was Malcolm Burnett, but you already know that. The other person I talked to? It was an interesting conversation but he's no one I would call a suspect."

"What he they say? What do you have?"

The waitress came and not so carefully set their plates in front of them. Beth didn't wait and tore into her breakfast. As she ate, she looked up at Sam. Her wide eyes telling him she was waiting for his answer.

"Questions," he said. "I have questions. And, like I said, maybe the beginnings of a person of interest."

Beth swallowed and wiped her mouth with a napkin. "Isn't that a suspect?"

"It might be. It might not be. It just means I want to look at that person a little closer and talk to him again."

She set her fork down. "Who is it?"

"You don't know him."

"How do you know?"

"Fine. Jerry Robinson. His name is Jerry Robinson"

"Who?"

"See? I said you didn't know him."

"Who is Jerry Robinson? What does he have to do with my father's murder?"

"I didn't say he had anything to do with it. I only said I want to look at him a little closer."

"Why did you talk to him in the first place? Who is he?"

"Lower your voice, Beth. People are looking at us."

"Screw them. Will you please just answer my question?"

"He was a cop. A Chicago cop. He was a boss, a deputy chief. He's retired now. I talked to him because, back when he was still on the job, he took an unusual interest in your father's murder."

"What does that mean?"

"He looked at the reports repeatedly during the course of the investigation and even after it stalled. He really didn't have any reason to. It was not in his area of responsibility. He wasn't part of the detective division chain of command. He also locked the computerized reports so that no one could open them without the authorization of someone of his rank or higher. That's why I talked to him."

"What did he say?"

"He claimed he knew your father. He met him a few times at social events. When he learned your father was killed, he became curious and followed the investigation through the reports."

"And what did you call it? Locking the reports? Why did he do that?"

"He said he didn't realize he did it. It was an accident."

"Is that possible?"

"I don't know yet. It seems plausible for someone who may not be adept with a computer. Our computer reporting system was still kind of new back then so it's possible he just didn't know what he was doing." Sam saw Beth's next question coming and said, "No, I don't know if Robinson is computer savvy or not."

"Can you find out?"

"Doubtful. But I can talk to some people and see how hard or easy it is to flag a file."

Beth seemed satisfied with Sam's answers. But he could see the wheels in her head working. She picked up her fork and started in on her breakfast again.

Sam did the same and they both ate in silence. Sam pushed his empty plate to the side and sipped his coffee while he waited for Beth to finish. When she finally sopped up the last of her eggs with a piece of toast, Sam said, "We should get back on the road."

"One more cup of coffee?" she asked.

"Let's get a couple of cups to go." He caught the eye

of the waitress. As she shuffled closer, Sam asked for the to-go coffees and the check.

When she shuffled off again, Beth said, "You said this Jerry Robinson is retired now."

"From the police department, yes."

"What's he doing? Just sitting around his house? Sitting on his porch and chasing kids off his lawn?"

"No. He started a business."

"Truncheon Security? Is that why you stopped there?" she said.

Sam sat back, disgusted with himself for forgetting she was tracking his phone. "You're playing me again. You knew about Robinson all along. You knew I did a search for him on my phone," he said.

"No, I didn't know anything about him."

"That's bullshit. You're lying to me again."

"No, I swear. I can't see your internet searches. I only get your phone calls, texts, and GPS location."

"I don't believe you."

Beth crossed her arms, turned her head, and stared out the window. Sam was having none of it.

"Quit pouting. You've manipulated me and lied to me from the minute I met you. And now, when I catch you doing it again, you lied again. I should walk out of here, get in my car and drive back to Florida."

"I'm not lying," she said. "I didn't play you. I didn't know about Robinson. I took a shot in the dark."

Sam ignored her. "I should just leave. But I won't. I'm going to do this for you but more for Dave. And I'm doing it my way, alone. You're going to stop tracking me and following me and you're going to unclone my phone or whatever you have to do to stop spying on me. You do it or I *am* going back to Florida. Understand?"

The waitress returned and set two foam cups and the check on the table. Sam grabbed the check and one of the cups. "Let's go," he said and walked over to the cash register.

CHAPTER
TWENTY-TWO

BETH FOLLOWED Sam out of the diner. As Sam opened his rental's door, Beth came up behind him.

"I wasn't pouting," she said. "I was angry with myself. You're right. I've lied to you and I'm sorry. But I didn't lie about Robinson. I didn't know anything about him until you just told me about him."

Sam turned to face her. "Do you think an apology is going to make me believe you?"

"No, I guess not."

"I want to. I really do. But I just can't trust you."

She pulled out her phone. "Here," she said, "check my phone. You'll see for yourself."

"I don't know anything about cloning phones or where the data would show up on your phone. Besides, you could have deleted everything already."

"What can I do to convince you?"

"I don't know, Beth," he said shaking his head. "I don't know." Sam settled behind the steering wheel and looked up at her. "We'll talk more when we get back. Let's get going." He pulled his door closed and started the engine.

The two hour drive ended at Beth's motel. She was packed and checked out in less than fifteen minutes. She followed Sam to his hotel where he checked her in. He left her to get settled in her room while he drove to the airport to swap out his car.

An hour later, he was back at his hotel. He parked the new rental in back, out of view from the street, and headed to his room. Once inside, he put the folder that held Walter Patterson's homicide file on the desk, locked his pistol in the room's safe, and laid down on the bed. He figured he deserved a short nap.

As he closed his eyes, his phone rang. He pulled it from his pocket and checked the display. He pressed the button to answer and held it to his ear.

"Gene," he said. "I'm glad you called. We have a few things to talk about."

————

Jerry Robinson sat behind his desk. He was not happy.

"I told you to follow him. That's all. I didn't tell you to take any action. Only to follow him and report back to me."

The man across from him lounged in his chair. He reclined so low, Robinson could hardly believe he was comfortable.

"I saw my chance and I took it."

Jerry's jaw tightened. "But you missed and now he knows Hermann wasn't an accident."

"So what?" the man said. "He can't prove it. The cops can't prove it."

"So what? You moron. It doesn't matter if he can prove it. He knows. And that means he knows he rattled someone. He's not going to give up now."

The man smiled. "He already did. I scared him off."

"What are you talking about?" Robinson said.

"He left. He took his rental car back to the airport. He's probably back in Florida already."

Robinson stood and walked around the desk. He perched himself on the edge of his desk across from the man.

"Sit up, you fool."

The man shrugged and did as he was told.

"Did it ever occur to you that he realized his car probably had a tracker on it and he went to the airport to get a different car?"

"Um," was all the man could come up with.

"Your problem," Robinson said, "is that you think everyone is as stupid as you are. Go back to his hotel and sit in the parking lot until you see him get into a car. You got it?"

"Yes sir. You want me to follow him if he leaves?"

"No," Jerry said. "After you make his new car, I want you to wait there in the parking lot until he comes back and then put a new tracking unit on the car."

———

Sam sat up and leaned against the bed's headboard. "You didn't need to put a tail on me, Gene."

"I know you too well, Sam," the Chief said. "I wouldn't have heard from you until, well, who knows when? And from what my detectives told me, it's lucky for you that I did."

Sam shrugged even though Kroll couldn't see it. "The shooter was probably gone by the time they showed up," he said.

"Maybe, maybe not."

"Are you going to keep the tail on me? If you are, you should know I swapped out my car at the airport."

"Yeah, Marcin told me. They should be getting a new subpoena right now. Do I really need to keep them on you? Are you going to tell me why you were in Galena? I suppose it's because of Dave Hermann."

"Yeah," Sam said. "I don't think his shooting was an accident."

"What makes you think that?"

"My client."

"The victim's daughter?"

"Yeah, Elizabeth Patterson."

"She was the girl with you in Galena, right?"

"Marcin told you about her, huh? I'm not surprised. He seems like a good detective. Anyway," Sam said, "she told me that her father's murder has been gnawing at her for years. And who could blame her? She had our names, me and Dave Herman. She went to Dave first and convinced him to take another look at her father's murder."

"And you're sure he was working on it?"

"Yeah, absolutely. He had the missing Walter Patterson homicide file. I've got it now."

"Hermann took it? Where did he have it?"

"At his place in Galena. Like I said, I have it now. It's safe."

"We need that back, Sam."

"You'll get it, don't worry."

"I do worry, Sam. Okay, so he had the working file. He was looking at the murder again. How does that prove Dave's death is a murder?"

"It doesn't," Sam said. "But do you think it's a coincidence that once I pick up the case and shake a few trees that someone tries to take me out the same way Dave was killed?"

"What trees did you shake?"

"Didn't your boys tell you?"

"Why don't you tell me, Sam?"

"Okay. I went to see Jerry Robinson."

"Truncheon Security, right?"

"Your boys figured that out, huh?"

"No. They don't know about Robinson. I didn't tell them about him. I only said that I wanted them to tail you. They tracked you there. I checked out Truncheon and Robinson came up as its president."

Sam nodded to himself. Gene was keeping his people out of the loop and that was fine with him.

"What did Robinson have to say?" Kroll asked.

"He told me he knew Walter Patterson socially and

became interested in the investigation because of that. He was only following the case out of curiosity."

"Why did he put the lock on it?"

"He said he didn't know he did. He said it must have been an accident and he hit the wrong key or something."

"Mmm-hmm. Well, that's bullshit."

"He's lying?" Sam said.

"Yeah. It's not easy to do. You have to jump through hoops to get it done. There are a bunch of check boxes and you have to enter your passcode before the system lets you do that. There's no way he did all that by accident."

"Then that moves him into the suspect column."

"Sam, I'm going to call Commander Kuchinski in Area Four. I want him to assign some of his people to this."

"Come on, Gene. Give me a chance to dig up a little more. All I have are a couple of coincidences right now. Let me find some real evidence. Plus, I already have a couple of your people following me. I don't want to have to work with a couple more on top of that."

"Sam, you're a civilian working on an open homicide. I cut you some slack for old times' sake. It was okay when I thought you were just going to poke around and see if you could come up with something. I really didn't think you would find anything. There's nothing in the reports I read that indicated anything but a robbery gone wrong. But now it looks like you found something. Even if it's pretty thin, I can't allow you to keep investigating an open murder."

"Allow me?"

"Yes. I'm telling you to stop. If you don't, you could be charged with obstruction of justice, interfering with an on-going investigation, concealing evidence, and who the hell knows what else. I want that file back, Sam. I want it today."

"Sure, you know where to find me. Send someone to get it." Sam ended the call without waiting for Kroll to respond. He picked up the hotel phone and dialed Beth's room. She answered on the third ring.

"Hello?" she said.

"Beth, it's me," he said. "Don't unpack. We're moving. I'll meet you down by the front desk."

"What's going on?"

"I'll tell you later. Hurry up. We have to move fast."

CHAPTER
TWENTY-THREE

"WHAT'S GOING ON?" Beth said. "Is this because you're still mad at me?"

Sam was standing at the front door scanning the parking lot. "Not now," he said. "There's a bank on the corner of Canfield and Devon. Look it up on your phone. It's a couple miles away. Meet me there. Park in the back. Watch for someone following you. If you spot a tail, call me and I'll think of an alternate plan."

"Who am I watching for?"

"Anyone, maybe the black Tahoe. I don't know. But keep your eyes open. Now go."

Beth hustled out the door and disappeared around the corner. Sam watched the parking lot exit until he saw her leave the lot. He stood there and watched for anyone following her. As far as he could tell, she was in the clear.

He went to a back door and poked his head out. He didn't see anything that raised the hair on the back of his neck. He hurried to his new rental, looked around one last time, and pulled out of the lot.

The spot he told Beth to meet him at was only ten minutes away. It took him twenty minutes. He cut through several residential neighborhoods, all of which were familiar to him from his days living in Chicago. He doubled back twice and pulled U-turns to ensure he wasn't being followed.

He pulled into the bank's lot, drove around the back, and spotted Beth sitting in her car. He pulled next to her, driver to driver, and lowered his window.

"What's going on?" she said.

"You weren't followed?"

"No. I was careful."

Sam nodded. "Remember last night when I told you my old partner gave me the okay to look into your father's murder?"

"Yeah, the detective chief."

"He called me today. His spies in the black Tahoe told him about us getting shot at in Galena. I explained what happened and that I think that whoever shot at us also killed Dave. I also told him I have the working file. No one knew Dave had it. Like I told you, it's not supposed to leave the office. The chief wants it back."

"Let's go to Kinkos and make a copy. He can have his file back."

"He also said he wants me to stop investigating your dad's murder. He's going to have the Area detectives take another look at it."

Beth didn't say anything. She turned her head and stared out the front windshield.

"Beth?" Sam said. "They have better resources. They have subpoena power, they can get search warrants, and they have a lot of really capable detectives."

She turned back, her eyes betraying her growing anger. "You're giving up. You don't want to help me any longer."

"I didn't say that. I'll keep working on it if you want me too. But I want you to know we're going to be playing hide and seek with the police if I do. I'll probably get arrested if they find me."

"Then there's no upside for you."

"But there is for you."

"What? All those things you said? The resources and search warrants and good detectives?"

"No, I meant there's an upside if I stay with this."

"What?"

"I'm not bound by all those legal constraints that the police are. There's no right to a lawyer when I talk to people."

Beth nodded. She understood. "You'd do that for me?"

"Yes. You and Dave."

"Thank you."

Sam nodded and started to roll up his window.

"Sam?" Beth said.

He turned back to her. "Yeah?"

"I'm really sorry I lied about, you know, all that other stuff."

"Forget it. I'm over it."

"No, I mean it. I'm sorry. I won't do it again. I promise."

"Never make a promise you can't keep."

Sam walked over to the bank's outdoor ATM and withdrew as much cash as it would give him. After, he had Beth follow him to a nearby side street. He parked the rental car and left the keys under the seat. He'd call them later and say it wouldn't start for him and that they should tow it in.

He had Beth drive them to Bruno's friend, Woz's bar. On the way, they stopped at a gas station and bought two prepaid cell phones. Burners. Sam transferred the contact list and the texts from Joyce from his phone to his burner and he and Beth exchanged their burner's phone numbers. At Woz's tavern, he dropped their phones with Woz and told them Bruno would be in to pick them up. Woz didn't even ask why.

Back in Beth's Jeep, they headed to the River North neighborhood in Chicago. Sam picked a lower end motel for them to crash. Beth used her ID – with the name Adamowski – to check in since Sam was confident Kroll was unaware of her name change. At least so far. Sam paid cash for two rooms, one night only. They'd switch hotels the next day.

Sam walked Beth to her room and waited as she opened the door. She walked in, looked around, checked out the bathroom, and turned back to Sam. Her face told him she was less than enthused.

"I didn't even get to shower in the other place."

"What's wrong with this place?" Sam said.

"The bathroom reminds me of that old movie 'Psycho'."

"I'll bet you've showered in worse places when you were in the service."

"I guess," she said. "Now what? What's the plan for the rest of today?"

"I've gotta call my father and let him know what's going on. Then Kinkos," Sam said, "and the post office."

———

Kroll answered his cell phone with a curt "Chief Kroll."

"Chief? This is Detective Alvarez."

"Did you get the file, Detective?"

"No sir. Laska checked out of the hotel."

"Son of a bitch."

"Sir? There's something else. There's another man registered here with the same last name. A Bernard Laska."

"I think I remember that's the father. He goes by Bruno but Bernard is his real name. I need you to stay on him, got it?"

"Yes, sir."

Kroll hung up and dialed a number.

Detective Marcin answered.

"Marcin, this is Chief Kroll. Did you get the subpoena for Laska's new rental car?"

"Yes, sir. We're already tracking him."

"Where is he?"

"We haven't seen him, sir. But the car is parked on a residential street on the northwest side of the city."

"Alright, good. Detective Alvarez called. Laska checked out of his hotel. We have to figure he's ducking us."

"He's not going to do that, sir. We've got his car."

"I'm not so sure we do."

"I don't follow, sir."

"Just let me know if he comes back to the car."

"Yes, sir. What do you want us to do if we get eyes on him?"

"Bring him to me. If he refuses, arrest him."

Kroll ended the call. He pressed a button on his desk phone.

Sergeant Williams' voice came over the intercom, "Yes, Chief?"

"Roy, see if you can pull Laska's old personnel file. Have someone do a background check on him. Full service. And I've got his cell phone number. Let's get moving on a subpoena."

"Yes, sir. Right away."

"And get me Commander Kuchinski from Area Four on the phone."

———

Sam and Beth stood in line at the River North post office waiting to mail the original file. Before copying the file, he made sure to remove the yellow sticky note Dave added. Sam addressed the heavy cardboard envelope he picked up at the post office to Chief Kroll at police headquarters. He thought about sending it express overnight delivery but decided to just go first class. That would give him a little more time before anyone could read it and catch up.

"What about your car?" Beth asked.

"What about it?" Sam said.

"Are you going to call the rent-a-car place and let them know where it is?"

"Sooner or later. The police are probably tracking it already. The longer I let them think they know where we are, the better for us."

A woman behind the counter waved them over. Sam paid the postage, took the receipt, and handed it to Beth. "Add this to the total you owe me," he said as they walked to her car.

"You're kidding, right?" she asked.

Sam only smiled.

They loaded themselves into Beth's Jeep. She asked, "What now?"

Sam said, "We eat. I'm hungry. It's too late to do much else today."

CHAPTER
TWENTY-FOUR

JERRY ROBINSON CHECKED the display on his phone as it rang. He punched at his phone. "What?" he said.

"Yeah, it's me."

"I know it's you. The phone tells me who is calling," Robinson said.

"Yeah, anyway, I'm over at the guy's hotel."

"Have you seen him?"

"No."

Robinson's jaw tightened. "Then why are you calling me?"

"There's cops over here. They look like detectives. You know, suits and ties and shit. They went inside and then came out. They were sitting in their car and one guy was on his phone."

"Are they still there?"

"Yeah. What you want me to do?"

"Stay there. Don't move until I call you back."

Robinson sat at his desk and pulled up the phone number for the hotel on his computer. He used his desk phone, registered to Truncheon Security, and dialed the number. The desk clerk answered, "DoubleTree O'Hare. How can I help you?"

"Yes, hello," Robinson said, "I'd like to be connected to Mr. Laska's room."

"One minute, sir"

Robinson drummed his fingers on the desk. He listened to a series of clicks and then the phone's ring.

"Yeah?" Bruno said, answering.

"Mr. Laska, please." Robinson asked.

"Yeah, that's me. Who is this?"

Robinson was confused. The voice on the other end was different in some way from the man he met. Similar but rougher, gruff. "Mr. Sam Laska?" Robinson asked.

"No. Who is this?"

Robinson hung up and redialed the hotel. When the clerk answered, he said, "I just called and asked for Mr. Laska's room. I was connected to someone else. I should have said Mr. Sam Laska's room."

"One minute, sir." Robinson waited. The clerk came back on. "I'm sorry, sir. Mr. Sam Laska checked out earlier today."

"Well, who was that other gentleman you connected me to? Maybe I could talk to him again."

"I believe the two are related. Shall I connect you?"

Robinson hung up without answering the clerk. He picked up his cell phone and dialed.

"Yo, what's up?"

"Is that how you answer the phone?" Robinson said.

"Sorry, man. I didn't see it was you. What's up? You want me to keep looking for that dude?"

Robinson spoke through clenched teeth. "No, he's gone. He checked out of his room. You lost him because you are a moron. Listen closely, I have a new job for you."

———

Bruno grabbed his cell phone. He dialed Sam's new burner phone.

Sam picked up quickly. "What's up, Dad?"

"Sam, someone called looking for you."

"Who?"

"I don't know. He called on the hotel phone, not my cell phone. He sounded black."

Sam closed his eyes and pinched the bridge of his nose with the thumb and index fingers of his free hand. "Dad, you don't know he was black. No one can tell what someone looks like by their voice."

"Don't start on me, Sam. I'm telling you, I can tell."

"Okay, Dad. What did he want?"

"I think he thought he was calling your room and the operator gave him mine."

"Why do you think that?"

"When I answered, he asked if I was you."

"What did you say?"

"I just said no. Nothing else. I didn't say you moved out."

"He probably knows it now anyway."

"I swear, Sam. I didn't say anything."

"I believe you, Dad."

"I think it might have been Jerry Robinson, Sam."

"Why do you think that?"

"Who else could it be?"

"The police. They're probably looking for me."

"But wouldn't they say they were cops? I'm telling you, Sam. I really think it was Jerry Robinson."

"Did you ever talk to him when you were still on the job? Do you know what Robinson sounds like?"

"No."

"Okay, Dad. Listen, just to be safe, maybe you should check out of the hotel. Find a different place."

"You think Robinson is a suspect then, huh?"

"Dad, I don't know yet. But the only people I can see looking for me are the police and the guy that took a shot at me. It probably was the police looking for me but, just to be safe, find a new hotel. Okay?"

"Yeah, Sam. Okay."

"Hey, Dad? Did you pick up the phones from Woz yet?"

"No, not yet. I'm gonna stop by there later tonight. I'll get them then."

"Okay, Dad. Talk to you later."

Sam slipped the burner back into his pocket. Beth was sitting across the table from him. They were in a pizza joint on Southport Avenue in the Lakeview neighborhood. She munched on a square of their pizza and said, "What's up with your father? I heard you say Robinson's name. He called your father?"

"My father doesn't know. He thinks he knows but the guy that called didn't identify himself. He was looking for me so Bruno thinks it was Robinson."

"You don't?"

"I don't know who it was. But the most likely answer is that the cops called looking for me. Kroll wants that file back."

"What if it was Robinson?"

"That would be interesting. That would mean he knows, or knew, where I was staying. How would he know that unless he was keeping tabs on me?"

"You mean following you."

"Yeah. And what reason would he have for following me?"

"Because you scared him."

"Right."

"Maybe he was scared enough to take a shot at us?"

"Maybe. It's interesting, isn't it?"

"You don't sound too concerned."

"I'd be more concerned if I was sure it wasn't the police that called my dad."

"Yeah," Beth said. "I guess it was a good move getting out of that hotel."

She took another bite of pizza. "You know," she said, "when you told me we were going for pizza, I half expected you to take me for deep dish Chicago style."

"That stuff is for tourists. This is real Chicago pizza.

Tavern style, thin crust and cut into squares, not wedges." He took a piece from the pie between them. "You should know that. You were born here."

"I spent my teenage years in St. Louis. Those are the prime going-out-for-pizza-with-your-friends years."

"I guess," he said. He held up his piece for her inspection. "What do you think?"

"I like St. Louis style better. It's the cheese here, it's bland."

Sam took a sip from his stein of beer. He thought about his father's phone call. Odds were, it was some police officer or detective who called Bruno. There was no doubt Kroll would send someone to retrieve the file from Sam. And that's just it. They would show up, in person. They'd check with the desk for the room number and learn Sam had checked out. And if by some weird chance they did call try calling, they would call Sam's cell phone they got from Kroll and not the hotel.

The more he thought about it the more he convinced himself that whoever it was that called Bruno was not the police.

CHAPTER
TWENTY-FIVE

"WHAT NOW?" Beth asked. She and Sam had finished dinner and were walking back to Beth's car.

"To the motel," Sam said. We can't do any more today."

"Alright, I guess." she said. They walked, with neither saying anything more until they sat in the car. As she started her Jeep, she said, "Can we pick a better place to stay tomorrow?"

"We can try, but we need to stretch my cash as far as possible."

"What if we shared a room?"

Sam turned and stared at her stone-faced.

Beth glanced at him as she pulled from the curb. "No, I'm not coming on to you. We'd get two beds. I just think that if we shared a room we could upgrade the hotel a little and still save money. When you think about it, it makes sense."

"I don't know."

"Hey, I was in the Army. I've shared sleeping quarters with guys before. It's no big deal. What do you say?"

"Alright, I guess. But I'm not changing my routine just because you're there. I sleep in a tee shirt and my shorts and I may make offensive noises in the bathroom."

"Same goes for me."

"And if I'm working, going over the file or making phone calls or something, you stay quiet and don't bother me. No questions."

"Deal. What's your room budget?"

"Less than two hundred. No, less than one-fifty."

"Okay, I'll look for a place." Beth steered the car south towards the River North neighborhood, passing through upscale Lincoln Park. "Are you going to work any tonight?" she said.

"I'm going to do more reading. Study up for the interviews I want to do tomorrow. I want to make a couple phone calls too."

"How about we stop somewhere and get a drink first?"

Sam answered quickly. "No."

Beth frowned. "Well, how about we just pick up a six-pack."

"That we can do," he said. "Domestic, not imported. And bottles, not cans."

.   .   .

Sam laid on the lumpy bed with a bottle of beer. The springs creaked every time he moved or shifted his body. *And what was that smell?*, he thought. Beth wasn't wrong about picking better motels from now on. He was trying to read over the statements of the three witnesses, Ronald Burke, Mae Lin Chan, and Darryl Wilcox. Burke was now deceased according to Joyce and Sam would have to rely solely on his previous interview. The others, Chan and Wilcox, would be interviewed again tomorrow. Finding Wilcox would be harder than Chan.

The statements of all three witnesses were similar but different enough to account for their unique perspectives. Slight differences due to perspective were expected. It would raise the hackles of any good investigator if their accounts were exactly alike.

What was strange, though, was their completely different description of the killer. Burke was unable to offer any description other than that the offender was an African-American man wearing dark clothing. He claimed, at the time, that when he realized what was happening, he put his head down and tried to disappear into his seat. Chan and Wilcox gave the only two detailed descriptions of the killer. But their varying descriptions of the killer was the primary reason a sketch artist wasn't called in to develop a composite drawing.

Sam remembered that Mae Lin Chan had difficulty speaking English. Sam spoke with her only briefly as Dave conducted the interview with her but from what

Sam could gather at the time was that Chan, being a recent immigrant from Taiwan, had only a rudimentary grasp of English. He hoped her language skills had improved since then.

Wilcox had no problem with English but he had one with the police. He had been arrested several times in the past, all for petty crimes. Sam felt, at the time, this was the reason for his uneasiness and nervous demeanor during the interview. After all, he was a young black man whose previous encounters with the police were negative. At least as far as Wilcox was concerned.

Chan and Wilcox gave similar accounts of the crime, both stating that a black man on the train car began going from passenger to passenger. He displayed a small black gun and demanded money from the passengers. He approached Walter Patterson, said something and thrust the gun against Patterson's chest and fired. When the train stopped at the next station, he fled out the door mixing in with the crowd of passengers who also ran off the train car.

Sam took a sip of his beer and looked over at the clock on the nightstand. It read three-thirty-four. He knew that was wrong and checked with his burner. The real time was eight-fourteen. The phone in his hand reminded him he had calls to make. He checked the contacts he transferred from his cell phone and hit the button to dial Joyce's phone.

The phone rang five time before Joyce picked up. "Hello?" she said.

"Joyce, it's Sam."

"Where the hell have you been? I've been trying to call you."

"Sorry, I had to ditch my phone. I've got a burner now."

"I was wondering. I didn't recognize the number and almost didn't answer."

"I'm glad you did. Write down this new number."

"It's on my phone now, you goof."

"Oh, yeah. Sorry. Do you have anything for me?"

"Yeah, I do. Hang on."

Sam waited and listened to the noise in the background. A television that was a bit too loud, some conversation he couldn't make out, and a baby fussing somewhere.

Joyce came back on. "Okay, got it. You ready?"

"Joyce, I didn't know you had a family."

"Yeah, imagine that. I have a life outside of work. Can we get on with this? I've got to get the baby down soon."

"Sorry. Go ahead."

"Okay, Jerry Robinson. Fifty-eight years old, unmarried—"

"Let me stop you there Joyce. You can text me his birthday and address when you get a chance. I know about his time on the police department. What I need is everything after he left there."

"Okay, let's see. After he left the police department he incorporated a company, Truncheon Security. That was in 2008. The company has good financials. They have security contracts with a bunch of malls, a grocery store chain, and bunch of odds and ends places. Their website says they do risk assessment too. I can't find who they might have been contracted with for that."

"Standard stuff for a security operation," Sam said, "but I know they're building some big campus. Where would they get the money for that?"

"Maybe if you gave me a chance to finish, you'd find out."

"Yeah, yeah. What do you have?"

"About eight months ago they were awarded the contract to run security for 420 Growers LLC."

"What do they do?"

"Really? The name didn't clue you in?"

"No. Why should it?"

"Medical and recreational marijuana is legal in Illinois. The 420 Growers company is just that. They grow and cultivate marijuana in Illinois."

"Damn, and that's an all cash business. Banks aren't allowed to do business with them because they're federally insured."

"Exactly. It's a perfect business to wash money," Joyce said, "if you were so inclined. But there's more."

"What?"

"Robinson isn't the only owner of Truncheon. He has a partner. Or partners."

"Who?"

"I don't know yet. Some company. But it makes sense. He had a shitty credit history and probably couldn't get a start-up loan. The trouble is the company is a shell company. I'm working it backwards but I'm not getting anywhere yet. This is complicated stuff, Sam.

"How much of Truncheon does Robinson own?"

"Forty-nine percent."

"Then he's not the boss."

There was a knock at Sam's door. "Is there anything else, Joyce?" Sam asked. "There's someone at my door."

"No, go ahead. I'll text you that other stuff on Robinson."

Sam pressed a button on his phone and walked to the door. He looked through the peephole, hesitated for only a second or two, and opened the door. Beth stood there holding up two bottles of beer. "Can we hang out?" she said. "I'm bored and I ran out of quarters for the magic fingers."

TWENTY-SIX

SAM SWUNG the door open and stepped aside. "Sure, come on in," he said.

Beth stepped through the door and handed Sam a bottle as she walked past. She spotted the pile of papers, copies of her father's homicide file, on the bed. "Are you working?," she said. "Am I bothering you?"

"No, I think I'm done for the night. I got everything done that I wanted to."

Beth twisted the cap off the bottle, sat in a chair at the desk and crossed her legs. She looked around the room. She spotted a silver metal urn sitting on top of the television. "Is that…is that Dave?"

"Yeah, it is."

"What are you going to do with him?"

"When this is over, I'm going to have a memorial service. He deserves that much."

"You're going to pay for that?"

"I'm going to ask for donations from the people that know him, worked with him."

Beth nodded. She raised her bottle, "Here's to Dave," she said and took a pull from her bottle.

Sam raised his bottle and drank with her. "To Dave," he said.

Beth sat quiet for a time. Feeling the need to lighten the mood, she sniffed the air and crinkled her nose. "What's that smell?"

Sam set the bottle in his hand down on the end table and began gathering up the papers scattered on the bed. He said, "I was wondering the same thing. I think something died in here."

"Eww, really?"

"I'm kidding. I don't know. But it does stink, right?"

Beth took a swig from her bottle. "Yeah. There's still time to get out of here and go to a bar or something."

He straightened the stack of papers and set them on his nightstand. "Nope," he said, sitting on the bed, "I want to get up and out the door early. And that reminds me, I need your car tomorrow. I'm going to reinterview the witnesses who were on the 'L' train."

"I can't go with you?"

"Absolutely not."

"You're going to leave me in this dump alone?"

"I told you in Galena, I'm doing this by myself. And you don't have to stay here. In fact, you probably can't. Check out is at eleven. I won't be back until after that."

"Where am I supposed to go without a car?"

"Take the bus or an Uber. Go to a movie or a museum. I'll call you when I'm done and pick you up."

"Well that sucks."

Sam shrugged and sipped his beer.

Beth stood and put her empty bottle on the desk. "I guess I should go. I didn't expect the evening to go like this."

"What were you expecting," he said.

"I don't know. Maybe that we'd get to know each other better."

Sam shot her a look. "That is never going to happen. We are never going to happen."

"That's not how I meant it, Sam. Geez, you're way too old for me. Why do men always go there? I guess I just thought we could be friends or something."

"I could do that," he said. "And what do you mean I'm too old? Marly is younger than me by eight years."

Beth sat again. "So, you naturally think all younger women should find you attractive? There's the male ego rearing its ugly head. But Marley, that's a conversation I'd like to have. Let's talk about you and Marley."

Sam drained his beer and set the bottle down on the end table. "Okay, what do you want to know?"

"How did you meet? Why did you break up? Joe the bartender said she dumped you."

Sam ran a hand through his hair. "Yeah, she did."

"Why?"

"I screwed up."

"How? Did you cheat on her?"

"No, I would never. You know what? I don't think I want to talk about this after all."

Beth ignored him. "If you didn't cheat, what did you do? It couldn't have been that bad."

Sam exhaled heavily. "I didn't think so either at the time. I thought I was doing the right thing. But now, I get why she broke it off."

"Come on, you've gotta tell me now. What happened?"

"I really don't want to get into it."

"Don't you want a woman's perspective? I can tell you whether I think you screwed up or she's blowing it out of proportion."

"I don't know."

"Come on. I'll bet I can help."

Sam thought about that. "Okay, maybe you can. Here goes. There was this guy in Florida, a dirty cop. He got caught and blamed me. He killed two federal agents and escaped. He was coming after me. I got a heads up from a friend, she's a deputy U.S. Marshal now, that the guy was after me. I got Marley and we came here to Chicago to put distance between him and me."

"Did Marley know about this guy?"

"Not at first, but I eventually told her. Anyway, the guy followed us to Chicago. I got caught up with some stuff with the police and Marley was alone in our hotel room downtown. She was safe, she had two deputy marshals with her. But she insisted on going to the police station to be with me and she left with the deputies in tow. The guy was waiting outside the hotel. He killed one of the deputies and almost killed the other one. He grabbed Marley. Kidnapped her."

"Holy shit."

"Yeah, holy shit. Marley is a tough girl though. She escaped as the guy was driving away by jumping out of the pickup they were in. Her pickup truck actually. She ran to a restaurant and called the police. By this time, the police and Marshals and FBI were in full search mode.

"I got to the restaurant with a couple cop friends. I made sure Marley was safe and unhurt and we were waiting for more help. As we're sitting there, Marley figures out how to track the guy and find out where he is."

"How?"

"She left her purse and phone in the truck when she jumped out."

"Pretty slick of her."

"I don't think she did it on purpose. But anyway, I told her to stay with one of the cops. I wanted to go get the guy myself. She told me to stay with her and let the cops handle it. She said she needed me to be with her. I didn't listen. I left."

"Why?"

"I wanted to make sure this guy never had another chance to hurt her."

"You were going to kill him?"

"Yes, if he didn't surrender first. I was going to give him that chance."

"I get that. But you left her when she needed you. She was just kidnapped. Do you realize how traumatic that was for her?"

"I do. But I wasn't thinking about that at the time. I was only thinking about keeping her safe."

"Did you talk to her about it?"

"I tried, a few times. She said that since then, she just can't trust me to be with her when she needs me."

"Trust is a hard thing to win back."

"Yeah, tell me about it."

Beth got out of the chair. "Well, this has been depressing."

"You asked for it."

"Yeah, I did." She dug into the pocket of her jeans and pulled out her keys. She tossed them to Sam and said, "I'm going to bed. Don't forget to call me when you're done tomorrow."

As she opened the door, she said, "Oh, and fill it up too. It's almost empty."

———

Jerry Robinson sat in his office sipping a bourbon. As late as it was, he couldn't leave until he got the phone call. His cellphone, on the desktop in front of him, stayed quiet for what seemed hours. He raised the glass to his lips again. The phone began buzzing. He checked the display, drained his glass, and pressed the button to answer. "I hope you have good news," he said.

"I did what you said," the voice answered. "I

checked all the license plates in the parking lot. There's one with Florida plates."

"Give me the plate number."

The man on the other end recited the letters and numbers as Robinson typed it into his computer. He read the screen and said into the phone, "That's it. His name is Bernard Laska. He has a Sarasota, Florida address. Stay on the car and let me know about any movement."

"Man, I've been here hours. How about I put a tracker on it?"

"That does us no good. We need eyes on the father's Cadillac. A tracker won't tell us if Laska comes back. You need to stay there and don't do anything but watch the car until I get back to you."

"When? I've been here all day."

"And you might be there all night. Understand this, you are going to be there until Laska comes back. We lost him because of your fuck up in Galena so suck it up and do this or we all are fucked. You got it?"

"Yeah, I got it."

CHAPTER
TWENTY-SEVEN

SAM WOKE before the sun came up. He showered and packed. With his Beretta tucked safely in the small of his back, he headed out the door. His first thought as he climbed into Beth's Jeep was coffee. His second thought was Marley and the mistake he made leaving her when she needed him to stay. If he didn't leave her at the hotel everything bad that followed would not have happened.

He found a Starbucks not too far away and paid cash at the drive-thru for two coffees. The sun was coming up as he stopped to gas up the Jeep. He drove back to the motel and parked in a spot in front of Beth's door. She answered his knock quickly. Beth stood in the open door, her wet hair hanging loosely around her shoulders, wearing blue jeans, a green turtleneck sweater, and a short leather jacket. A green Army duffle sat on the unmade bed.

"I brought you coffee," he said.

She took the to-go cup from him. "Thanks," she said.

"You gonna invite me in?"

Beth stepped aside and let him pass. She closed the door behind him.

"You're up early," he said.

"I was going to go find coffee and then, I don't know, find something to do, I guess."

"How about I buy you breakfast?"

"And then? You'll drop me at a bus stop?"

"I've reconsidered. I think it would be better if we stayed together. We'd be safer together."

Her mouth curled into a little half smile. "Are you worried about me?"

"I just think we should stay together."

"Okay, breakfast it is."

"One condition," he said as Beth grabbed her duffle from the bed, "and this is non-negotiable, you wait in the car when I'm talking to people. I told you, I need to do these things alone."

"You're the boss," she said. "You got a place in mind for breakfast?"

They ate at a Waffle House in the western suburb of Oak Park, Beth's hometown. They sat in a corner booth and Sam picked the seat with a clear view of the front door. It was an old habit.

"Why did you bring me here?" Beth said.

"It has nothing to do with it being your hometown,"

he said. "The first person I want to talk to owns a nail salon not too far away in Forest Park. She was on the train car when your father was killed."

"Then she can identify the person?"

"I don't know for sure. First, there was a language problem. She spoke very little English at the time. I'm hoping she's better at it now. Next, and this is a big problem, her description – as much of it we could understand – is different from the other witness. The only other witness we now have."

"How many witnesses are there?"

"Like I said, only two now. There were three but one passed away. Natural causes. He really didn't get a good look at the killer anyway."

"How was it that there were only three witnesses? The train car must have been full, right? It was rush hour."

"I think I told you back in Florida, people panicked when the train stopped. They all ran away, afraid they'd be next."

"But a man was murdered."

"And they didn't want to be next. I'm not defending them, but I understand why they ran. What I don't understand is why no one came forward later when we asked. We had it on television and in the papers. We didn't get one person who was on that train get in touch with us. People just don't want to get involved."

"They're all a bunch of cowards," Beth said, her arms crossed over her chest and a with look on her face

Sam remembered from her high school yearbook picture.

"I can't argue with you on that," Sam said.

He took a sip of coffee. He studied Beth and saw the rage in her. He needed to get her thinking about something else. "Last night," he said, "you also asked how I met Marley. Do you still want to know?"

———

Chief Kroll got to his office early. Sgt. Williams wasn't at his desk yet. He started a pot of coffee and fired up his computer. His wall clock read eight-ten. Commander Kuchinski, the commanding officer of the Area Four detective unit, probably wasn't at his desk yet either. Kroll dialed his cell phone.

"Kuchinski," he answered.

"Stan, this is Chief Kroll. Where are you?"

"I'm in my car on the way into the office, Chief. What do you need?"

"Any update that you have."

"Okay, but this is probably a few hours old. Since you called yesterday, I had Lieutenant Spiros assign a team to the Patterson homicide. I don't yet know what progress, if any, they made. It probably took them a few hours just to read and catch up on the file. By the way, did you get the working file back?"

"No. The retired detective that has it is in the wind. And that's my next question. What about his rental car? Did you assign anyone to relieve my people last night?"

"Yes, sir. They were assigned right out of the afternoon roll call yesterday. I checked with them at ten last night. The retired detective, what was his name? Laska? Yeah, Laska had not yet returned to the car."

"And relief for my detectives at the hotel?"

"Same thing, detectives assigned to their relief from the afternoon crew."

"Alright. Area Four will maintain those assignments until further notice. Lt. Spiros will be responsible for his own people's reliefs."

"Yes, sir. Anything else?"

"Yes. When you get to your office, give me a call back. I want an update on the progress in the Patterson case and anything new from your people sitting on the car and the hotel."

"Yes, sir."

Kroll ended the call and dialed Det. Marcin.

Marcin answered. "Yeah?" he mumbled into the phone.

"Detective Marcin. This is Chief Kroll. Did I wake you?"

"No, sir. I mean, yes. But I should get up now anyway."

"Good. I want you and your partner in my office ASAP. And get ahold of Alvarez. I want him and his partner here also. You got it?"

"Yes, sir. Right away, sir."

Kroll hung up and sat back. All he could do now was wait, and that was the worst part of being the

Chief. Waiting for others and having to trust that they do the job as well as you yourself could.

————

"You're just trying to change the subject," Beth said.

"I am. So, do you want to hear the story or not?"

"Yeah, sure. Tell me."

The waitress interrupted before Sam could begin his story. She dropped their plates in front of them along with the check and left without a word.

Sam grabbed the check, read it over, and said, "You're getting this one." He handed it to Beth who glanced at it, dropped it back on the table, and said, "You're not buying this time?"

"This isn't a date, Beth. You might not be able to afford a good hotel but I know you can afford the Waffle House."

"Yeah, okay. Go on," she said, "tell your story."

Sam shoveled a forkful of scrambled eggs into his mouth, swallowed, and began. "Bruno had a friend, Josie. Her grandson was found dead from an apparent overdose. I told her I'd look into it. I didn't expect to find anything but, just to help her get through that tough time, I did it.

"I went to the morgue and guess who was working there? Marley. She was a medical examiner's assistant back then."

"You're kidding?" Beth said. "Why would she take that job? Did she go to school for it?"

"No. She needed a job and her uncle – he's a detective in Sarasota – he helped get her the job."

"She did autopsies and stuff?"

"No, but she assisted the ME with them."

"That's gross. So, you hit on her? Right there in the morgue?"

"No. When I first saw her I thought she was out of my league."

"She is."

"Thanks for that. What happened is that she asked me out."

Beth laughed and almost choked on a piece of toast she was munching on. "You're kidding?"

"Why is that funny?"

Beth held up her hands in mock surrender. "Hey, sorry. Yeah, it's not funny. She obviously saw something in you that eludes me."

"Yeah, cute. I should have left you at the motel."

Sam checked the time on his phone. "Okay, we have to finish up. The nail salon opens soon. I want to catch this woman before it gets too busy there."

"Wait a minute," Beth said, "that's the whole story? That's it? The only thing mildly interesting is that Marley actually asked *you* out."

Sam pushed his plate to the side and scooted out of the booth. He stood and looked down at Beth. "Funny girl," he said. "I'll be waiting in the car. Don't forget to leave a good tip. These people depend on them."

CHAPTER
TWENTY-EIGHT

MALCOLM BURNETT STEPPED off the train onto the platform at the Ogilvie Transportation Center on the west end of downtown Chicago. Every day, every workday, he boarded the train near his home in the far northern suburb of Highland Park and rode the Metra line downtown. He would then walk the remaining three-quarters of a mile to his office.

Today was no different than any other day. Except that today Jerry Robinson was waiting for him on the platform near the escalators.

Burnett passed him and stepped on the escalator. Robinson followed and stood behind him as the moving stairs took them up to street level.

"What are you doing here?" Burnett said without looking back at Robinson.

"We need to talk," Robinson answered.

"So, you picked the one place that has hundreds of cameras covering every square inch?"

"You told me never to use the phone."

"And that should have clued you in. You don't contact me, I contact you."

"We have a problem," Robinson said.

"I know. The retired detective, Laska."

Burnett stepped off the escalator and walked to the station's exit. Robinson followed and fell in step beside him once they were out of the building.

"How do you know about him?" Robinson said.

"He came to my office."

"What did he want?"

"What else? To talk about Walter."

"What did you tell him?"

"Nothing, of course. At least nothing we didn't talk about sixteen years ago."

"He came to me also. He knows I knew Walter."

"I know. He told me he paid you a visit."

"What did he say?" Robinson said.

"Like I just said, he told me he talked to you. What did he say to you?"

"He asked me about Patterson. Someone in the police department is helping him. He knows I was looking at the electronic case file. Everyone who opens it leaves a digital footprint. He asked why I was looking at it. I told him I knew Walter and that we had met at parties and such and I was following the investigation out of curiosity."

Burnett stopped and turned to Robinson. "That's a reasonable answer. That's how you and I met. He also asked me if I knew you. I denied knowing or meeting you."

Robinson drew a breath. "He also asked me why I locked the file."

"You did what?"

"When it looked like the investigation went cold, I put a restriction on the digital file so that I would be notified if anyone tried to look at it again."

"Is that normal to do that? What did you call it? Restrict a file?"

"No, it's not normal. And that's the problem. Restriction permissions are usually reserved for only the most sensitive investigations. And Walter's case was definitely not that. At least, it didn't look like that."

"What did you tell him about doing it?" Burnett asked.

"I said I didn't know I did it and that it must have been an accident. I hit the wrong key or something."

"Did he believe you?"

"I think so. I don't know. I can't be sure."

Burnett started walking. Robinson, again, fell in next to him.

"As I see it", Burnett said, "Laska is a problem of your making. If you hadn't left your, what did you call it? Your digital footprint all those years ago, he would get no further. His investigation would again end just like it did sixteen years ago."

"That's not true, and you know it. What about the other one? Hermann. He never learned about me."

"But he did learn about your nephew."

"And I had Andre take care of that."

"If you deal with Laska the same way, we risk even more people becoming suspicious. Someone on the police department knows that Laska and Hermann both worked on Walter's case. It won't be hard for them to put two and two together. Don't do anything about him yet. I need to think about it."

"My nephew made a mistake."

Burnett again stopped and turned to Robinson.

"What kind of mistake?" he said.

"Once Laska showed up at the office, I had Andre follow him. We put a tracker on his car. Andre followed him out to Galena."

"Laska went out there?"

"Yes," Robinson said. "Andre, and this is without my permission, I had no idea he was going to do this, Andre took a shot at him."

Burnett's face turned a shade of crimson Robinson had never seen before. Burnett moved in closer to Robinson and spoke through clenched teeth. "You idiot. Why would you act before consulting with me?"

"I didn't. Andre did. I only wanted Andre to follow him."

"Did he hit Laska?"

"No, he missed."

"You know what this means? Laska knows Hermann's death was no hunting accident."

"We can't be sure of that."

"We can't take the risk that he doesn't."

"What do you want me to do?"

"Are you still following Laska?"

"No. Andre lost him. But he's here with his father. I have Andre watching the father. Laska will come to him sooner or later."

"Alright. Stay on the father for now. If you see Laska, you stay on him again. Do nothing else until I contact you."

"There's one more thing."

"Jesus. Now what?" Burnett said.

"The daughter was with Laska in Galena."

"Elizabeth?"

"Yeah. You know, all this started with her. She just couldn't leave it alone. If she just went away--"

Burnett poked at Robinson's chest with a finger. "You do nothing to that child. Do you understand?"

Robinson looked down at the finger in his chest then back up at Burnett. "Yeah, I understand."

CHAPTER TWENTY-NINE

SAM SAT behind the wheel of Beth's Jeep with his phone to his ear as she climbed in. "Okay, thank you," Sam said. He pressed a button and put the phone back in his pocket.

"Who was that?" Beth asked.

Sam gave her a none-of-your-business look but answered her anyway. "The car rental place."

"You told them where the car is at?"

"Yes."

"Cool," she said and buckled her seat belt.

"Did you leave a good tip for the waitress?" he said.

"Fifteen percent."

Sam shook his head. He unbuckled himself, got out of the car, and walked back to the restaurant. Beth watched him through the Waffle House's window as he walked over to their waitress and handed her something.

When he came back, she asked, "How much did you give her?"

"Enough," he said and started up the Jeep.

"Hey, what's your problem?" she said.

"I told you to leave her a good tip. Fifteen percent is not a good tip."

"That's why you're being a dick? Because I didn't leave enough of a tip? Oh, wait. That's not it. You're pissed because I was busting your balls about Marley."

"Leave it alone," he said as he maneuvered the car out of the parking lot.

"Hey, I'm sorry. I didn't mean anything by it. I was just joking."

Sam gripped the steering wheel tightly. He said nothing.

"Really, Sam. I'm sorry," she said. "I won't do it again. I guess I didn't understand what she means to you."

Sam opened his window and stuck his elbow out.

"I've never been in a serious relationship myself," Beth said.

Sam looked over to her. "Why not?"

"I guess I was always afraid of getting close to anyone. My father was taken from me, my mother died and left me alone. I didn't want to get close enough to anyone and have them leave me again."

"It hurts, right?"

"Yeah."

"So, who's being the dick again?"

Beth laughed. "Yeah, okay. I've been a dick. But, come on. You have too."

"Maybe just a little."

Sam pulled to the curb. "We're here," he said. He looked down the street through the windshield. The salon, 'Mae Lin's Nails and Spa' was just a few doors down. From his angle he couldn't tell if it was open. He stepped from the car, leaned in the window, and said, "Remember our deal. You wait here."

"Yep, that was the deal," Beth said.

Sam walked down the block to the salon. A neon sign in the window declared the salon was open. He pulled on the door and walked in.

The room was long and less wide than he imagined it would be. The left wall was lined with odd looking tan recliners. Small backless wheeled stools sat in front of each recliner and short two-drawered cabinets separated each recliner from its neighbor.

Sam stood next to a glass counter. Behind the counter stood a slight Asian woman, the only other person in the salon. She looked up at him and said, "You got an appointment?" She looked down at a book on the countertop.

If she was Chan, Sam thought, her language skills had definitely improved.

"Ms. Chan?" Sam asked.

"Yeah, yeah. You got an appointment?"

"Mae Lin Chan?"

The woman's head fell to the side. "What you want?"

"Ms. Chan, I'm Sam Laska. I hope you remember, we met many years ago. You were on an elevated train car on the Green Line. There was a man shot on the train."

Sam saw the recognition in her eyes as she remembered.

"You one of the detectives," she said. "I remember you now. You get old."

"Yes, I know," he said. "I'd like to talk to you about that day again."

"Where the other guy? I talk to him already."

"Detective Hermann? You talked to him?"

"Yeah, more than month past. And I talk to you long time ago. Same thing today. You go now." She waved a hand as if shooing away a fly.

Sam was encouraged hearing that Dave Hermann talked to Chan again. "Detective Hermann won't be working on this any longer. I'm taking over again. So, please, I need to speak with you."

"What happen to him? Why he not work?"

"Detective Hermann passed away suddenly."

Chan shook her head from side to side slowly. "That too bad. He nice man." She checked her watch. "Okay. We talk and then you go?"

"Yes. I only have a few questions."

"Okay," she said. "You gotta talk fast. I get customers soon." She stepped out from behind the counter, motioned Sam to get out of her way, and locked the door.

"You come," she said, and walked to the back of the salon.

She led Sam to a small back office that probably was once a closet. She squeezed behind a desk and waved Sam into a chair.

"Ask," she said.

Sam had her describe what she saw on that day sixteen years ago. He let her speak without interruption. When she finished he began his questioning to fill in the blanks. He asked where she was seated on the train car, where Walter was standing, and where the killer was when she first noticed him.

Chan said, just as she had sixteen years ago, that she sat on a bench than ran laterally along one side of the car. She was positioned at the end of the bench near the center of the car and adjacent to an exit door. Walter was standing on the opposite side of the door only a few feet away. Because the car was full, it being rush hour, she did not have a direct view of Patterson. The man who would be the killer was seated at the back of the car in an aisle seat.

"And you said he was a black man, correct?"

"Yeah, skinny black guy. Not tall, not short."

"Did you notice anything else about him?"

"Black coat, black hat. Like baseball guys."

"A baseball cap. Did it have a logo on it? Writing?"

"No, just black."

"Anything else? Did he have a mustache or beard?"

"No, clean face."

"Glasses?"

"No."

"How about his shoes? Did you notice his shoes?"

Chan looked up and away. Her brow wrinkled and she closed her eyes as she thought. Her eyebrows arched and her eyes opened. She looked back at Sam. "Yeah, I remember. Nice shoes. Like with suit."

"Dress shoes?"

"Yeah, black. Nice polish. He a clean guy."

Sam straightened in his chair. It was not a detail they knew before and it was not what he expected.

His face must have shown his surprise. Chan said, "You don't believe me?"

"Yes, I believe you. It's just something I didn't know before today."

"No one ask me before."

Sam nodded. Dave never asked.

"And you're absolutely sure that is the man who did the shooting."

"Yes, I'm sure."

Sam inhaled and exhaled deeply. He ran a hand through his hair. "Is there anything else about him you can remember? Did you hear his voice?"

"No. Too far away. He talk soft."

"He was whispering?"

"Yeah, whisper."

"Do you think you'd recognized him again?"

"I think yes, maybe. But I don't want to see him again."

"I don't blame you. What about the gun? Did you see his gun?"

Chan nodded. "Oh, yes. Black gun, small. Round in the middle."

"A revolver." No ejected brass to worry about.

"Yeah, that's it."

Sam went through a few more details with Chan. He had her describe what she saw as the killer picked people to rob before he got to Walter Patterson and then his confrontation with Patterson.

"He say something to the man I can't hear. Then he shoot. The train stop and he run away with everyone else."

"How many times did he shoot?" Sam said.

"Don't know. I'm too scared. One time, maybe two."

"I understand. Did he take anything from the man he shot?"

"I don't think so. He talk and then he shoot."

Sam asked, "Why did you stay on the train when everyone else ran?"

"Safest place. Killer out there, I'm safe where he is not."

Sam nodded. She was exactly right, he thought.

"You done now?" Chan asked.

"Almost," Sam said. "I need to ask you, are you absolutely sure about your description of the man with the gun?"

"Yeah. I'm sure."

"Because another witness described the man as tall and heavy set."

"You mean fat?"

"Yes, I guess so. He also said the man was wearing sunglasses and his clothes were very dirty."

"Who say that?"

"Do you remember the other witnesses?"

"Yeah, white guy and black guy."

"It was the black guy."

Chan began shaking her head. "Why he say that?"

"I don't know. that's why I'm asking you if you're absolutely sure."

"I'm sure. He lies."

"Why do you think he's lying?"

"Because he sit next to killer man."

"What?"

"He sitting next to killer man before killer man get up. They talk together."

"They were talking?"

"Yes. I see them talk."

"Did you hear what they were saying?"

"No. Just see them talk together."

"Did you tell this to Detective Hermann?"

"When he come last time. Yes."

CHAPTER
THIRTY

SAM WALKED BACK to Beth's Jeep. He was lost in thought. As he saw it, there were only a couple of possibilities. Mae Lin Chan was mistaken. She didn't see the offender sitting with Darryl Wilcox. The sixteen years since the murder could have distorted her memory. Time will do that. Next, she didn't make a mistake and she did see Wilcox and the killer sitting together. That wouldn't be that odd. The killer had to be somewhere on the train car. He'd be standing or sitting next to someone. And it was also possible that, while sitting next to Wilcox, the killer engaged Wilcox in a casual conversation. He could have been biding his time, waiting for the right time. Or he could be working up the courage to pull his weapon and rob the passengers,

"What's up?" Beth said. "Did you talk to her?"

Sam looked at her. He had been concentrating on Chans' statement and no memory of climbing into her car. "Shhh," he said. He stared out the front windshield.

The last possibility was that Wilcox and the killer knew each other. They may even have been partners. The plan would be for one to commit the robberies and one to stay behind afterwards to claim to be a witness and furnish the police with a bad description to throw them off the scent. Maybe, even, the robberies were just part of the ruse and the true goal was the murder of Walter Patterson.

Sam now understood why Dave put the sticky note over Darryl's interview in the file.

"Don't shush me," Beth said. "What did she say?"

Sam started the Jeep and pulled from the curb. "Interesting stuff," he said. "Very interesting stuff."

"Damn it. Are you going to tell me or not?"

"Yeah, I'm going to tell you. First, I need you to get our copy of the file out of my bag in back seat."

"What for?"

"I need Darryl Wilcox's address. He's the other witness."

"The live one?"

Sam looked over to her. "I'm not gonna visit the dead guy, Beth. Pull out the file and look for Darryl Wilcox."

Beth unlatched her seatbelt and twisted around in her seat. "I can't reach it. Pull over."

"Climb over the seat."

"Pull over!" Beth yelled.

Sam yanked the wheel and stomped on the brake pedal forcing Beth throw her arms out to brace herself against the dashboard. He threw the car into Park, jumped out and opened the back door. He unzipped his suitcase and grabbed the file.

Back in his seat, he flipped through the pages. He found the page with Wilcox's address, the address he gave sixteen years ago. He handed the stack of papers to Beth and said, "Here, hang on to this." He pulled out his burner and double checked the address with Wilcox's information texted to him by Joyce. He stashed the phone and pulled from the curb, headed to the highway.

"Are you going to tell me what's going on?" Beth said as she secured her seat belt.

"The nail salon lady, Mae Lin Chan, she told me Wilcox was sitting next to the man the that killed your father. They were sitting there on the train and talking."

"They knew one another?"

"I don't know."

"What were they talking about?"

"Chan said she couldn't hear them."

"They had to know each other. No one talks to random people on the El."

Beth's words came faster and faster, and her voice's volume higher and higher.

"I know you're getting excited, Beth. I'm excited too. But we both need to step back a bit. There are some reasonable explanations for them talking."

"What? What possible reason can there be for them talking that doesn't involve them knowing each other?"

"First, Chan could be mistaken. It was sixteen years ago. Her memory might be playing tricks on her. Next, it could just have been a casual conversation. Something like, 'Move over, I need more room' or something like that." He looked over at Beth. "Sometimes, people do talk to random people."

Beth crossed her arms across her chest and slumped down in the seat. Her face showed disappointment with the sensible explanation.

"The last possibility," Sam said, "is that they did know each other and Wilcox never told us."

"You mean he lied."

"Yes, and there are two possible reasons for that if it's true they knew each other. It was a chance meeting and Wilcox had no idea what the guy was going to do. After, he decided to protect the guy by lying to us."

"Or he was part of it all along."

"Yes. And if Wilcox was part of it, was it still just a robbery that went sideways or—"

"Or were they targeting my father."

"Exactly," Sam said.

Beth sat up and turned in her seat to Sam. "How are we going to figure that out?"

"We aren't. I am," Sam said. "Remember our deal."

Beth turned back, clearly unhappy. She sat quietly as Sam steered the Jeep onto the highway headed into the city.

The highway, I-290 also known locally as the Eisenhower expressway, cut through the middle of the city east to west, from downtown Chicago to the western suburbs. Sam got on at Harlem and drove eastbound. A little more than midway to the Loop was his exit. He pulled off and headed north to Darryl Wilcox's last known address, 136 S. Hamlin Blvd.

Sam pulled to the curb in front of the address and looked at an empty lot where a house should be. "Crap", he said. The lot was strewn with rubble, patches of weeds, discarded tires, and assorted garbage.

"This is it?" Beth said.

"Yeah, this was the address he gave when we interviewed him."

"Do you know if he has any others?"

Sam checked his phone for Joyce's text. "A couple, but this is the most recent."

"Sixteen years and this is the most recent? We should still check the others."

"We will," he said as he put the car in gear. He glanced up at the street sign on the corner. "But I think they're going to be bogus as well."

"Why?"

"Look at the street sign. We're on the corner of Hamlin and Wilcox." He looked at Beth. "Wilcox. His last name. I don't think that's a coincidence. He gave us a bogus name sixteen years ago. He used the street name as his last name."

"You didn't check on him back then?"

"We did. I remember that he told us he didn't have any ID on him. We always ask for it. But he had a criminal history, fingerprints on file, under the name Darryl Wilcox. So, we thought if we needed him he wouldn't be that hard to find again."

"What do we do now? Are we going to check the other addresses?"

Sam threw his head back against the headrest and stared at the roof liner above him. He ran it through his head. He turned back to Beth. "Give me that," he said pointing to the file in her lap.

He paged through the file until he came to Darryl Wilcox's criminal history. She scanned each entry and the name Darry gave each time he was arrested. He stopped midway down the page.

"Son of a bitch," he said.

"What?"

He showed Beth the photocopied page. "Darryl Wilcox used aliases on some of his arrests. Here," he said pointing to one entry, "read the name."

"Andre Robinson," Beth said.

CHAPTER
THIRTY-ONE

FROM HIS DESK outside the Chief of Detectives' office, Sgt. Roy Williams buzzed his boss's phone.

"What's up, Roy?" Kroll asked.

"Commander Kuchinski for you on line two, Chief."

"Thanks, Roy," Kroll said and pressed the second button on his desk phone. "Stan?" he said into the receiver.

"Yes, Chief."

"What do you have for me?"

"My people tell me Laska's rental car was towed this morning. While they were sitting on it waiting for Laska, a tow truck from the rental agency pulled up and hooked it. The detectives talked to the tow driver and he told them that the person who rented it called in and said it wouldn't start and that they should go get it."

"I expected something like that," Kroll said. "What about your people sitting on Laska's father?"

"The father changed hotels last night. They watched

him leave the hotel with a suitcase and they followed him to the Marriott out by the airport. They checked with the front desk and got his room number."

"Any other movement from him? He never met with his son?"

"No. But he did leave the Marriott at one point. He drove over to a bar, Woz's Tap, on Higgins just east of Harlem. He stayed there about an hour and then went back to his hotel."

"I take it he wasn't making a meet with his son," Kroll said.

"My guys say they stayed outside but did leave their car to take a peek in the front window. The father was sitting by himself having a beer."

"And they stayed on him after he left?"

"Yeah, he went back to his hotel. He didn't go out again all night. He's still there."

"Okay. Keep your people on the father. If Laska shows up, they grab him and call me immediately."

"Yes, sir. Anything else?"

"Yes. Are your people getting anywhere on the Patterson homicide?"

"They worked on it all last night. They're gone now, but they left a note. They finished reading through the file and, when they get back in, they'll recontact the witnesses and do new interviews. They asked about the working file, Chief. They're working from the digital file but they could really use the working file."

"I know that. Tell them to do the best they can for

right now. We won't get that working file until we find Laska."

"Alright, Chief."

"You've only got one team working it?"

"Yes, sir. Do you want more?"

"Yeah, I want it worked around the clock. All three watches."

"You got it, Chief."

"I also have some people I'm assigning to find Laska. I'll have them coordinate with your detectives today."

"Yes, sir," Kuchinski said.

Kroll hung up and hit the intercom on the phone.

"Yes, Chief?" Sgt. Williams said.

"Did you hear from Marcin and Alvarez and the others?"

"They're standing right here waiting for you, boss."

"Send them in," Kroll said.

The four detectives stood in front of Kroll's desk. "Good morning, detectives," Kroll said. "It's time you got the whole story so here is the situation. Retired detective Sam Laska has been privately working an old open murder. He was the original lead detective on the investigation sixteen years ago. He has the working file and we want it back. He is in the wind and you are going to find him. Detective Marcin and – what's your name detective?" Kroll said, pointing to Marcin's partner.

"Calvin, sir." The detective said.

"Detectives Marcin and Calvin have been following Laska for the last few days on my orders. They followed him out to Galena where someone took a shot at Laska. That may be related to the homicide he's unlawfully working on. The detective who originally worked it with Laska sixteen years ago, Dave Hermann, was killed in an apparent hunting accident on his property out there. That's the same place someone took a shot at Laska. Laska believes Hermann was reinvestigating this old homicide also. He believes Hermann's death was not a hunting accident but a homicide because of that."

"Excuse me for asking," Alvarez said.

Kroll anticipated his question. "I spoke with Laska yesterday and that is what he told me. That is also when he told me has the working file. He found it in Detective Hermann's home in Galena."

"Yes, sir," Alvarez said. "Sorry for interrupting."

Kroll nodded. "I also told him to end his investigation and return the working file. Obviously, he decided not to listen to me."

"Sergeant Williams pulled his personnel file and also obtained a subpoena for his cell phone records. Start with his phone. But I suspect he knows we'll try to find him that way and ditched it. Go through his personnel file and see what you can do with it. Maybe there's an old address or relative listed in there you can check on."

"Anything else, Chief?" Marcin said.

"Yes. Commander Kuchinski from Area Four has people taking another look at the homicide Laska's been digging into. I want you to meet with them and coordinate your efforts. Everyone got it?"

In near unison, the four detectives answered with a "Yes, sir."

"Good, get going." Kroll said.

Three of the detectives walked through the door. Marcin stayed back. "What is it, Detective?" Kroll asked.

"Chief, I think we have more than enough to get a warrant for Laska's arrest."

"We do. I don't want to go there yet," Kroll said.

"Can I ask why?"

Kroll drew a deep breath and let it out again. "We were partners way back when. He's a good man and an even better detective. His only motivation is to solve the murder. In his mind, he is doing the right thing. I want to give him another opportunity to voluntarily return the file and end his investigation."

"Yes, sir. I understand," Marcin said.

CHAPTER
THIRTY-TWO

"YOU DIDN'T NOTICE the name Andre Robinson before?" Beth said.

"No," Sam said.

"How could you not. It's right there," she said, slapping at the file in Laska's hand.

"Lower your voice, Beth. I was only working with a copy of the electronic file. I didn't have his criminal history until I took the working file from you."

"I gave it to you."

"No, I took it. And once I had it I was more interested in rereading the reports and interviews and our notes. Mine and Dave's. That was more important. I knew Wilcox had a history of petty offenses and didn't think going over it again was important."

"You were wrong."

"It looks like I was. But better late than never."

"Sixteen years later."

"Beth, the name Andre Robinson meant nothing

sixteen years ago. It's only because of the possible connection to Jerry Robinson that it becomes important. And sixteen years ago, there was no way for us to know about that connection or even Jerry Robinson."

"I guess," she said, and turned to look out her side window. "Now what?"

"We do the most important part of detective work. We knock on some doors."

She turned back to Sam. "What doors?"

"Wilcox's other addresses."

"How do you know they're not vacant lots like this one?"

"I don't. I was just trying to teach…you know what? Never mind. We'll drive by and check them out."

One by one, Sam drove to the remaining three addresses. None were vacant lots but all were abandoned buildings. "That was a waste of time," Beth said.

"No, it wasn't," Sam said. "Negative results are still results. We know all the addresses are no good. Now we move on."

"How? What do we do now?"

"We find a hotel, pick up some lunch on the way, and I make a couple phone calls."

Beth had a list of hotels and motels from a search she did on her phone. Sam chose one in the northwest suburbs, a Best Western near two major highways. On the way, they picked up take-out from a hot dog stand.

Beth again used her ID to check in and Sam paid in cash, requesting a first floor room near an exit.

Sam double locked their door and claimed the bed nearest the door by tossing his bag on it. Beth made a beeline to the bathroom while Sam plopped back on the bed. He closed his eyes and tried to process the day's developments and resulting questions.

Was Darryl Wilcox a witness to a murder who happened to speak casually and innocently with the eventual killer? Or was he a participant in a murder who pretended to be a witness and lied to cover his co-conspirator's crime? These were the two extremes and everything in between them fell within the realm of possibility. And the big question whose answer would fill in a lot of the blanks: was the name Darryl used, Andre Robinson, just a coincidence or was he related to Jerry Robinson? Dave Hermann seemingly wondered the same thing.

Beth came out of the bathroom. "Hey, are you sleeping? Let's eat."

Sam sat up and rubbed his eyes. "No, not sleeping. I was just thinking."

"About what?"

"Today." Sam pulled out his burner. "Go ahead and eat," he said. "I've got to make a few calls." He grabbed his phone and dialed Joyce first. She answered on the first ring.

"Hey you," Joyce said. "I still haven't gotten anything on that shell company."

"I'm not calling about that. Where are you?" Sam looked at the time on his phone.

"Still at work, it's three-thirty here."

"Good. I've got a big favor to ask."

"Bigger than all the crap I'm already doing for you?"

"Yeah, this is a rush job. I need you to run a name and get right back to me. It can't wait."

"I can try. I've got to finish a few things for Larry and Jack but I can squeeze you in."

"Do mine first. I'll take any heat they give you."

"Yeah, like that would work. What do you have?"

"Run the name Andre Robinson. Use the same birthday you have for Darryl Wilcox. I want anything and everything you have."

"Got an address?"

"Any of the addresses Darryl Wilcox used. But I don't think any of those are good."

"You think Andre is Darryl's alias?"

"I think Andre is his real name and Darryl is the alias."

"Oh, I got it. Okay, I'll see what I can find and call you right back."

"Thanks, Joyce. I owe you big time."

"And I'm gonna cash in. I can always use a babysitter."

Sam ended the call and dialed his father. It rang until it went to voicemail. Sam redialed quickly and Bruno picked up on the first ring.

"Hey, kid," Bruno said. "Sorry, I was in the bathroom."

"I hoped you washed your hands," Sam said.

"Yeah, yeah. What's up? Where are you?"

"Not far. I don't want to say, just in case."

"Sure, I get it."

"How about you? Did you change hotels?"

"Yeah, I'm at the Marriott now. Listen," Bruno said, "I think there are some cops out in the parking lot."

"I'm sure there are. They're probably waiting for me."

"I'll bet. Oh, I got your phones. You and the girl."

"Thanks, Dad. I expect the police are tracking mine now. They probably already figured out you've got my phone. Otherwise, they'd be knocking on your door looking for me. Hey, I just got an idea. Do you want to have a little fun with them?"

"Yeah. What do you have in mind?"

"Leave my phone in the room but take Beth's with you. Take a drive up to Wisconsin."

"Ha! That'll be fun. Where should I go up there?"

"I don't know. The Brat Stop in Kenosha?"

"Yeah, I like that. You want me to bring you back anything?"

"Cheese curds. What else?"

"Okay kid. I'll call you and let you know what happens."

"Hopefully it'll be an uneventful trip. Take it easy, Dad."

"See ya."

Sam tucked the burner back in his pocket. Beth said through a mouthful of French fries, "You done with your calls? You better eat or I'm gonna take your hot dog."

Sam got up and grabbed the greasy paper bag that held his lunch. Or was it dinner? He sat on the corner of his bed nearest to Beth and started in on the fries.

"We're waiting for a call back?" Beth asked.

"Yeah," he said. "hopefully we won't wait too long."

"Then what?"

"It depends on what we learn."

Beth nodded. The room went quiet except for the sound of Beth slurping the last of her Pepsi through a straw. She tossed the foam cup in the trash, crumpled her paper bag and tossed it on top of the cup. She sat back in her chair and said, "Who's this Joyce dame?"

"Dame?" Sam asked.

"It's a habit. I watch lots of old movies."

Sam smiled. "Joyce is an assistant at the law firm I work at. Well, I don't actually work there. I do investigative work for them sometimes. Run down witnesses, process service, stuff like that."

"What's process service?"

"Serving subpoenas, delivering notice of a lawsuit, legal documents. Stuff like that."

"Okay, I get it," she said. "And Joyce can look all this stuff up for you?"

"Yeah, there are services, companies, on the internet that, for a fee, can look people up. They can get lists of addresses, phone numbers, credit histories, driver's licenses and car registrations and stuff like that. They can also direct you to other paid services for things like criminal histories. It's all legitimate. Law firms and other companies use them. Some police departments too."

"Wow, that's cool. And—"

Sam's phone began buzzing. "Hang on," he said to Beth. He punched a button on his burner, held the phone to his ear and said, "Joyce?"

"Yeah, Sam. It's me."

"Did you find something?"

"Oh yeah. You were right on the money."

"Don't keep me waiting," he said.

"I've got an Andre Robinson with the same birth-date as Wilcox, an Illinois driver's license, an address current as of three months ago, and an employment history. Well, not so much a history as a current employer. Guess who he works for?"

"Truncheon Security?"

"Bingo. I'll text it all to you."

CHAPTER
THIRTY-THREE

ANDRE SAT in his car across the street from the Marriott's parking lot. He had a clear view of the front end of Bruno's Cadillac and he was tired of staring at it. He had been sitting in the same spot watching the car since the old man moved it here from the other hotel. And he had been watching it over there even longer. He was bored, tired, and he had nothing to eat except shitty takeout burgers from the Micky-D's next door.

He took another sip from the extra-large cup of Coke which was nothing but melted ice now. He squirmed in his seat. He had to take another piss. He took a look around and stepped out of his car. He took one last look at the Cadillac and ran down the street to the McDonalds.

Less than ten minutes later he was opening the door to his car. He looked over to the Cadillac to make sure it was still there. It wasn't. Panic set in. He turned to the left and right and left again. He caught a flash of its rear end accelerating down the street. He jumped into his car, cranked the engine, and sped from the lot.

————

Sam looked at the burner in his hand. He shoved it into his pocket, grabbed his suitcase and started rifling through it. He found the plastic bag of Hermann's belongings. He pulled out Hermann's phone and tried to switch it on. It was dead.

He held it up for Beth to see. "Do you have a charger that fits this phone?" he said.

She looked over. "Is that an iPhone?"

Sam checked. "Yeah."

"In my car."

"Go get it."

"A 'please' might be nice to hear," she said as she got up and walked to the door.

She returned and handed the cord and plug to Sam. "Is that Dave's phone?"

"Yeah. I want to check his most recent calls."

"Why?"

Sam hooked up Hermann's phone to the cord and plugged it in. "I think he might have been thinking the same thing I am. I think he was on to Andre also."

Sam and Beth stared at the phone waiting for enough of a charge to power on. The phone dinged and Sam hit a button on its side.

"His passcode is 1-4-0-6," Beth said.

Sam looked up at her. "How do you know that?"

Beth shrugged and her mouth curled into a half smile. "I kind of hacked into his phone too."

Sam shook his head in disgust, punched the code into Dave's phone and the home screen popped up. He navigated to the recent calls screen and quickly scanned the page. "There," he said, "the sixth call down."

Beth leaned over and read the screen. "Who's number is that?" Beth said, reading.

"I think it's Truncheon Security," Sam said. He quickly checked the number using the Google app on his phone. "Yeah," he said, "Truncheon Security. The calls above it are all your number. One completed, four missed." Sam tossed the phone on the bed. "I think Dave figured out Darryl Wilcox was Andre Robinson. He probably ran a background on him and got his employment history. He called Truncheon looking for Andre. That's how they got on to him."

"And they killed him."

"Yeah," Sam said.

"That settles it," Beth said. "Jerry Robinson killed my father and Dave."

"It definitely looks like it," Sam said.

"Looks like? He did it!" Beth was out of her chair and pacing around the room. Her hands and arms flailing to emphasize every word out of her mouth. "That son of a bitch killed my father."

"Beth," he said, "sit down. We have to talk about this."

Beth whipped her head around at stared at him.

There was that yearbook photo face again, Sam thought. It sent a chill down his spine.

"Talk? I'm not going to talk." She marched to the desk, grabbed her purse, and pulled out her Sig Sauer nine millimeter pistol. "I'm going to kill him."

Sam laid back on his bed and propped himself up on his elbows. "Okay. You'll spend the rest of your life in prison but, hey, it'll be worth it. Right?"

"They won't catch me. I'll make sure of it."

"I guess that means you're going to kill me too."

"What?"

"We spend all this time together and you don't know anything about me yet? I can't let you do that. I can't let you kill him and just do nothing about it. I'll turn you in. The only way you'll stay out of prison is by killing me too."

"You think I'm wrong? You were going to do the same thing to that guy that kidnapped Marley."

"And fate intervened so I wouldn't have to. But sometimes I think I was punished for my bad intentions anyway." He pointed to a chair. "Put the gun away. Let's talk. There's some things we need to figure out."

"Like what?"

"Exactly what involvement did Jerry Robinson have in your father's murder? Who pulled the trigger? And the big one, why?"

"It doesn't matter why."

"Yes, it does. Think about this, what would make Jerry Robinson even consider killing someone? Not just your father, but anyone. He was a deputy chief on the police department. If he stuck around, he probably would have gotten another promotion if not several more. What makes a man with all that going for him want to involve himself in a murder? And even more, why kill your father?"

"I don't know."

"Yeah, me either. But I want to. Don't you? Don't you want to know why your father was killed?"

Beth sat down on the bed next to Sam and stared at the wall. "I don't know," she said. "Now that I know it wasn't just over a few dollars, I'm not sure I want to open that door." She walked over to the desk and deposited the pistol in her purse. She turned back to Sam. "What do we do now."

"Let's talk this out. Like I said, we don't know for sure how much involvement Jerry Robinson has in your father's murder but we can assume he has some. We want to know how much involvement and why. What was his motive?"

"In my Criminal Justice classes, we talked about motives. One of my professors broke it down to only four. He called it the four 'L's'. Love, lust, loathing, and loot."

"We had something like that in Area Four when I worked there. Ours was a bit more…offensive. I guess that's the word for it. But after years of working murders, I came to understand that there is only one motive, desire. Everything bad about people flows from desire."

"Okay, what did Jerry Robinson desire?"

"That's what we have to find out."

"How do we do that?"

"We could ask him," Sam said.

"You're kidding, right?"

"Yeah, we're not there yet. I think we have to talk to someone else first."

"Who? Andre or Darryl or whatever his name is?"

"It's not going to be easy finding him without going to Jerry Robinson. No, I'm thinking I need to talk to Malcolm Burnett again. When I talked to Jerry Robinson he told me he knew your father. He met him socially and then went to him for legal advice on starting a business. He said that's why he was following the investigation. Burnett told me he didn't know Robinson but maybe he remembers your father mentioning a problem with some client. Something he might have been afraid of."

"Okay, let's go. Let's go see him."

"It's too late today. It's almost five. I'll go in the morning."

"*We'll* go in the morning," Beth said.

"You can drive us downtown and wait with the car, but I'm talking to him alone. That's the deal, remember?"

"I haven't seen him since I was a little girl. I used to call him Uncle Mal. Maybe seeing me again will—"

"Will what, Beth? All seeing you again is going to do is stir up a bunch of emotions in him. Probably in you too. That's not what I would call an appropriate environment for an interview."

"You've got a point. Okay, I'll stay away. But I do want to see him again."

"After this is over, okay?" He pushed himself off the bed. "After this is over."

———

Chief Gene Kroll had his hand on the doorknob when the phone on his desk rang. He walked back and pick up the receiver. "Chief Kroll," he said.

"Chief, Commander Kuchinski. I'm glad I caught you."

"Did any of our people find Laska?"

"No, sir. Not yet."

"Then what's going on?"

"A couple of things. Your guys have a location on Laska's cellphone. They have it at the Marriott by O'Hare. It hasn't moved since they picked up the signal."

"That's the same hotel his father is at, right?"

"Yes, sir. And the father, Bernard, he left his hotel. He's northbound on I-94 nearing the Wisconsin border."

Kroll plopped down on his chair. "Let the father go. It sounds like he knows he's got a tail and he's taking them for a ride."

"There's more, Chief. Our detectives think they aren't the only ones following him. There's a silver gray BMW on the father also."

"Are they sure it's following him?"

"They're telling me they're pretty sure."

"Any idea who's in the BMW?"

"The guys got the plate number. The car is registered to Truncheon Security in the city."

"That's interesting."

"Why? Who's Truncheon Security?"

"There could be a connection with Truncheon and the cold case Laska is working." Kroll paused momentarily while he figured out what to do next. "Okay," he said, "tell the detectives to stay on the father. Just keep him under surveillance and make sure nothing happens to him."

"You think the BMW has bad intentions?"

"I don't know, but let's be careful."

"Got it. Anything else?"

"Yes. I think Laska's cellphone is probably in the father's room and Laska is nowhere around. He probably handed it off to his dad and is using a pay-as-you-go phone."

"Do you want us to go in and make sure?"

"We don't have a warrant, Paul."

"I think we could convince the hotel to let us in. We can use the old 'well-being check' excuse."

"Sure, go ahead. But tell your people to leave the phone alone. Just verify it's there and that Laska isn't."

"Yes, sir."

"And Paul?"

"Yes?"

"When the father returns, have your people give me a call on my cell. I'm going to try to talk to him myself."

"You got it, boss."

CHAPTER
THIRTY-FOUR

AFTER DINNER at the Brat Stop in Kenosha, Bruno headed back to the Marriott. It was nearly a two hour drive in the dark. He kept checking his mirrors, on the way up and now driving back, trying to pick out the tail he knew he had. But they were pretty good and he never made them.

He made it to his hotel by ten o'clock, parked his Cadillac in the lot, and headed inside. Chief Gene Kroll was waiting for him in the lobby. Kroll, flanked by two detectives, walked up to Bruno as he passed through the sliding glass entrance doors.

"Mr. Laska," Kroll said, "I'm Chief of Detectives Eugene Kroll. I need to speak with you about your son."

Bruno stopped and looked over the detectives on either side of Kroll and then Kroll himself. "What about him?" Bruno said.

Kroll glanced around the lobby then back to Bruno. "Can we talk somewhere private? Maybe your room?"

"You got a warrant?" Bruno said.

"Of course not, Mr. Laska. I just want to talk to you. If you're not comfortable in your room we can find a private place somewhere near here."

Bruno looked at the detectives again. "Okay," he said to Kroll. "You and me can go to my room but these two stay here."

Kroll nodded to his people. "Okay, Mr. Laska. They'll wait here."

Kroll followed Bruno to his room. Once inside, Bruno claimed the sofa and pointed Kroll to an easy chair.

"You've got the floor," Bruno said.

Kroll positioned himself on the edge of the seat, leaning forward with his forearms resting on his knees and his hands clasped together. "I need to find Sam," Kroll said.

"You gonna arrest him?" Bruno asked.

"I don't want to. But he has property that belongs to the Chicago Police Department and we want it back."

"What property?"

"You don't know?"

"Why don't you tell me?"

"He has a homicide file. I've asked him to return it and he refused. Well, he didn't really refuse but he's playing hide-and-seek with me."

"What do want me to do?"

"I need to talk to him."

"Don't you know his number?"

"His phone is here in your room. Calling it would do me no good."

Bruno grinned.

Kroll continued. "I'd like you to give me the number of the phone he's using."

"I can't do that," Bruno said. "But I'll let him know you want to talk to him."

"Can you do that now? Maybe you can call him and I can talk to him."

"Do you know my son?"

"We were partners back in the day."

"Yeah," Bruno said. "But do you know him? Because if you do, you'd know that talking to him is not going to do you much good. When he gets something in his head there's no moving him."

"I'd like to try."

"The best I can do for you is let him know you want to talk to him."

Kroll stood. "Mr. Laska, I could arrest you for interfering with our investigation. I'm pretty sure a search of your person incident to arrest is going to turn up your cellphone. And I'll bet Sam's new phone number is on that phone. I don't want to do that."

"Good. Because I'll sue your ass."

"For what?"

"Going into my phone without a warrant. Yeah, that's right. I know you can't look at it without a warrant."

"We can get a warrant pretty easily."

"That'll take you hours. And do you really want to go through all that trouble for an old homicide file that no one has looked at for sixteen years?"

"No, I don't want to do it. So, why don't you just call him now and make both of our lives a little easier?"

Bruno wiped a hand across him mouth. Kroll could see Bruno was debating what to do. "Maybe this will help you make up your mind," Kroll said, "you're being followed."

"Yeah, I know. I made your guys already. They were sitting in the parking lot outside. I took them for a ride up to Wisconsin today."

"I'm not talking about our detectives. There's someone else following you also."

"Who?"

"You can try to guess or you can call Sam and I'll tell you."

Andre filled the tank of his BMW at a gas station down the block and around the corner from the Marriott. He drove back to the hotel and took a circuit around the parking lot to confirm the Cadillac with the Florida plates was still there.

He backed into a spot with a less than ideal view of the car and called his uncle.

"What is it?" Jerry Robinson said.

"This fucking old man."

"What about him?"

"He decided to go for a drive. He went all the way up to Wisconsin."

"I saw that."

"You're tracking me?"

"Every company car is LoJacked. What did he do in Wisconsin? Did he meet someone?"

"No, he stopped at a restaurant and had dinner then came right back."

"Did he make you? Does he know he has a tail?"

"No, I was careful."

"Alright. Do you have enough gas in case he decides to go out again?"

"Yeah, I just filled up."

"And you have eyes on his car?"

"Yeah."

"Okay. Call me back if there's any change."

———

Sam was propped against the headboard on his bed, his hands behind his head. As he promised Beth, he wore only boxer briefs and a tee shirt. Beth was on her bed and was wearing, as she promised, an oversized tee shirt. It came down to her knees so he couldn't tell if she had anything on underneath. He tried not to think about it.

They were watching an old Cary Grant film on the television, North By Northwest. Cary was running through a field trying to dodge a World War I era biplane when Sam's phone began buzzing.

He grabbed it off the nightstand and checked the display. "It's my father," he said without looking over to Beth. He punched the button to answer.

"Hey, Dad," he said. "What's up? Are you back from Wisconsin?"

"Yeah, I am," Bruno said. "I got back about half an hour ago."

"Did you get my cheese curds?"

"I did," Bruno said. "Listen, Sam. I'm here in my room with Chief Kroll."

"Kroll? What's he doing there?"

"He wants to talk to you. But there's something else. He says someone is following me. Not just them but someone else."

"Who?"

"He wouldn't tell me until I called you."

"Give him the phone."

There was a pause while Bruno made the handoff to Kroll. When he came on, Kroll was nothing but business.

"Chief Kroll," he announced.

"Gene?" Sam said. "What kind of game are you playing?"

"You want to talk about games? How about the game of hide-and-seek you're playing? I want that file back and I want it tonight."

"I can't do that, Gene. I don't have it."

"You told me you did. Hermann had it and now you do."

"I did have it. I put it in the mail to you. You'll probably get it tomorrow or the day after."

"You put a homicide file in the mail? Are you crazy?"

"You don't trust the USPS? They're highly efficient, Gene."

"Stop with the jokes. Are you serious? Did you really mail it to me?"

"Yes."

"Alright. You're returning the file. Now I need you to come in and talk to us. I want you to tell us everything you've done so far and what, if anything, you've learned."

"Why should I do that? When you get the file your people will have everything I did. If they're any good, they'll be able figure out everything I have."

"Sam, you can't keep working this homicide. You know that."

"No, I don't. My client wants me to continue and I intend to do just that."

"Your client? You're not licensed as a PI in Illinois, Sam. And even if you were, you know PIs can't work active police investigations."

"I can be licensed tomorrow. Jerry Robinson said he'd hire me."

"I don't think you'd want that. He's the one following your father. Well, someone from Truncheon anyway. There's a guy in a silver BMW sitting out in the parking lot now."

"No kidding?" It didn't surprise Sam one bit, but

Robinson wasn't interested in Bruno. Like the detectives tailing Bruno, Sam knew that Robinson figured watching Bruno was the best way to find Sam.

"They're probably waiting for you to show up, Sam," Kroll said.

"I wonder why," Sam said.

"Knock it off, Sam. Are you going to come in or not?"

"Yeah, tomorrow. I'll call you. Is that good enough?"

"Yes, I'll take it. Don't fuck me on this though."

"I won't, I promise. Are you going to pull your people off my father now?"

"Is your father going to be safe if we do?"

"Yeah. As long as we have a deal, I'll go back to the Marriott and stay with him."

"Robinson's people will make you. Unless you want us to scare them off."

"No, leave them where they are. Let them follow me to your office tomorrow. It'll shake them even more."

"Then you've got something on them?"

"I'll give it all to you tomorrow."

CHAPTER THIRTY-FIVE

"WHAT IS IT NOW?" Jerry Robinson took a sip from his glass as he answered his phone. The brown liquid warmed him and took the edge off these phone calls.

"Cops were here. I didn't see them at first but I think they were waiting for the old man to get back."

"Are they still there?"

"No, they all left."

"Did they see you?"

"No, man. They never even looked over by me."

"Okay, let me think a minute." Jerry took another sip from his glass. This was the second time the police had gone to old man Laska's hotel. There were only two possibilities. One, they were looking for Sam Laska for some reason. And two, Laska was using his father as an intermediary to relay information to the police. But why wouldn't Laska just call them himself? They must want him for some reason and he doesn't want them to find him.

"Okay," Jerry said into his phone, "I don't like that the police are involved. We need to find Laska and find out what he knows and what he told the police. Stay on the old man. He's our only connection to Laska. The old man will either go to him or Laska will come to him."

Sam rolled off the bed. "Get dressed," he said to Beth. "We're going out."

"What's going on?" she said. "Are you really going to the cops tomorrow? What's up with Robinson? I heard you say his name."

Sam grabbed his jeans and pulled them on. "Robinson has someone following my father." He looked at Beth still on the bed. "Come on, get moving. Unless you want to stay here."

Beth jumped off the bed. "No way. I want to go with you." She started towards the bathroom. "Where are we going?"

"To the Marriott where my dad is staying. I want to get a look at the guy following Bruno."

Sam finished dressing while Beth was in the bathroom. He tucked his Beretta in the small of his back and slipped on his sweatshirt. He checked his phone and reread the last text from Joyce. He slipped the phone back in his pocket and turned to the bathroom door. He was about to call out to Beth to get her moving when the door opened.

"Okay," she said, "I'm ready." She looked around the room. "Are we coming back here? Should I pack up?"

"We're coming back. Anyway, I think we are," he said. "Toss me your keys. I'm driving."

Beth dug into her purse, pulled out the Jeep's key and tossed it to Sam. He started for the door then stopped. He turned to Beth behind him. "You got your Sig with you?"

She patted her purse. "Right here. Locked and loaded. You think I'll need it?"

"You never know," he said and opened the door.

On the drive, Sam updated Beth on his call with Kroll. There wasn't much to tell her that she already didn't glean from listening to his side of the conversation.

"Are you really going to go to the police tomorrow?" she said.

"No," Sam said. "But I might call them. I haven't decided yet."

"You are going to keep working my father's case, right?"

"Yeah, don't worry about that. I told you I would and I'm going to see this through to the end."

"But they don't want you to."

"No. It's actually illegal for me to work on an open homicide but screw it. It was mine from the beginning and it's still mine now."

Beth looked out her side window. Another thought came to her. "Did Robinson really offer you a job?"

"Yeah, he did. I thought it was fishy when he did it and now, when I think about it, he probably did it hoping to keep tabs on me."

"Or bribe you with a great offer."

"There's that, too. At any rate, I never seriously considered doing it."

Beth nodded, more to herself than to Sam, and the car got quiet. Neither Sam nor Beth spoke. Beth reached over and turned on the Jeep's radio. Some female singer's voice flooded the Jeep with an ear-busting techno song Sam didn't recognize. He reached over and turned it off.

"Hey," Beth said, "my car, my radio. Don't touch." She reached for the radio again but Sam caught her hand.

"Come on," he said. "I'm trying to think." He glanced over to her. "Please?"

Beth sat back. "Okay, fine." She folded her arms across her chest. "What are you thinking about? You got a plan?"

"I'm trying to put one together."

"What do you have so far?"

"Well, I'm hoping the guy in the car is either Jerry Robinson or Andre, or whatever his name is. I walk up, pull him out of the car, and beat him until he tells us what we want to know."

"Subtle. What's Plan B?"

"You beat him until he tells us what we want to know."

"I like Plan B better," Beth said.

"But I think we can come up with something a little less drastic."

"You got an idea?"

"Yeah. We're gonna need to make a stop before we get to the Marriott."

CHAPTER THIRTY-SIX

THE RED JEEP pulled under the covered entrance to the Marriott's front door. Andre watched as Laska got out and walked inside. He was too far away to see who was in the passenger's seat of the car left idling under the portico but he could tell someone was definitely there.

He pulled out his phone and dialed his uncle. Jerry Robinson answered on the first ring.

"What is it?" Jerry said.

"You were right. Laska just showed up," Andre said. "He pulled up to the front door of the hotel and went inside."

"The son?"

"Yeah. What do you want me to do?"

"Is he with anyone? What kind of car?"

"It's a Jeep, a red Jeep. I think someone is waiting in the car and the Jeep is still running. I can see the exhaust. I don't think they're gonna stay here long."

"Who's in the car? Is it the girl?"

"I don't know. But it's the same Jeep the girl had in Galena."

"If it's the girl, you do nothing but follow them if they leave. Got it?"

"Yeah, I got my eyes on the car now. Hey, wait a minute. He's coming back out now. Yeah, he's getting back in the Jeep. No, he just opened the door. Now someone's getting out of the passenger's side. It's the girl. Yeah, he's with the girl. They're switching drivers. She's gonna drive and he got in the passenger's side."

"You stay on them and let me know where they go. I want updates from you. Regular updates. You got it?"

"Yeah."

"I'll let you know if I need you to do more than just follow them."

"Okay."

"And Andre?"

"Yeah?"

"Do not lose them."

Andre watched as the Jeep pulled from under the portico and out the driveway of the Marriott. He slipped his phone into his pocket, dropped his BMW into gear and followed the Jeep onto the street.

"I don't know where I'm going," Beth said.

"You're fine," Sam said, "stay on this street. You'll be making a left soon so get over into the next lane."

The street they were on, westbound Higgins Road,

was a four-lane primary street. Daytime traffic was normally heavy but, this late at night, it was sparse. Yet there were enough cars for the silver-gray BMW to follow with some concealment. At least Sam hoped the BMW thought so.

Beth slid the Jeep into the left lane. Sam turned and looked out the back window.

Beth checked the rearview mirror. "Do you see him?" she said.

"I think so. He's staying pretty far back." He looked over at Beth. "Don't lose him."

"I won't, don't worry."

Sam pointed up ahead. "Put your signal on and take a left at the light."

Beth nodded and pulled the Jeep into the turn. She checked her mirror again.

"Did he make the light?" Sam said.

"Not yet…wait, there he is."

"How far back is he?"

"Maybe two, three hundred feet."

"Okay, get into the right lane. The entrance is coming up pretty quick."

"I see it."

"Kill the headlights when you turn in."

Beth turned onto the asphalt road, a long winding lane banked on either side with a dense growth of trees. They had turned onto an access road which led deep into a heavily forested recreational area of the Forest Preserve District of Cook County. The road led to large open picnic areas dotted with covered pavilions, picnic tables, and barbeque pits and protected from the intrusion of the city's eyes and noise by the thick woods. There were no streetlights along the way and a moonless sky and the dense canopy of branches shrouded them in near total dark.

"I can barely see the road," Beth said.

"Good," Sam said. "Slow down. I think we're coming to the parking area."

Beth squinted trying to make out the road in the dark. Sam noticed and told her to kill the dashboard lights.

"Yeah, that helped," she said.

Sam looked over his shoulder and through the back window. "I don't see him yet," he said.

Beth checked her mirrors. "Yeah, I don't…no, there he is. He's still got his headlights on."

"Okay, good. You know what to do, right?"

"Yeah. You sure this is a good idea?"

"No, but it's the best I could come up with on short notice. Slow down a little more."

"He's gonna see the brake lights."

"Good."

Beth tapped the brakes. She looked over at Sam. "Good luck."

Sam nodded, opened his door, and rolled out into the blackness of the night.

Andre turned into the Forest Preserve and stopped. He saw nothing but trees and darkness beyond the reach of his headlights. The taillights of the Jeep had disappeared. His only thought was that there was a curve in the road ahead that hid them from his view. He debated backing out and trying to pick them up again at the Marriott but quickly dismissed the thought. His uncle warned him not to lose them. He was also confused. He didn't understand why Laska and the girl turned into a Forest Preserve. He wondered if they were looking for a private place to do the big nasty. No, he quickly decided, they would just get a motel room. The only other reason he could think of was that they were meeting with someone. A meeting they wanted to keep very private. If that were the case he wanted to know who they were meeting.

A pair of taillights flashed ahead and he smiled to himself. He switched off his headlights and crept ahead slowly. He had a thought and stopped his car. His BMW would be easy for them to spot, even in the dark. After switching his phone off, he reached across the car and popped open the glove box. He withdrew his new Glock 9mm and exited the car. He set off on foot, using the cover of the woods, to find the red Jeep.

Laska's eyes adjusted to the pitch black of the night. Still, he could only make out the vague shapes of the trees and bushes of the forest. Anything further away than twenty or so feet was a guess. However, he was confident spotting a car would be no problem.

Crouched behind the trunk of a large elm a few feet

from the road, he was further concealed by an over-growth of brush and saplings. He stayed low to the ground and listened for any approaching sound.

Laska crouched there for what seemed like hours. The BMW should have reached him by now. He wondered if it had backed out knowing he'd be made if he kept on. He shifted slightly, preparing to move to the entrance to check it out. The crack of a dried twig and a rustling of leaves stopped him. He flattened himself to the ground. The rhythmic crunch of dried leaves and rustling branches drew nearer to him. Whoever was in the BMW was now on foot and the plan Sam concocted was out the window. He had no choice but to improvise.

Laska's heart pounded in his chest. The sound was coming straight at him. He pulled his Beretta and thumbed off the safety. He stared into a sea of black as his body tensed and the rustling drew nearer.

Andre pushed through the brush and under a low-hanging branch. He stumbled over a fallen limb and cursed the woods under his breath. His home was the city and its streets and alleys. He'd take concrete, brick, and asphalt over grass and trees any day. He kicked at a clump of leaves and caught his foot on a gnarled tree root. He cursed again as he fell to his knees, sticking out a hand to prevent a face plant into the ground. He righted himself, brushed the dirt off his knees, and looked at the pistol in his other hand. He shoved it into the front of his pants and pressed on.

He paused every so often, getting his bearings by keeping the road on his left. He squinted, peering ahead trying to get a glimpse of the red Jeep. He saw nothing but black. He moved forward, pushing aside the spindly branches of a bush and maneuvering around a large tree. As he stepped forward a twig snapped behind him. Sensing movement, he whipped his head around and grabbed at the pistol in his waist.

CHAPTER
THIRTY-SEVEN

SAM PRESSED himself low against the elm tree, away from the dark figure passing on the other side. He heard his footsteps tramping through the underbrush from his left to his right. His Beretta at the ready, he turned his head to the left and peeked around the tree. The man was past him and moving slowly forward.

Sam slowly stood and scanned in front, across the road, and behind the man. It was stupid to assume the man was alone. He saw nothing but the black of the night made it impossible to be sure. He looked around the tree again at the back of the man moving away from him. He stepped out and cautiously began closing the gap between the man and himself.

Sam moved silently, step after step. He was drawing closer and less than ten feet from the dark figure. As he took another step his foot slipped on a slick patch of ground. A quick step with his other foot saved him but snapped a small twig.

The figure ahead of him stopped and began to turn, his right hand moving to his waist. Though still shrouded in the shadow of the night, Sam glimpsed the man's face. A memory from sixteen years ago flashed through his mind. The man was older now but Sam had no doubt this was Darryl Wilcox, or Andre Robinson, or whatever name he went by.

With his Beretta already in hand, he knew he could rip off a least three shots before Darryl drew his pistol. But he needed Darryl alive. Sam rushed ahead, closing the gap between them, and threw his body at Darryl. He grabbed for Darryl's right hand. The two men fell, with Sam landing on top of Darryl. Sam locked onto the hand at Darryl's waist and shoved the business end of his Beretta under Darryl's chin.

"You're gonna want to let go of the gun," Sam said. He increased the pressure of his pistol on Darryl's chin, pushing his head back. Darryl's grip on his pistol relaxed. "Good," Sam said, keeping his grip on Darryl's hand. "Now slide your empty hand out slowly. And in case you're having second thoughts, know that your quickdraw isn't faster than my bullet travelling through your brain."

Darry withdrew his hand and Sam pulled the pistol from his waist. He stood, keeping his Beretta trained on Darryl, and took a single step back. "Now roll over onto your stomach and put your hands behind your head."

Darryl, still on his back, glared at Sam. "You can't do this. You got no right."

"Why are you following us, Darryl?"

"I'm a private detective. I'm just doing my job."

"For Truncheon Security."

Darryl's eyes went wide.

"Were you doing your job out in Galena too?" Sam said. "That was you who took a shot at me, right?"

"Fuck you."

"I'll take that as a yes." Sam gave Darryl an easy kick to the ribs. "On your stomach, hands behind your head. Now."

Darryl did as he was told. He strained to turn his head and keep his eyes on his captor. Sam put a foot on his back. "Eyes down, Darryl. You'll see plenty of me later." Sam looked at Darryl's pistol, a Glock 17. He tucked it into his waist. His right hand still held his Beretta. With his left hand he pulled his phone and dialed Beth.

"Yeah?" she answered. "What's going on?"

"Bring up the car. I've got him."

Sam heard the Jeep's engine start up and the headlights flare. Beth was tucked far off in the parking area two hundred feet or so ahead. He kept his eyes on Darryl as the Jeep's headlights lit up the area. When he heard the Jeep draw near he raised his arm to alert Beth.

Beth jumped from the Jeep and Sam called out to her. "Bring the bag." On the stop they made on the way to the Marriott, Sam and Beth did some shopping at a 24 hour grocery store and bought two rolls of duct tape, several rolls of elasticized bandages, and a box of foam earplugs.

Beth ran over carrying a plastic grocery bag. Sam

said to her, "Meet Darryl Wilcox." Sam looked down to Darryl. "Or is it Andre Robinson?"

Darryl said nothing. Sam handed his Beretta to Beth and took the bag. To Beth, he said, "If he makes any move at all, shoot him. Start at his ass and work your way up to his head."

Sam began wrapping Darryl's hands with the duct tape, binding them tightly behind his back. Before Sam moved to bind his feet, Darryl said, "This is kidnapping. You gonna pay for this."

Sam moved close to his ear. "It's not kidnapping if they never find your body, Andre. I'm gonna call you Andre from now on, because that's your real name, isn't it?"

"Fuck you, mother fucker."

"Again, I'm going to take that as a yes."

After Andre's feet were bound with a heavy wrap of duct tape Sam rolled him over. He ripped off a length of the tape and covered Andre's mouth. He shoved the foam earplugs into Andre's ears and wrapped the bandage around his head, covering his eyes. He searched Andre, head to foot, and took his wallet, keys, and cellphone. He tossed the keys to Beth and pocketed the wallet and phone. "Go get his car," he told Beth. "It's down the road. We'll use it to take him out of here."

"What's wrong with my Jeep?" she asked.

Sam smiled. "It doesn't have a trunk."

Beth drove the BMW over to Sam and made a three-point U-turn on the narrow road. She stepped from the car and over to the trunk. Before opening it, she looked over to Sam. "Are we really putting him in the trunk?"

"You bet," he said.

Beth shrugged and used Andre's keys to open the trunk. "Hey," she said, "come look at this."

Sam walked over and peered inside. A long, zippered soft sided case lay on the bottom of the trunk. Sam unzipped the case and exposed the Ruger Mini-14 rifle inside. He looked over to Beth. "Let's get Andre out of here. We've got a lot to talk about."

Sam zipped up the bag and put it into Beth's Jeep. They carried a struggling Andre over to the BMW and locked him in the trunk. "Now what?" Beth asked.

Sam motioned her away from the BMW with a nod of his head. They stepped over to her Jeep and Sam said, "We need a good place to talk to him. Someplace secluded and out of the way."

"With no nosey neighbors," Beth said.

"Exactly. What about that motel you had earlier in the week? The place with the hourly rates."

"It might work," she said. "It's a single story. The rooms have a kitchenette with doors in the front and back of each room."

"Good for a quick get-away in case a jealous husband or wife showed up."

"That's what I thought too. There's plenty of

parking in the back out of the view from the street and the office is on the far end. If we get the unit on the opposite end it could be perfect."

"Good. I'll drive the BMW and follow you."

CHAPTER
THIRTY-EIGHT

BETH ASKED for the end unit and paid cash for the room with money she got from Sam. She used a fake name to register and the old man behind the desk never asked for ID. That would be bad for business, Beth figured.

Sam had already backed into a spot in the back and waited. He did a quick look around the exterior of the motel for cameras. There were none. It was not a place people wanted to be photographed.

It was only five minutes or so before the door popped open and Beth stepped out. They carried Andre into the room and set him on an old wooden chair.

Once they had Andre settled, Sam nodded Beth back outside. "You follow my lead on this," he said. "You're gonna hear me say things but it's all a bluff, okay? I want him scared and intimidated and feeling hopeless. I don't have any plan to act on anything I say. Got it?"

"I understand. But what if he doesn't give us what

we want?"

"We'll cross that bridge if and when we get to it."

Beth nodded and the two headed back in with Andre.

Sam walked around the room, locking the two doors and drawing the faded curtains across the windows. The room and it's furnishings could only be described as shabby. The hotel itself, fronted on an old thorough-fare and probably built in the 1940s before the advent of the federal highway system, was brick and frame construction and hadn't seen any serious attention since then. The floor was uncarpeted linoleum, yellow and black, and was peeling away from the floor along the seams and corners. The furniture certainly hadn't been upgraded in at least forty years. And, after checking out the bathroom, Sam thought it hadn't been cleaned since then either.

Beth sat on the bed behind Andre. Sam pulled a threadbare upholstered chair over and sat in front of Andre.

Sam removed the plugs from Andre's ears and unwrapped the bandage covering his eyes. "I'm gonna take the tape off your mouth and we're going to talk, Andre," he said. "Now, you can try to yell for help but, I guarantee, no one is going to hear you. Plus, I have sensitive ears so any loud noises will greatly disturb me. I'll have to shut you up and I'll probably do that by beating the dog shit out of you. Do you understand?"

Andre nodded. Sam reached over and ripped the duct tape from his face.

Andre immediately leaned forward towards Sam. "You can't do this, man. This shit ain't legal."

"Yeah, it probably isn't. But we really don't care. Do we, Beth?"

"Nope. In fact, I think we should soften him up a bit before we start talking."

Sam smiled. "Beth, you might be right," he said. He looked at Andre. "What do you think? Do you need to be softened up?"

Andre stiffened. "You can't. You were a cop. You know you can't do this."

Sam leaned in, resting his arms on his legs. "Exactly, Andre. I was a cop. Past tense. I'm not a cop now. Those rules don't apply to me."

Sam stood quickly. Andre flinched and pushed himself as far back into the chair as he could. He reached into his pocket and Andre's eyes grew wider. "Relax, Andre," Sam said and withdrew Andre's phone and wallet from his pocket. "Let's start with this," he said, showing Andre's wallet to him.

Sam sat down again and flipped the wallet open. Inside was an Illinois driver's license in the name of Andre Robinson, a gas credit card and a Visa credit card both in the name of Truncheon Security Services, and an employee ID for Truncheon in Andre's name. On the back of the card was a black magnetic strip.

Andre saw the ID in Sam's hand. "See, I told you. I'm a private cop. I was just doing my job, man."

"Who told you to follow us, Andre?" Sam asked. "Who gave you that job?"

Andre puffed his chest out. "I can't tell you. Confidentiality."

"Client confidentiality, huh?"

"Yeah."

"There is no client, Andre. You know that and we know that. Jerry told you to follow us, right?"

Andre turned his head away.

Sam continued. "Let's talk about Jerry, Andre. How is he related to you? Is he your daddy?"

Andre turned back to face Sam. "You know what? I don't got to tell you nothing. I ain't talking to you."

"Do you really want to go that route, Andre?" Sam asked. "Because that means you take the fall for everything by yourself."

"You ain't got nothing on me."

"You're forgetting the Mini-14 in your trunk, Andre. The one I'd bet you used to take a shot at me. I don't have to guess that your fingerprints are all over it. And it's gonna be easy comparing it to the bullet they pulled out of the pickup's tailgate in Galena."

Andre glared at Sam. "You put that rifle in my car. I never had no rifle."

Sam laughed. "Andre, who owns that rifle? Is it registered to Truncheon Security? How would I get my hands on a Ruger Mini-14 owned by Truncheon Security?"

Andre stared straight ahead.

"And there's more," Sam said. "You had a Glock 17 on you. I'll bet anything it registers to David Hermann. You know, the Chicago cop that was killed in Galena."

Sam saw panic in Andre's eyes. He hit paydirt. "Did you take it off his body or from his house, Andre?"

Andre struggled against his duct tape bindings. His eyes were wide and his head flipped left to right, back and forth, searching for any way out.

Sam tossed the wallet and cards onto the bed next to Beth. He hitched his chair closer to Andre. "Andre," he said, trying to get his attention again. "Andre, look at me."

Andre continued to struggle and searched the room with his eyes. Sam stood and put his hands on Andre's shoulders. "Andre," he said. "Look at me."

Andre stopped and looked up at Sam.

"Andre," Sam said, "we don't want you. We don't care if you walk away from this. We're here to get the man that killed Walter Patterson. That's all we want."

Sam sat again. "Do you understand me, Andre? That's all we want."

"I don't know nothing about that," Andre said.

"Sure, you do, Andre. You were on the 'L' train. You used the name Darryl Wilcox and said you were a witness."

"So what if used a different name? I just didn't want to be no witness. It ain't no crime to lie to the police in Illinois."

"Why did you stay on the train, Andre? Why didn't you run with everyone else when the train stopped? It's because you wanted to be a witness. You gave a bad description of the shooter to throw us off the scent, Andre."

"I saw what I saw. You can't say I didn't."

"Andre, you were sitting next to the shooter. You talked to him. You looked right at him."

"Who said I was sitting by him? Who said I talked to him?"

"You know it's the truth, Andre. And because you know it's true, that means I've got someone who saw it who had no problem telling me about it."

Andre said nothing. Sam could see the wheels turning in his head trying to grind a way out of this.

"Here's what I think, Andre," Sam said. "You and the shooter knew each other. Still know each other. This was a set up. This was a targeted killing. You both got on that train knowing you were going to kill Walter Patterson. The whole robbery-gone-bad thing was just a cover." Sam sat back. "You're in the shit now, Andre."

Andre began shaking his head. His face was covered in a film of sweat. "I want my phone call. I want a lawyer."

"I'm not a cop, Andre," Sam said. "Remember? You don't get a phone call. You don't get a lawyer. Not with me. No one is coming to help you. There's only me and Beth. We're the only ones who can help you."

"How? How you gonna help me? You got me all tied up here, threatening me. How you gonna help me?"

"By giving you a choice. Do you want to go to prison for the rest of your life or do you want to be a witness? You tell us who killed Walter and you testify in court. You become a witness."

Andre was sweating profusely now. He licked his lips over and over again.

"You thirsty, Andre?" Sam said.

"Yeah, man. I need something."

"We'll get you some water." Sam nodded at Beth who got up and headed to the bathroom. Sam knew Andre was close. He had seen this hundreds of times before back when he was one of 'us'. Once they got to that stage, drowning in a sea of hopelessness and truths they could not deny, they needed someone to throw them a rope. Sam was the one offering that lifeline.

Beth returned with a plastic cup of water and held it to Andre's lips. She exchanged a glance with Sam as Andre gulped the water. She didn't look happy.

Sam directed her back to her seat on the bed with his eyes and his expression told her to give him a few more minutes. He turned his attention back to Andre.

"You okay now?" he said.

Andre swallowed hard and nodded.

"Andre," Sam said, "I'm all you've got. I was a homicide detective. I know how all this works. I know what you need and how to help you."

"How?"

"I can get you a deal. And all you need to do is tell me who killed Walter Patterson."

"What kind of deal?"

"The kind where you don't die in prison."

"I don't want to go at all."

"All I can promise you is that I'll do everything I can to help you. Come on, Andre. Take my help."

CHAPTER THIRTY-NINE

"WHO KILLED WALTER PATTERSON, Andre? Who was the man on the 'L' train with you?"

"You promise to help me?"

"I promise," Sam said.

Andre's head dropped and his eyes closed. A single tear ran down his cheek. *Here it comes*, Sam thought.

"Uncle Jerry," Andre said, barely whispering.

"What was that?" Sam said.

"My uncle Jerry."

"Jerry Robinson?"

"Yeah, he did it. He shot the man."

Beth jumped off the bed and out the back door into the rear parking lot. Sam stood and patted Andre on the shoulder, his eyes on the open door. "Good man, Andre," he said.

"You're gonna help me, right?"

"I promised you, didn't I? Rest up for a minute. I'll be right back." Sam went out the back door. Beth had walked off and stood, her back to Sam, in the middle of the lot.

Sam walked over to her. "You okay?" he asked.

Beth glared at him. "No, I'm not fucking okay. That son of a bitch in there helped kill my father and you're promising to help him."

"He killed Dave too. I lied to him, Beth. I lied to get him to tell me what he knows."

"You said you'd help turn him into a witness."

"I told you that you would hear things from me that you might not like. It's all just a ploy. You have to hang tough, Beth. Andre's going to prison for the rest of his miserable life. I needed him to tell us who killed your father and I said what was necessary to get him there."

Sam saw Beth's expression soften and the tension slowly leaving her body. He continued. "Now, I got him past the hardest part but I need more from him. Are you going to be okay in there? Because if you're not, I want you to stay out of the room. Go get coffee or something."

"What else do you need? He told you Jerry Robinson pulled the trigger."

"Details, I need details. I want to know how they planned it and why. The more he gives me, the more I have to hand over to the police and the tighter their case will be. And then there's Dave Hermann's murder. He has to give that up too. I'm confident the Glock is Dave's missing gun but Andre can always say we put it on him. We were in Dave's house in Galena. He can say we found it there and put it on him. Even the worst defense attorney can win that one."

Beth nodded slowly.

"You're okay, then?" Sam said.

"Yeah, I'm okay."

"Good," Sam said. He checked his phone. "It's a little after midnight. Can you go find us some coffee and maybe some food. Bring some for Andre too. It's going to be a long night." Sam was happy he got Beth to calm down but knew it would be hard for her to hear what was coming next. He couldn't take the chance of her losing it in front of Andre.

"I'd rather stay and hear the rest."

"I going to record Andre on my phone. You'll hear it all on the playback later. Take a break and cool down a little more."

"Okay. Maybe I do need a little time."

"You've waited sixteen years for this, Beth. I can't imagine what that was like. But we're getting it done."

Beth nodded. "Okay," she said. "I'll be back in a few minutes."

Sam walked back to their room. Andre was still where he left him, head down and chin resting on his chest. Sam took his seat in front of Andre and saw tears streaming down his face. "I know this is tough, Andre," he said, "but this is the best way, the only way for you. You're cleaning the slate."

Sam pulled his phone out, hit a few buttons, and set it on the floor between them. "I'm going to record us, Andre. Is that okay with you?"

Andre looked up. "Why?"

"It's the only way to prove you're cooperating. It's your own proof."

"Yeah, okay. Go ahead."

Sam needed to hear those words from Andre. Illinois was a one-party State when it came to recording someone. That meant the recording was legal if one party consented. Unless the other person had a reasonable expectation of privacy. Andre's permission was slightly better but Sam didn't think his recording would pass muster even with Andre's permission. The recording probably wouldn't make it into evidence. Sam's methods of obtaining it made that clear. At least, with Andre's permission, he was giving the prosecution a leg to stand on in their court arguments. It also gave leverage to the detectives who would be interviewing Andre later. Andre wouldn't be able to recant when they played his own voice detailing the murders to him. Andre would have no choice but to stay the course and repeat his confession to them and pray Sam would keep his word to help him.

Andre," Sam said, "a few minutes ago, you told me Jerry Robinson, your uncle, killed Walter Patterson on the Lake Street 'L' train. Isn't that right?"

Andre mumbled his reply.

"A little louder, please," Sam said.

Andre picked his head up. "Yes."

"Okay, do you remember when that was?"

"I don't know. A long time ago."

"It was sixteen years ago on Friday, April 14th, 2006."

"Yeah, I guess."

"Okay, now let's talk about how it happened and why."

Sam and Beth stood outside the back door of the motel room sipping the coffees Beth brought. Sam had finished with Andre a bit before she returned from her errand. They fed Andre and, his hands and feet still bound with duct tape, helped him onto the bed to get some rest.

Beth peeked into the room at Andre. "Look at that bastard. He's asleep. He killed two people and he's sleeping like a baby."

"I've seen it before," Sam said. "It seems weird but it's really not. It actually makes sense. After giving it all up, he has nothing to fear any longer. There's no sword hanging over his head. He's done worrying about looking over his shoulder."

"You're saying his conscious is clear?"

"No. I don't think people like him have a conscious. Or at least they're able to suppress it so deeply it's never in play. This?" He flicked his head towards Andre, "This is something else. This is relief that the worst is over. He's accepted his fate and so now he can relax."

Sam took a sip of his coffee and pulled the phone from his pocket. "Do you want to hear what he said?"

Beth drew a breath and blew it out. "No, I don't want to hear that asshole's voice. Just tell me what he said."

Sam gave her the short version.

"Your father's murder was a contract killing, Beth," Sam said. "Jerry was hired to kill your father. He recruited Andre to help him. Andre claims he doesn't know why or who hired Jerry but there was a big payday for Jerry. That's where he got the money to start up his security company.

"It was Jerry's plan. Jerry pulled the trigger and Andre stayed back to give false information to the police."

Tears were streaming from Beth's eyes. She turned away and wiped her checks with a single finger. She spun back around the threw her coffee into the lot. "I want to see these rotten fucks hang," she said.

"I know," Sam said. "I get it. You will. At least metaphorically. There's no capital punishment in Illinois. But they'll both spend the rest of their lives in prison. That can be worse. Especially for an ex-cop like Jerry Robinson."

Beth was still fuming, fists clenched, staring into the room at Andre on the bed.

"Hey," Sam said as he looked over his shoulder into the parking lot, "that was a good throw. Not like a girl throws at all." He looked back to Beth. "Did you play ball in high school?"

Beth glared at him.

Sam held up his hands in surrender. "Sorry, I'm just trying to lighten the mood."

"This isn't the time for that," she said.

"You're right." Sam stuck his hands into his pockets and leaned against the wall. "Do you want to hear the rest now?"

CHAPTER
FORTY

THE REST WAS Andre telling Sam about Dave Hermann. It took Sam a while to convince Andre to admit to killing Dave. This was all about Andre proving himself, Sam told him. Proving he could be trusted. He had to tell the truth, all of it, if he was to be believed about everything else. It was the only way Andre would get Sam's help.

When it finally sank in and that it was all part of the deal, Andre grudgingly admitted to killing Dave Hermann. Jerry told Andre that Hermann had come to Truncheon asking about Andre. He knew Andre was Darryl Wilcox, the witness on the train. Hermann was told Andre no longer worked at Truncheon and he left without any information on Andre. But Jerry Robinson couldn't trust Hermann wouldn't uncover more.

Jerry had Andre follow Dave who eventually led him out to Galena. Andre saw his chance. He set up in the woods, like he did with Sam and Beth, and shot

Dave. Dave wasn't as lucky as Sam. There was no wind the day Dave was killed.

"And that's where we're at," Sam said. "We've got enough on Andre and Jerry. Well, almost. A second witness who can identify Jerry would seal the deal on him."

"The nail salon lady?" Beth said.

"Yeah. Let's hope she can still identify him after sixteen years."

"We don't need her."

"I know they probably didn't cover this in your Criminal Justice classes, but no State's Attorney is going to approve charges on Jerry with just Andre's word. And right now, we've got nothing else connecting him to all this."

"I mean, I could just go kill him."

"We talked about this already, Beth. I can't let you do that."

"Then you better hope the salon lady can ID Robinson."

"We need Robinson alive, Beth. According to Andre, someone hired Jerry to kill your father. Jerry Robinson is the only one who can tell us who that was."

"Then I'll kill him after he tells us."

Sam knew arguing any further was pointless. It was just another bridge to cross when he got to it. "Come on," he said walking into the room, "we need to get some rest. Daybreak is only an hour or so away."

Beth followed him inside and closed the door. She

looked around the room. "I'm not sleeping here. There's only one bed and that asshole has it."

Sam sat in the crappy upholstered chair and put his feet up on the wooden chair he had Andre in earlier. "Grab a pillow and sleep in the bathtub."

Beth walked over and looked at the tub. "I think it's worse than sleeping on the floor."

"Your choice," Sam said.

"How about if I go back to the other motel. All our stuff is there anyway."

"No, we stay together. We'll get our bags in the morning."

"You don't trust me?"

"After what you said earlier? No." Sam, stretched out in the two chairs, crossed his arms and rested his head on his chest. "Please just take the tub, Beth."

"You're going to sleep there?"

"I'm not going to sleep. One of us needs to stay awake."

Beth nodded, more to herself than Sam, and headed off to the bath. "I don't think I'll be able to sleep either."

"Get the lights," Sam said as she walked away.

The night passed with Sam still lying across the two chairs. The sun would be coming up soon. Soft, regular breaths came from Andre and Beth in the bathroom. She fell asleep after all, he thought. Now he needed to consider his next moves. His plan was to call Gene Kroll in the morning and have him meet them at Area Four

HQ. With Andre in tow, he'd turn him over along with the recording of Andre's confession. They were best equipped to run with this now. There was not much more he could do without them.

Sam would have them check the registration on the Glock and the Mini-14 and give Det. Hatfield a call at the Jo Daviess county sheriff's office. Dave's murder was in their jurisdiction and they would handle it. But, they'd have to wait in line. Chicago would want Andre for his participation in Walter Patterson's murder first.

He would leave Jerry Robinson up to the police. If they were as good as Sam thought they should be, the detectives would get Jerry to give up the person or persons who contracted the murder.

And that bothered Sam. Why would whoever hired Jerry approach him? What possible reason could there be that a former deputy chief in the police department would agree to commit murder. If it was money, it had to be a handsome sum.

Sam looked over to Andre still sleeping on the bed. Whatever reasons Jerry Robinson had, Sam thought, he pulled his nephew into it and destroyed his life too. His eyes wandered over to the bedside table where he placed Andre's wallet and phone. His eyes fixed on the cellphone. He went through Andre's wallet earlier but not the phone.

He walked over and picked it up. It was either switched it off or out of a charge. He was barely familiar with the model but, after fumbling with it for a few minutes, it sprang to life. The first screen told him there were seven missed calls, all from 'Uncle Jerry'. The last coming in thirty minutes ago.

He checked the phone's voicemail. Andre's phone had a cool feature. The voice mails were transcribed into text and Sam began reading, starting with the oldest. There were only six messages – the last missed call had no voicemail attached – and all said about the same thing, each more urgent than the previous one: Where are you? Call me. Are you still following them? What are they doing? Answer me.

Sam next checked the contacts list in the phone for Uncle Jerry. Other than the phone number there was no further information for Uncle Jerry listed, no address, no last name, no email address. None of that mattered, though. Uncle Jerry's identity was no mystery.

Sam continued to page through the contacts, moving through them alphabetically. He stopped when he reached the L's. The only listing read 'Lawyer MB'. Sam's pulse quickened as he read the entry.

He remembered he called Malcolm Burnett's office earlier in the week. He could compare the number on Andre's phone to the number he called. But he used his cellphone and not the burner currently in his pocket.

Laska's train of thought was broken by the sound of a car outside. He checked the time display on Andre's phone. It was 5:42 am, a not so unusual time for someone leaving the motel. But Sam didn't hear a car start up.

The disadvantage of old, shabby motels was their paper-thin walls. Even the exterior walls let in the slightest sounds from outside. But at this moment, Sam took the porous walls as a lucky break. He stood still and concentrated on the sound of the car. His head moved with the sound of the vehicle as it passed their end unit, around the corner, and into the lot behind where Andre's BMW and Beth's Jeep were parked right outside their door.

Sam listened as the sound told him the vehicle stopped and stood motionless, its engine still running. He quickly moved to the bathroom and shook Beth. "Get up," he said barely above a whisper.

"I'm already awake," she said. "I hear it too."

"Got your Sig?"

"Right here," she said displaying the weapon. "I kept it with me."

Sam nodded. "Help me get Andre into the tub."

The sound of the car's engine stopped.

"Too late," Beth said.

Sam nodded. "Stay here," he said. "Cover the door. I'm going to roll him onto the floor."

"How do we know if someone isn't coming through the front door too?"

"We don't."

Beth gave him her best wide-eyed what-the-fuck expression.

"Odds are we only have to worry about the back-door," he said. "But be ready for a front door entry too. That's your job. I'll be exposed so you have to have my back."

"You gotta be shitting me."

"You got a better idea? I'm all ears."

Beth shook her head and knelt in the doorway between the bedroom and the bath with her pistol trained on the front door. Sam moved to the bed, covered Andre's mouth with a hand, and shook him awake. Sam put a finger to his lips and whispered to Andre to stay quiet. He then helped him onto the floor on the side of the bed. The bed wouldn't be much protection but it was better than nothing.

Sam crouched next to Andre, his Beretta in his hand. He looked back at Beth. She stared at the door with that same yearbook face. Sam smiled to himself and turned back, hoping they were ready for whatever came through the door.

CHAPTER
FORTY-ONE

THE FIRST BLAST of the shotgun ripped a hole through the door at the lockset. Sam wasn't expecting it. He figured on a kick to open the door and the intruder entering armed with a suppressed pistol. He was lying on the floor, his head sticking out past the foot of the bed only far enough to see the door. His right arm and hand holding his Beretta were extended toward the door.

The first blast was followed by a second into the room through the now open doorway. Sam felt the shudder of the mattress and bed as the pellets struck. A snowfall of foam and fabric fluttered around him. Staring at the door he saw the silhouette of the shooter in the doorway backlit by a far off streetlamp. He fired at center mass, squeezing off the rounds as quickly as he could pull the trigger. The sound of the gunshots from his and Beth's pistols rang in his ears and the flashes from their pistols lit up the room like a strobe light.

The man staggered back but, instead of falling, he moved to his left. A wild blast from the shotgun hit the ceiling above the bed sending chunks of plaster and wood flying. The man was gone, out of Sam's line of sight, disappearing somewhere along the back of the motel.

Sam yelled to Beth. "You okay?"

"Yeah," she answered.

"Check on Andre," he said. "Stay with him."

Sam jumped to his feet and ran to the door. His Beretta at the ready, he bobbed his head out the door and quickly moved it back again. What he saw registered quickly and he stepped out. Jerry Robinson was hobbling towards a black Lincoln, breathing heavily and using the shotgun as a makeshift cane as he dragged his left leg behind him. Sam leveled his pistol and began walking toward him.

Sam stopped. "Robinson," he yelled, "drop the shotgun. Hands on your head."

Robinson stopped but held onto the shotgun.

"Do it," Sam said.

Robinson stood unmoving, his back to Sam.

"Last chance, Jerry."

"You'd shoot me in the back?" Robinson called out.

"Maybe he won't," Beth said, "But, sure as shit, I will."

Sam hadn't noticed her walk up behind him. She

stood only a few paces behind him and far off to his left, her Sig also leveled at Robinson.

"Beth," Sam said.

Her eyes moved to Sam and back again to Robinson. "Only if he give me a reason, Sam."

Robinson turned his head and looked over his shoulder. He let go of the shotgun and it clattered on the asphalt. Sam rushed over and forced him to his knees. He tucked his Beretta into his pants in the back and put Robinson face down on the pavement.

He frisked Robinson quickly. Robinson flinched as Sam's hands moved over his left leg. The leg suffered a through-and-through wound above the knee. It was serious but not life threatening. Sam rolled him over and searched him a second time. As his hands ran over Robinson's torso, Sam recognized the firm stiffness of a ballistic vest. He eyes fell to Robinson's chest. Five shots, all center mass, had ripped into the vest.

Sam tore at the Velcro that secured the vest and pulled it off Robinson. The vest had done its job but Robinson's labored breathing revealed it did not do so without some damage. Broken bones from the impacts on Robinson's chest were likely.

Robinson's eyes asked a question. "You'll live," Sam answered. He flipped Robinson back onto his stomach and stood. He looked over to Beth.

She stood frozen in position, staring at Robinson with her hands locked onto her lowered pistol. Tears streamed down her cheeks.

"You okay?" Sam called to her.

She didn't move.

"Beth!" he yelled.

Her eyes found him. "Yeah," she said.

"What about Andre?"

"Uninjured," she said.

"Go back and stay with him," Sam said. "I've got this."

Beth nodded and slowly turned back to their room.

The sound of yelping sirens drawing near pierced the early morning air. Sam pulled out his phone and dialed quickly.

"Gene?" he said, "It's Sam. Time to go to work."

Sam sat alone in an interview room on the second floor of the Area Four Detective Division HQ. He was sitting at a steel table in the center of the room, the wrong side. That being the side farthest from the door. He looked around the small room and at the graffiti scratched into the surface of the putty colored walls. He knew the room hadn't seen fresh paint since he last worked here sixteen years ago.

He had undergone hours of interviews with Det. Marcin and his partner, detailing the events of last night and this morning. He told them of his interview with Mae Lin Chan and explained how he figured out Darryl Wilcox was Andre Robinson. He told them how he and Beth found the Ruger Mini-14 that was used by Andre to kill Dave Hermann and take a shot at himself, and of the Glock he took from Andre which, Andre admitted, belonged to Dave Hermann. He told them about the murder for hire scheme engineered by Jerry Robinson as explained to him by Andre and how it went down on the 'L' train.

Marcin and his partner were good, Sam thought. They asked all the right questions at the right times and went over Sam's story more times than Sam could remember. But the one thing they asked, who hired Jerry Robinson, Sam couldn't answer. Not yet anyway.

They finished with Sam, for the time being they said, and left him alone. Sam sat for over an hour waiting until the door opened and Chief Gene Kroll walked in, closing the door behind him. He took a seat across from Sam.

"What's up?" Sam said.

"I don't know if they told you, but your father's here. He's sitting out by the front desk. I stopped by his hotel on the way back from the scene. I figured he deserved to know what was going on. He followed me in."

"Thanks for that."

"We're keeping your Beretta for the time being. It's getting booked into evidence. The girl's Sig Sauer also. Oh, and your burner phone with the confession on it."

"I figured," Sam said. "Are you making any progress?"

"Some," Kroll said. "The detectives listened to your recording and are talking to Andre Robinson now."

Sam nodded. "And Jerry Robinson?"

"Still at the hospital. We've got a police guard on him. He's not talking. He already asked for his lawyer."

Sam was confident he knew who that lawyer was, but he said nothing. "What about the Glock? Did the registration come back?"

"Yeah, we confirmed it belonged to Dave Hermann. But you knew it would, right?"

"Andre told me he found it in Dave's house in Galena. That's all on the recording. Did you call the Jo Daviess Sheriff's office?"

"They're sending a team out here." He looked at his watch. "I'm surprised they're not here yet."

Sam pointed to Kroll's wrist. "What time is it?"

"A little after two."

"I could use some lunch. We missed breakfast."

"I'll see if I can get you something when we're through here."

"I'd rather go out, and I'd like to take Beth with me."

"I can't allow it."

"There's that word again, Gene. Am I under arrest?"

"I haven't decided yet."

"And that means, right now, I'm not." Sam stood.

"Sit down, Sam."

Sam looked down at Kroll.

"Please," Kroll said.

Sam shrugged and sat.

"We *should* arrest you, Sam. You were in possession of police department property and refused to return it—"

"That's a bullshit charge. I mailed the file to you."

Kroll held up a hand to silence Sam. "You were actively investigating an open homicide and kept pertinent facts from us. You kidnapped Andre Robinson and held him against his will. And you got into a gun battle in a motel room causing thousands of dollars in damage."

"Okay, I'll give you the interfering charge for investigating a murder. But kidnapping? Come on, that was a citizen's arrest of a homicide suspect. My plan was to bring Andre to you in the morning. And the gunfight was self-defense. I had no idea Jerry Robinson would track us down."

"Andre's company car had a GPS tracker on it."

Sam shrugged. "I guess I'm getting rusty."

"And 'citizen's arrest' is a bunch of bullshit, Sam. Don't con me."

"Yeah, okay. You're right." Sam leaned forward and put his hands on the table. "So, are you going to arrest me?"

"No, we're not."

"Then I can go get lunch?"

"Are you going to come back? The Assistant State's Attorney is going to want to talk to you too."

"Yeah, I promise."

"Today?"

Sam smiled. "Yeah, today."

CHAPTER
FORTY-TWO

SAM WALKED out to the front desk. Bruno jumped out of his chair when he saw him.

"Hey, you okay, son?" he said hurrying over to Sam.

"Yeah, Dad. I'm good. Did they tell you what happened?"

Bruno nodded as he said, "Yeah. Jesus, Sam. I'm glad you're safe."

"Thanks. Listen, did you bring my phone?"

"Yeah," Bruno said, digging into his pocket, "I've got it right here."

"Thanks," Sam said, taking the phone from his father. "Did you see Beth?"

"She was over there sitting by one of the detective's desk. But another guy came and took her somewhere into the back."

"Probably to an interview room. I guess they're going over some stuff with her." Sam walked his father a little away from the front desk. "Listen, Dad, I've got something I need to do. Can I use your car?"

"Yeah, sure. Where you going?"

"I don't want to say yet. If anyone asks, I went to get us a sandwich."

Bruno nodded and handed his keys to his son. "What kind of sandwich?"

Sam smiled. "I'll stop and get us a couple of Italian beefs on my way back."

"No hot peppers. My stomach can't take them anymore."

Sam found his father's Cadillac on the top level of the parking garage and, once behind the wheel, he pulled out his cellphone and dialed Joyce.

"Sam?" she answered.

"Yeah, it's me. I got my phone back."

"Unless you've got some new request, I've got nothing for you. I can't get anywhere on that shell company."

"That's exactly what I was calling about. Let me ask you this, though. Did you pull up the Articles of Incorporation?"

"Yeah, but the names of the company's directors are all bullshit. I can't find a thing on any of them. That's how a shell company works. Everything is a dead end."

"Is the law firm who handled the incorporation listed?"

"Yeah of course. But they won't give up any information. They can't. Not without a court order anyway. That's just another dead end."

"What's the firm's name?"

"Hang on a sec."

Sam waited as Joyce pulled up the information on her computer.

"Sam?" she said, coming back on. "The firm is Burnett, Styles, and Price on Washington Street in Chicago."

"I'm gonna take a shot in the dark. The attorney who signed the papers, his name is Malcolm Burnett."

"Yeah, that's it. Hey, you got something?"

"Yeah, I do. Did the same law firm do the incorporation for the 420 Growers company?"

"Hang on again."

Joyce came back on. "Yup, and the same lawyer, Malcolm Burnett, signed the papers."

"One last question, Joyce. You told me Jerry Robinson had a bad credit history and probably needed help starting up his business."

"Yeah, he had a personal bankruptcy. That was a little before he left the police department."

"That's all I need. Thanks, Joyce. Tell Jack I'll be back in a day or two in case he needs me."

"Okay, Sam. Good luck."

Sam pocketed his phone, cranked up the Cadillac, and pulled out of the garage.

. . .

Sam stepped off the elevator and into the outer office of Burnett, Styles, and Price. The blonde woman sitting behind a large half-circle reception desk looked up. "Can I help you?" she asked

Sam walked over. "Is Mr. Burnett in?" he said.

"Do you have an appointment?"

"You know what?" Sam said. "I'll just go back there and take a look." He turned and headed off down the hall.

The woman called after him, "Sir! You can't go back there!"

Sam quickened his pace. He pulled out his phone and hit the voice recorder app. The woman, now out of her spot behind the desk, chased after him.

"Stop," she called out. "Sir, you must stop."

Sam reached Burnett's office before the woman caught up to him. Without knocking, he pulled open the door and walked in. Malcolm Burnett was behind his massive desk talking on the desk phone. He looked up at Sam and spoke quickly into the phone, "I have to go." He hung up and stood. "Mr. Laska, what—"

The receptionist followed behind Sam. "Mr. Burnett, I'm sorry. I told this man he couldn't come back here."

"It's alright, Diane," Burnett said. "Go on. You can go back to your desk. And please close the door behind you."

Diane left the two men and Sam walked over and sat in one of the Queen Anne's chairs in front of Burnett.

"What's this about, Mr. Laska?" Burnett said. "Do you have information about Walter's case?"

"I do," Sam said. "The police have made an arrest. Two arrests actually."

"Two? I thought Walter was murdered during an armed robbery by a single killer."

"Well, that initial assessment was wrong. I guess you'd have to blame me for that mistake. I was the lead detective back then."

"Who are the men?"

"Jerry Robinson and Andre Robinson. But you know that already. I'll bet that call you were on was from Jerry Robinson in the hospital. You're his attorney, right? And Andre's attorney too."

Burnett sat back. Resting his elbows on the arms of his chair, he steepled the fingers of his hands in front of him. He stared at Laska. When he finally spoke, he said, "I think we're done here. Thank you for the information, Mr. Laska. But now you need to leave."

Laska stood, more for comfort than effect. The Queen Anne's chair was killing his back already. "Oh, we're not done. Not by a long shot. We have a lot to talk about."

Burnett reached over to his desk and picked up the phone's receiver.

"I hope that's one of your partners you're calling," Sam said. "You're going to need a good attorney."

"I'm calling the police. I'm going to have you arrested for trespassing."

"Good. Call them. It'll save me from doing it."

Burnett put the receiver back in its cradle and sat back. "Alright, Mr. Laska. You go right ahead and talk. But don't expect me to say anything."

"Fine with me," Sam said. "Let's start with Jerry Robinson. You lied to me. A few days ago, you told me you didn't remember ever meeting Jerry Robinson and you acted surprised when I told you he and Walter were well acquainted. But you do know him. You know him well enough to have incorporated Truncheon Security for him. In fact, I'm willing to bet you're his partner. Now, I can't prove that. Not yet at least. But some shell company owns the controlling interest in Truncheon and I'm pretty sure you own that shell company. And then there's Truncheon's big new client, the marijuana business. You handled that incorporation also. I'm also betting that, if you aren't the sole owner, you at least have a big piece of it.

"But back to Robinson. Here's how I got on to him. I first became interested in Robinson because of his unusual interest in Walter's murder years ago. I didn't know about it then and only found out when I started poking into this again. Anyway, I went to ask him why. He told me he was acquainted with Walter and his interest was only curiosity. But that wasn't true, was it? He didn't know Walter at all.

"When you talked to Jerry a few minutes ago, did he tell you his nephew Andre confessed? Probably not, I don't think he knows yet. Andre told us, both me and the police, that his uncle fired the shots that killed Walter. He also said that Jerry was hired to kill Walter.

That means Jerry couldn't have cared less about Walter. But someone else did. That someone else is you."

Burnett pushed himself out of his chair. "You're crazy. This is crazy. I'm not going to listen to this nonsense."

"Yes, you are. Sit down."

Burnett hesitated and then sat. Sam could see the fear in his eyes. It wasn't a fear of Sam, but fear for what he knew was coming.

"I asked myself," Sam said, "why would you care? Why would you want your partner killed? Then it came to me. You told me Walter was bringing in a big client and that client was only interested in Walter representing them. When Walter was murdered, they didn't stick with you. I've got a feeling that Walter was leaving your partnership and taking the big new client with him, leaving you with nothing. That's called motive.

"But then I realized there was another problem. With Walter gone, how does a young attorney with barely any client list afford to hire someone to commit murder? It would take a boat load of money to convince someone to take a chance like that. Then it came to me. You picked Robinson to approach because he wanted to start a company but he was broke, bankrupt. And an easy mark for you. All you needed to push him over was to dangle big money in front of him. But where would you get the money from? I'm thinking it was insurance. I'll bet both you and Walter had insurance policies with the beneficiaries being the other partner. Lots of partnerships and businesses do it. I had a case involving something similar years ago when I was still a cop. How big was the payout, Malcolm? You know, they're gonna want their money back when they find out about all of this."

"You'll never prove that. You'll never prove any of it."

"Actually, it will be pretty easy. Just a check of the court records sixteen years ago to figure out who that company was that wanted Walter. Then it's a simple matter of a few interviews to prove Walter's intent to dump you. Same thing with the insurance company. The police will find out."

Walter sat silent. He looked out the window and the view of the city outside. "You expect me to admit to any of this? Is that why you came here?"

"No, if I thought you were going to confess I would have brought someone with me. A prover. I was actually hoping you'd do the honorable thing and take a leap out that window. But I don't think you will. You have no courage and no honor." Sam walked around and stood between Burnett and the window, blocking his view. "When you first planned this, did you ever consider Walter's wife and child? Did you go to Walter's funeral and tell Amanda, the woman who died of a broken heart, how sorry you were for her loss? And Beth, what did you say to her? You destroyed her life."

"I never wanted to hurt them. Especially Elizabeth. I loved that child as if she was my own. But Walter betrayed me. We were supposed to be partners forever."

Sam nodded. "Thank you for that," he said. He pulled his phone out and showed it to Burnett. "That's good enough."

Burnett's eyes went wide. "A recording? You can't use that. I never consented. That will never be admitted into court. And if you testify, it will just be your word against mine."

"I didn't intend for it to be used in court. Besides, the police won't need it. I suspect when Jerry realizes he's going to be charged with murder for hire, they're not going to be able to shut him up."

Sam turned and looked out the window to the street below. "Wow, that is a long way down." He backed away. "You know, I can't stand heights myself." He turned away and walked to the door.

Burnett called after him. "Are you going to play that recording for Elizabeth?"

Sam stopped and looked back at Burnett. He turned away and walked out.

CHAPTER
FORTY-THREE

THE ROOM WAS quiet except for the sound of the recording on Sam's cellphone. When it ended, Sam reached over to the center of the conference table where he had placed the phone and switched it off. Sitting around the table with him were Chief Gene Kroll, Commander Stan Kuchinski of Area Four, detectives Marcin and Calvin, and two people from the state's attorney's office.

"We can't use this." The man speaking was Robert Sanderson, a Cook County Assistant State's Attorney. Sitting next to him was his boss and the head of the Felony Review unit, William O'Brian.

"You had no consent and Burnett had a reasonable expectation of privacy in his office," O'Brian said. "Besides that, it's only a half-assed admission."

"Hold on," Kroll said.

Sam butted in. "It's okay, Gene. I knew they couldn't use it. I made the recording for your benefit. You needed to know who hired Robinson and now you do. And you know the how and why of it."

"Hardly," O'Brien said. "Burnett didn't admit to any of your theories. It's all supposition on your part."

"But it gives us a direction to go in," Marcin said. He looked over to Kroll. "Chief, we can run with this and build a case but Calvin and I don't have any experience working financials and shell companies and that kind of stuff."

Kroll nodded. He looked over to Commander Kuchinski. "Let's give a call over to Financial Crimes and get a couple of their people over here to work this." He looked back to O'Brien. "What charges are you looking at for Jerry Robinson?"

"For starters," O'Brien said, "two counts of attempted murder for the shooting at the motel. And once we get a formal statement from Andre and a positive ID from Ms. Chan, we'll charge him with Walter Patterson's murder."

"Solicitation of Murder for Hire?" Kroll asked.

"I want more than just Andre's word on that," O'Brien said. "I want an admission by Jerry Robinson implicating Burnett."

Kroll looked over to Marcin and Calvin. "Go over to the hospital and inform Mr. Robinson of the pending charges. Let's see if he changes his mind about talking to us. I'll bet he doesn't want to take the fall alone."

"I'll go with them," Sanderson said. He looked over to his boss, O'Brien, who nodded his assent.

Sam pushed away from the table and stood. "You

don't need me any longer. It's on all of you now." He left the conference room and walked over to the front desk where his father and Beth were waiting. Sam had played the recording he made with Burnett for Beth earlier. He knew it would break her heart but she deserved to know the truth.

He took a seat next to Beth and told her what the ASAs said about the recording. Sam explained Burnett would likely be charged. It would take some work and probably a little time but they'd get him. She said nothing. She just sat and wept.

Sam put his arm around her. As she fell against his shoulder, he said, "Don't worry, it's almost over."

"No," Beth said. "It will never be over for me."

It was late into the night when Sam and Beth were told by Gene Kroll they could leave. Bruno dropped Sam and Beth at her car and Beth drove them to pick up their bags. As they collected their belonging, Beth looked over to Sam. "Thank you," she said. "For everything."

Sam nodded. "I'm glad you finally learned the truth, as hard as it is." He picked up the steel urn that held Dave's ashes and carefully placed it on top of the clothes in his suitcase. "What are you going to do now?" he asked.

"I was thinking about paying Burnett a visit."

Sam froze. He stared at Beth.

She smiled. "Relax, I was just kidding."

"I hope so."

"Honest," she said. "I think maybe I'll go back to St. Louis. Maybe Los Angeles."

"Okay," he said. "You know, the weather is nice in Florida this time of year. I could ask the lawyer I work for if he needs some help."

"God's waiting room? I'll pass." She looked over to Sam and the urn lying on top of his open suitcase. "What about Dave's funeral? Are you going to make plans?"

"I talked to Gene Kroll about that earlier. He's going to press the Superintendent for an Honor's funeral. Dave was killed doing his job. It's a line of duty death."

"Will you let me know when it is? I'd like to be there."

"I will. I'm going back to Florida but as soon as I get the word from Gene I'll come back with Dave's ashes."

"Thank you."

They finished packing in silence. After, Beth drove Sam back to the Marriott. As she pulled under the portico, Sam said, "If you want, I'll get you a room here tonight."

"Thanks for the offer but I'll pass."

"You have to stay somewhere."

"I decided to go to St. Louis. I can get there in a few hours."

"More than just a few."

Beth nodded and gave him a weak smile. It wasn't enough for Sam.

"One last thing," he said, "Gene Kroll told me the

comparisons on the rounds that hit Jerry Robinson came back. I win, three to two."

Beth laughed. "Bullshit. I know I hit him more than that."

"The science doesn't lie."

"What about his leg?"

"It was a through-and-though wound. We'll never know."

"I'm claiming it."

"I don't know about that."

"It's mine. We're officially tied." She gave him a big smile this time.

That was the smile Sam wanted.

Sam and Bruno left for Florida early the next morning. Sam again insisted they drive straight through. Some-where around Bowling Green, Kentucky, Sam got a call from Gene Kroll. Jerry Robinson suddenly found his voice when he was told he was looking at a life sentence. He gave up Malcolm Burnett, telling Marcin, Calvin, and Sanderson that Burnett promised Robinson a big payday. Big enough to get him out of debt and help him start his own company.

Sam was right about Burnett being the owner of the shell company that partnered with Robinson and, though he was only a small shareholder in 420 Growers, Burnett was given his owner's shares for using his political influence to get the company their license to operate. Securing the contract for security with Truncheon was the cherry on top.

Robinson claimed he didn't know where Burnett got the money to pay him for Walter Patterson's murder, but Robinson said it took several weeks after the murder before he got paid.

"The State's Attorney's office took written and video statements from Andre and Jerry. They approved multiple counts of first degree murder on both." Kroll said. "I figure they'll argue for no bail at their first appearance in court."

"What about Burnett?" Sam asked.

"Burnett solved all our problems for us," Kroll said.

"He confessed?" Sam asked.

"No. This morning he went to the Metra station in Highland Park like he does every morning on the way to work. Only today he jumped in front of a train. He killed himself, Sam."

"Jesus, you're kidding."

"Not at all. He saved us a lot of work. He saved his family and partners a whole lot of embarrassment also."

"Highland Park Police handled it, I assume."

"Yeah. We found out about it when Marcin and his partner went to knock on Burnett's door to arrest him."

"So, the witnesses said he just jumped in front of a commuter train?"

"He was standing in a large crowd. Next thing they know, he's on the tracks. That's what the witnesses said."

"No one actually saw him jump? And they're sure it was a suicide?"

"The Highland Park police are satisfied, Sam. Especially after hearing Burnett knew he was about to be arrested for murder. What are you getting at?"

"Nothing," Sam said, "nothing at all."

Sam ended the call. He sat and stared out the side window as his father steered the Cadillac down the highway.

It was over, Sam thought. Walter Patterson's killers were found out and jailed or dead. Some might say that balance was restored. But Sam knew that was a lie. There is no 'getting even' when it comes to murder because what was stolen was more than one life. There are always others who must go on living with a hole carved out of their soul. Others like Elizabeth Patterson.

He hoped she didn't let it ruin her more than it already had.

CHAPTER FORTY-FOUR

"WE'RE GETTING CLOSE NOW, KID." Bruno was behind the wheel for the last leg of the drive. Sam was awake but just barely. Slumped against the door in the front passenger's seat, he opened his eyes and sat up.

"Where are we?" Sam asked as he scanned the road ahead for a familiar landmark that would answer his question.

"Mile 215," Bruno said, "ten miles out." Their exit was at mile marker 205. From there, it was only a few more miles westbound to Siesta Key and Bruno's small villa.

Sam rubbed his eyes and pulled his phone out to check the time. It was a little after eight in the morning. He debated with himself only briefly before dialing Marley's number.

Aunt Vicky answered Marley's phone. "Hello, Sam.'Bout time you called again."

It took Sam a few seconds to adjust to Vicky's Jamaican accent. Once he did, he said, "Hi, Vicky. Is Marley awake?"

"No, Sam. She's still sleeping. Where you at, son?"

"We're almost home. Fifteen minutes away."

"Good. You should come to the house."

"Is everything okay?"

"Yessir, but she needs you to be here. Me too. I ain't been home in days and you know I can't leave Uncle Nosmo alone for this long. He probably eatin' and drinkin' hisself to death these last couple of days."

"Is Marley going to be okay with me stopping by?"

"You ain't stopping by, son. You moving in and gonna take care of your woman. And you gonna be here until your baby come. I'm going home. I been here long enough."

"There's nothing I'd like more, Vicky. But does Marley want me there?"

"I know that girl's heart. She wants you."

"Okay, I'll have my dad drop me off there. But if Marley says anything I'm blaming you."

Vicky let go a laugh. "You just get your skinny butt here."

Sam sat in a chair next to Marley's bed paging through a magazine. She had been sleeping since he arrived at her house and tiptoed into the bedroom.

He heard her stir and looked over. Her head fell to the side and her eyes slowly opened. She blinked and blinked again. "Sam?" she said and grunted as she pushed herself up onto her elbows.

"Hi, Marley."

She covered her mouth as she yawned and said, "When did you get here?"

"About an hour ago. Vicky went home. She asked me to take over."

"Good. She was starting to get on my nerves."

"She's a good woman."

"I know, but…I don't know. Maybe I'm just being cranky." She tried to push herself up even higher, grunting with the effort. She looked over to Sam. "Help me get up, please."

Sam stood. "Are you sure that's a good idea? Vicky said—"

"I have to go to the bathroom, Sam. It's either that or go right here in the bed."

"Okay, sorry," he said and helped her to her feet. He walked with her to the en suite bathroom and waited outside for her. When she came out, she told Sam she wanted to sit for a while instead of going back to the bed. He helped her to a large, overstuffed chair in a sitting area of the large bedroom.

Sam pulled up a chair and sat opposite her. "How are you feeling?" he asked.

"Better now," she said and smiled. She shifted in the chair to get comfortable. "When did you get back from Chicago?"

"About an hour ago. I called and Vicky answered your phone. She told me to come right over."

Marley nodded. "I'm glad you're here. Did everything go okay in Chicago?"

"Yeah. Do you want to hear about it?"

"No. I think I've decided I don't want to know about your work."

"Marley, if I have to choose between what I do and you, I choose you. I'll find something else to do. Anything else. You can even put me to work washing dishes in your restaurant."

"But you wouldn't be happy. You'd eventually come to resent me for asking you to choose."

"I won't."

"Sam, you need to do what you do. It's who you are."

"I can change. I can find something else."

"Sam," she took his hand in hers, "I'm not asking you to change. I'm saying I've accepted it."

Sam was still unsure of what she meant. Marley saw the confusion on his face. "What I'm saying, Sam, is I want us to be together. You, me, and the baby. A family."

Sam squeezed her hand. "Back in Chicago, when I left you in that diner—"

"I understand why you did it," she said.

"And I understand why you needed me to stay. I'll never do that again." He moved in closer to her. "Are you sure you're good with it?"

"Yes, Sam. I love you." She pulled him in and kissed him.

"I love you too," he said.

"I want to be married before the baby comes."

"I'll make it happen." He smiled. "Somehow." He moved in to kiss her again but she stiffened and sat back.

"What?" he said.

Marley grimaced. "I think…I think that was a contraction." She looked at Sam and smiled. "We're going to meet our daughter today."

————

ACKNOWLEDGMENTS

Many thanks to all the usual suspects and a few new ones: Bill Shepherd, Bob Weisskopf, Christie Sergo, Jack Hodges, and Gene Roy. Also Patrick O'Donnell who hosts the outstanding *Cops and Writers* podcast. Thanks to all for the alpha and beta reads, suggestions, advice, fact-checking, and insight. Also a big thank you to the love of my life Sharon Rybicki.

To my readers, thanks for reading and for your patience. It's been a few long years but Sam and Marley are back.

ABOUT THE AUTHOR

Richard Rybicki, a former police officer and detective, is an emerging author of crime fiction. This is Richard's fourth novel in the Sam Laska Crime Thriller series. Learn more, connect with the author, and sign up for the author's newsletter at www.rrybickiauthor.com , on Facebook at https://www.facebook.com/RybickiAu thor , and Twitter at @rybicki_richard

ALSO BY RICHARD RYBICKI

The Pain Game

Where the Road Leads

Bottom Feeder Blues

The Suits - A Short Story Collection

Made in the USA
Columbia, SC
06 March 2023

13207832R00200